2020

BERKELEY NOIR

EDITED BY
JERRY THOMPSON & OWEN HILL

BROOKLYN, NEW YORK, USA

Published by Akashic Books
©2020 Akashic Books

Series concept by Tim McLoughlin and Johnny Temple
Berkeley map by Sohrab Habibion

ISBN: 978-1-61775-797-6
Library of Congress Control Number: 2019943609

Akashic Books
Brooklyn, New York, USA
Twitter: @AkashicBooks
Facebook: AkashicBooks
E-mail: info@akashicbooks.com
Website: www.akashicbooks.com

To the memory of Anthony Boucher.
O.H.

To the memory of my mother, and to the memory of Susan Tircuit (Cody's Books alumna), and to my teachers Lucille Clifton and Ntozake Shange, beacons of light, love, and inspiration.
J.T.

ALSO IN THE AKASHIC NOIR SERIES

MONTREAL NOIR (CANADA), edited by JOHN McFETRIDGE & JACQUES FILIPPI

MOSCOW NOIR (RUSSIA), edited by NATALIA SMIRNOVA & JULIA GOUMEN

MUMBAI NOIR (INDIA), edited by ALTAF TYREWALA

NAIROBI NOIR (KENYA), edited by PETER KIMANI

NEW HAVEN NOIR, edited by AMY BLOOM

NEW JERSEY NOIR, edited by JOYCE CAROL OATES

NEW ORLEANS NOIR, edited by JULIE SMITH

NEW ORLEANS NOIR: THE CLASSICS, edited by JULIE SMITH

OAKLAND NOIR, edited by JERRY THOMPSON & EDDIE MULLER

ORANGE COUNTY NOIR, edited by GARY PHILLIPS

PARIS NOIR (FRANCE), edited by AURÉLIEN MASSON

PHILADELPHIA NOIR, edited by CARLIN ROMANO

PHOENIX NOIR, edited by PATRICK MILLIKIN

PITTSBURGH NOIR, edited by KATHLEEN GEORGE

PORTLAND NOIR, edited by KEVIN SAMPSELL

PRAGUE NOIR (CZECH REPUBLIC), edited by PAVEL MANDYS

PRISON NOIR, edited by JOYCE CAROL OATES

PROVIDENCE NOIR, edited by ANN HOOD

QUEENS NOIR, edited by ROBERT KNIGHTLY

RICHMOND NOIR, edited by ANDREW BLOSSOM, BRIAN CASTLEBERRY & TOM DE HAVEN

RIO NOIR (BRAZIL), edited by TONY BELLOTTO

ROME NOIR (ITALY), edited by CHIARA STANGALINO & MAXIM JAKUBOWSKI

SAN DIEGO NOIR, edited by MARYELIZABETH HART

SAN FRANCISCO NOIR, edited by PETER MARAVELIS

SAN FRANCISCO NOIR 2: THE CLASSICS, edited by PETER MARAVELIS

SAN JUAN NOIR (PUERTO RICO), edited by MAYRA SANTOS-FEBRES

SANTA CRUZ NOIR, edited by SUSIE BRIGHT

SANTA FE NOIR, edited by ARIEL GORE

SÃO PAULO NOIR (BRAZIL), edited by TONY BELLOTTO

SEATTLE NOIR, edited by CURT COLBERT

SINGAPORE NOIR, edited by CHERYL LU-LIEN TAN

STATEN ISLAND NOIR, edited by PATRICIA SMITH

ST. LOUIS NOIR, edited by SCOTT PHILLIPS

STOCKHOLM NOIR (SWEDEN), edited by NATHAN LARSON & CARL-MICHAEL EDENBORG

ST. PETERSBURG NOIR (RUSSIA), edited by NATALIA SMIRNOVA & JULIA GOUMEN

SYDNEY NOIR (AUSTRALIA), edited by JOHN DALE

TEHRAN NOIR (IRAN), edited by SALAR ABDOH

TEL AVIV NOIR (ISRAEL), edited by ETGAR KERET & ASSAF GAVRON

TORONTO NOIR (CANADA), edited by JANINE ARMIN & NATHANIEL G. MOORE

TRINIDAD NOIR (TRINIDAD & TOBAGO), edited by LISA ALLEN-AGOSTINI & JEANNE MASON

TRINIDAD NOIR: THE CLASSICS (TRINIDAD & TOBAGO), edited by EARL LOVELACE & ROBERT ANTONI

TWIN CITIES NOIR, edited by JULIE SCHAPER & STEVEN HORWITZ

USA NOIR, edited by JOHNNY TEMPLE

VANCOUVER NOIR (CANADA), edited by SAM WIEBE

VENICE NOIR (ITALY), edited by MAXIM JAKUBOWSKI

WALL STREET NOIR, edited by PETER SPIEGELMAN

ZAGREB NOIR (CROATIA), edited by IVAN SRŠEN

FORTHCOMING

ACCRA NOIR (GHANA), edited by NANA-AMA DANQUAH

ADDIS ABABA NOIR (ETHIOPIA), edited by MAAZA MENGISTE

BELGRADE NOIR (SERBIA), edited by MILORAD IVANOVIC

JERUSALEM NOIR, edited by DROR MISHANI

MIAMI NOIR: THE CLASSICS, edited by LES STANDIFORD

PARIS NOIR: THE SUBURBS (FRANCE), edited by HERVÉ DELOUCHE

PALM SPRINGS NOIR, edited by BARBARA DeMARCO-BARRETT

TAMPA BAY NOIR, edited by COLETTE BANCROFT

123

GILMAN
DISTRICT

WEST
BERKELEY

WEST
BERKELEY
FLATS

BERKELEY
MARINA

SAN FRANCISCO BAY

580

YACHT HARBOR

KENSINGTON

BERKELEY

BERKELEY HILLS
INDIAN ROCK

TILDEN
REGIONAL
PARK

GOURMET GHETTO
NORTH BERKELEY

DOWNTOWN BERKELEY

SOUTHSIDE

BERKELEY PUBLIC
LIBRARY

HO CHI MINH PARK

CENTRAL BERKELEY

OCEAN VIEW

24

TABLE OF CONTENTS

PART III: COMPANY TOWN

INTRODUCTION
The Other Side of Piedmont

From the Top

This is not Oakland. This is a swing-shift sistah on the 51B moving from Rockridge, down College Avenue and Telegraph, to let Thursday night meet Friday afternoon / this is a song of ritual and tradition sung soft and hard by a downtown with two mouths / one that chews and one that swallows.

Is it pretentious to claim that a Bay Area college town can be a breeding ground for noir? For that certain kind of shadow and light, but mostly shadow? Where's the noir in that perfect view of the Golden Gate, cutting-edge lettuces served in a ghetto dubbed "gourmet," the parking lot with reserved spaces for Nobel Laureates?

This place is red wine and beer spilling over pepperoni cheese pizza and late-night final exams living on the edge of every new beginning. This is a bullet on a cloud dancing around the Berkeley Marina, or a week of wet kisses and PhD applications, love poems, and broken promises on the page / a slice of the pie for everyone running with the promise of chutney, chopsticks, toothpicks, and bottles of Tabasco dangling from preconceived notions of a city that wiggles itself between hot and spicy / get-down or takeout.

A town named after a British philosopher doesn't exactly evoke visions of Goodis or Highsmith. Grifters? Dames? Cops? In Berkeley? On the surface the alleys don't seem that dark, until we look a little closer. Possibly the most iconic visual image of Berkeley does involve cops. It's from a film with activist Mario Savio, atop a police car, declaring, "There's a time when the operation of the machine becomes so odious, makes you so sick at heart, that you can't take part!" Now *there's* a statement that sums up the spirit of noir.

Berkeley Noir asks, *If not here, where?* When pulling together this outstanding list of authors, we were constantly reminded of Berkeley's rich literary history, one that swerves through varying shades of noir. Those who helped pave the way for this collection include Anthony Boucher, Janet Dawson, Margaret Cuthbert, Ellen Gilchrist, Linda Grant, Jonathan Lethem, and Barry Gifford. There will always be a place in the heart of this city where even outcasts can feel at home. From legends like Philip K. Dick setting his stories here, or Chitra Banerjee Divakaruni working out marital bliss in her early novels, or Linnea A. Due tackling teenage alcoholism in the 1970s in *High and Outside*. The search through darkness for an authentic, eclectic voice is the most important ingredient in the rich stew that is Berkeley, California.

FROM THE BOTTOM

The fix is in, and the grifters, the cops, the profs, the students, and the unsheltered are aware of that, and play the game they choose (or don't choose). And what of the cops of the BPD, whose squad car once became a stage for Berkeley radicalism? Susan Dunlap gives us a police procedural, gourmet-ghetto style, that serves as a kind of equalizer: "'Citizens of Berkeley,' Shelby grumbled as the siren faded away, 'they bitch about everything. But a guy guns a man down and trots off and not a single concerned citizen bothers to follow him.'"

Yet the spirit of Berkeley, at least as perceived by most Berkeleyites, is in opposition to cops. Berkeley has been famous for its resistance mentality for at least fifty years. When the fix is in they shine some light on it, fight it, sometimes to the point of political correctness, but who cares?

When we began discovering the noir landscape, we went to the UC Berkeley campus, to University Avenue. We ventured into the hills, and of course Telegraph Avenue, for its wild and complicated dreamlike characteristics. There is a careful hand in the mix of dark tales in this volume that makes Berkeley's mystical water landscape the perfect crime accomplice. Jim Nisbet's nautical opus "Boy Toy," and Lucy Jane Bledsoe's "The Tangy Brine of Dark Night," play a wicked duet on the dreamy waters that embrace the Berkeley magic, and the dark, slow-burn, brown-gravy world of Kimn Neilson's "Still Life, Reviving" reminds us that even the stillness in shadows can destroy, distract.

The stories in this book skew left of center, even left of left. There's crime, as we witness in J.M. Curet's "Wifebeater Tank Top," there's corruption, there's the double cross, but always with some political context (well captured in Shanthi Sekaran's "Eat Your Pheasant, Drink Your Wine" and Thomas Burchfield's "Lucky Day"). The bottom is the bottom, even in the People's Republic, and it's as hardscrabble as Gary, Indiana, or Pittsburgh.

All that sunshine can be cruel if you're sleeping in the park, or trying to finesse a place for your kid to go to school (check out Aya de León's excellent story, "Frederick Douglass Elementary"), or dealing with an aging parent.

Noir is at its best when it comes up from the bottom, fighting that losing battle to do a little better. The faces in this book reach beyond careful politically correct glances and song.

This is a city of curtains and kisses / keys and six degrees of separation.

Poets and prophets, and farmer's-market physicists.

Fallen ideals on the back of sun-dried tomato peels and pizza slices / chasing CBD and Telegraph / University Avenue got you wondering what's in the back pocket of this *Berkeley Noir* song.

This is Berkeley!

Here, too, the fix is in. But, jeez, is that the sun shining through the fog across the bay? What a view!

Jerry Thompson & Owen Hill
Berkeley, California
February 2020

PART I

FROM THE PEOPLE'S REPUBLIC

HILL HOUSE

BY LEXI PANDELL

Berkeley Hills

I arrive at the hill house and pull out my phone to double-check the address. A droplet of sweat clings to the tip of my nose and I blow it off. It splashes on the screen, just missing the jagged crack across the front.

It's the right place.

Patrick Bloom's house is smaller than I'd expected, only two stories high. But when I peer through a gap in the massive wooden fence, I can tell that it's nice—one of those Berkeley homes with old bones, scaled all over in brown shingles. This whole street is stacked with unassuming multimillion-dollar houses.

I lock my bike to a *No Parking* sign and try to catch my breath. When I moved back to Berkeley from New York, everyone told me I should get a bike. Unfortunately for me, I'd forgotten why I never biked when I was growing up here. Worse than the shitty drivers are the hills, like the one up to this house. I had to get off my bike after nearly keeling over backward.

October has brought its unseasonal, and unfortunately named, Indian-summer heat. While my friends back east are bundling up for autumn, I'm wearing a tank top featuring the leering Cal mascot, Oski, and my dark hair is twirled in a bun, and I'm still pouring sweat. The wet strap of my duffel bag bites into my shoulder.

I unlatch the gate and walk through a garden to get to

the front door. Tomatoes on tangles of vines, plumes of herbs, beans racing along trellises like string lights, fireworks of green leaves belonging to carrots, kale, lettuce, beets. There's even a raised bed with corn—who the fuck grows corn at home?

Patrick Bloom, I guess.

I knock, willing my stomach to untie itself from its knot. After a moment, Patrick Bloom, the world's most renowned health writer, opens the door and looks out, not in an un-friendly way, just a little blank, until he sees my shirt and bag and realizes that I am the grad student there to house-sit.

"Mariana?"

I nod and he lets me in. It's the kind of house designed to feel like a home. I'd seen it featured in a magazine before. In addition to Patrick Bloom's writing, his wife designed book covers, a few of them famous. Their home has long been the subject of public interest.

Patrick Bloom shows me how to work the oven, where to find the bathroom, how to access the deck with a view of San Francisco. His famous mop of curly white hair is even bigger in person; a thin spot burrowed at the back of his head makes it look a little like a halo.

Patrick Bloom stands for something that intrigues me. Cleanliness. Health. Wholesomeness. The idea that your life can be better if you eat quinoa and listen to your body and walk more. Not that his work isn't based on science, just that the resulting advice is so simple and smart that you hate your-self for not thinking of it first. I devoured all of his books while I was living in New York, bartending and filing the odd music review for an alt-weekly. I applied to journalism school at Cal, where Patrick Bloom is a professor, with the assumption that I wouldn't get in. When I showed up for the new student tour, the admissions officer flashed a crocodile smile and told me that she thought my essay was excellent. I don't remember what I wrote, though I do know that I mentioned Patrick Bloom.

Patrick Bloom's assistant is a second-year student named Eloise. She's blond and so skinny that the bones of her knees show through her jeans. She snacks on baby carrots and hummus while she uses the school computers to plow through research for Patrick Bloom's upcoming book. She must use the printers ten times as much as any other student. She delivers his reading material in hard copy. Hulking scientific studies, long articles, entire e-books.

There are only a handful of teaching assistants in our program. Most of them, well, *teach*. But Eloise is entirely dedicated to Patrick Bloom. The university covers her tuition. That's how much he's worth to them.

Eloise was handpicked by the TA before her and someday she, too, will pass the torch. It's competitive—rumor has it that a recommendation from Patrick Bloom will snag you a job at any top magazine. Eloise was the one who suggested my house-sitting for Patrick Bloom when she was called away for her grandfather's funeral in Connecticut.

"Is that something you do a lot?" I asked. "House-sitting?"

"Yeah, but it's not weird. And his house is *amazing*. So it's, like, fun."

Patrick Bloom leads me upstairs. Photos of him and his wife posing with various celebrities, feminine touches in a throw pillow here or a watercolor painting there. We walk past his children's rooms. Nautical theme for the boy, with model ships lining his windowsill. The girl's is painted ballet-shoe pink.

It looks like a family of four still lives here, but his children are off at college and his wife died three years ago. I know this because he wrote an award-winning memoir about cooking for her as she was dying. She designed the book cover as her last major piece. I thought it was kind of ugly and maudlin, if I'm being honest, but the writing was some of his best.

We pass a room with a big wooden door. His study. The door is locked. He doesn't have to tell me that it's off-limits.

I think he's going to show me to a guest room, but instead he leads me to the master bedroom.

"This is where you'll stay."

I drop my duffel. The walls are painted brown and there are wide windows with no blinds. It's like the mouth of a cave.

"A little unconventional, I know," he says. "The design of the room is based on scientific research on the optimal sleeping environment. I'm writing about it in my next book."

He doesn't seem to think it's odd that I just smile and nod at everything he says. I'm a terrible journalism student—I don't ask nearly enough questions.

Downstairs, he drums the refrigerator with his fingers and tells me to eat anything I like, he doesn't mind. He shows me back out to the garden and tells me to harvest.

"Whatever you don't pick will go bad." He considers a zucchini, small but plump. He yanks it from the vine. "It will rot. Especially in this heat . . ."

A car pulls up out front and honks lightly. Patrick Bloom dashes inside for his luggage. He can't possibly be leaving already, I barely know anything about his home. But, indeed, he is. He shakes my hand and thanks me. His skin is still sticky from the zucchini.

"If anything comes up, my number is on the fridge," he tells me.

And then he is gone.

I go inside. The zucchini remains on the table where he left it. I pick it up and sniff. It smells green. I hate zucchini. I put it down and retrace my steps from the tour, exploring for a second time at my own pace. I realize I'm holding my breath. No one is here monitoring me. I don't know why I'm afraid.

I go to the bathroom and see a flash of highlighter-bright urine in the bowl. Jesus. I flush the toilet before sitting down. A rack of magazines flank the toilet. Food, lifestyle, travel. Do all rich people keep their magazines in the bathroom? Has he ever run out of toilet paper and had to rip off a page to use on his ass?

It's nearly dinnertime and the sun streaming through the windows turns orange. I only brought two things to eat—a jar of peanut butter and a box of granola bars. I had planned to bike to the grocery store. I'm grateful I can eat his food. Fuck dealing with that hill again. Plus, how many people can say they've eaten something from Patrick Bloom's garden?

I text a photo of it to my brother Jack. We are not related by blood, but we grew up together and I'm an only child, so he's the closest thing to a sibling I have.

Got any tips about picking this stuff? I write.

I know zilch about gardening, but Jack does, in a way.

When Jack was fifteen and I was eleven, my mom found pressed pills in his backpack. He told me they weren't for him, just something he was selling. I don't know what explanation he gave my mom, but it wasn't good enough. She went ballistic. The next day, we woke up and Jack was gone.

Two weeks later, a farm worker visiting family in Oakland saw the poster with Jack's face and called us with a tip. We drove an hour and a half to Gilroy, where we found Jack kneeling in a strawberry field. He had grown tan enough that, with his bandanna and hoodie, he fit in with the dozens of scrawny Mexican guys out there. The biggest difference was that, while they wore steel-toed work boots, he had on his scuffed-up Doc Martens.

The car ride back to Berkeley started out quiet. Even from the backseat, I could see that his hands were dirty and blistered.

"You stink," my mom said finally. It was true. A cloud of stench, sweet and earthy.

"If you're not going to let me make money my way," Jack said, "I'll make it another way."

"I don't give a fuck about what you do on the street, you're not my kid. But don't bring that shit into my home. I find anything else and you're out."

After that, Jack took odd jobs doing yard work for frat houses and rich professors near campus, though I'm fairly certain he kept dealing on the side.

Now in Patrick Bloom's garden with the late-day sun beating on my bare shoulders, I stare at my phone. I know Jack isn't going to respond to my text, but I wait for a few minutes anyway.

I guess I'll have to do it myself.

I pull a cucumber off the vine, pluck some late-season tomatoes, and rip a head of lettuce from the ground.

In the kitchen, I find some knives. Japanese. Very sharp. I cut open the cucumber to discover that it's disgusting. Pulpy and warm. The lettuce is okay, though I find dead winged insects lining the crotch of the leaves. I wash it five times. I slice into the tomatoes but miscalculate and catch the end of my finger. It spurts. Shit. I wrap it in a paper towel and then wipe the little droplets of blood from the cutting board.

It's not until I'm eating the salad that I taste the metallic tang of the blood I missed. The cutting board I used is made of a porous wood and, by the time I rinse it after dinner, it's stained.

It seems atmospheric to read Patrick Bloom's books at his house during my first night there, and he has copies on the bookshelf with uncracked spines. I take a couple to the living room and flip to my favorite sections. A preface about foraging for mushrooms in the wilds of Humboldt County. A chapter about our genetic similarities to flies. A passage that compares Gatorade with the sugar water left out for hummingbirds.

Normally, I read his books and feel excited about the possibility of language and how bizarre the world is. Tonight, it just exhausts me.

It's stuffy in here. It feels like my insides are stewing. I fight to keep my eyes open. The words swim on the page. I need to sleep.

I go upstairs and lie down on Patrick Bloom's bed, but I can't drift off. This room gives me the creeps. It's the kind of room where someone would go to die, dark and primitive.

Every time I roll over, I catch my reflection in the shade-less windows and my heart jumps, certain that I'm seeing a ghost. I almost pass out, but the howl of a distant Amtrak jolts me awake.

It is shockingly, terribly hot. I jump out of bed and rattle the windows, but there's no way to open them. There are no fans, either. I swing the door open, praying for circulation.

I pluck my iPhone off the bedside table. No response from Jack. Not that I've gotten one from him in months, but still. Nighttime is Jack's time. My mom always hounded him about staying up until three, four, five in the morning and then sleeping all day long.

If he'll ever respond, it's now.

My mom met Jack's dad, Dez, when I was four and she was a freshman at Cal. She had recently returned to school after my birth derailed her life; Dez managed a Top Dog. When Dez replaced my spot in my mother's bed, I moved to a cot in the living room. Jack slept on the couch. We weren't supposed to have more than two people in the apartment, but nobody ratted on us. Our neighbors had all kinds of things they weren't supposed to. Pets, drugs, massage businesses, subletters.

Jack was twice my age and a mystery to me even then. He had a sullen, boyish beauty. At night, if I turned over toward the couch and opened my eyes, I'd usually find him awake and staring back. I began to think of Jack as nocturnal; something other than human.

Just before finals week of her junior year, a crushed-lilac bruise appeared around my mother's eye. She made Dez pack his bags while she was off in some lecture hall filling in the bubbles on a Scantron. She ended up getting an A.

After that, I moved back into the bedroom with her. Jack stayed on our couch and Dez sent money every month. What kind of guy dumps his kid with an ex like that? A guy like Dez. He wasn't a junkie or a criminal, just the world's biggest asshole. Still, in turn, my mom cared for Jack. In turn, Jack cared for me.

When a girl pushed me down on the playground, he followed her after school, shoved her against the wall, and said that if she ever touched his little sister again he'd break her arm. He walked between me and the homeless folks we passed on the street; when they hassled us, he covered my ears and cussed them out. He always shared his candy, panicked if I ate it too quickly, watched me chew as if he were afraid I might choke. He stole pretty things for me—origami paper, hot-pink erasers, stickers.

My mother ignored the ways Jack grew stranger and darker. As a teenager, he came home with a lip pierced in the school bathroom with a safety pin and tiny, squiggly shapes pricked into his skin by a friend's shaky hand using a sewing needle dipped in pen ink. But that was the Bush era, a time for Bay

Area teens to go to punk shows and rage against The Man. Besides, I may have called Jack my brother, but my mom never called him her son. Her responsibility to him, as she saw it, was to make sure he survived to adulthood, no more and no less.

I hadn't heard anything from Jack for more than a decade when I got a call from my mom in March.

Jack had gotten in touch to tell her he was back in Berkeley. He gave her a phone number, which she read to me.

"I have nothing to say to him," I snapped. But I still remembered the number long after I hung up. Memory works in funny ways.

When the acceptance letter came for journalism school, I said yes, even though I'd never wanted to move back to Berkeley and even though it felt too much like following in my mother's footsteps. This was different. It was grad school. Patrick Bloom was an instructor there. And I had applied before I knew Jack was back.

I hadn't made my decision for him.

But I had called him the first week of classes.

"Jack?" I said after he picked up. When the line went dead, I was certain that it was him.

I've been texting him since, but I haven't heard a thing.

I roll over to face the ceiling. I angle my phone toward my face and it lights up. Spots flood my vision. No wonder I can't sleep when this shit is so bright.

The house I'm watching is cool, you should swing by, I type. And then I add the address. Not that he'd ever come. Not that I'm certain I'd want him to, anyway.

I leave my iPhone faceup, but it does not illuminate with a message that night. I don't fall asleep until sunrise.

I wake in the afternoon. In the master bath, I examine the

deodorant-crusted stains ringing the pits of my shirt. I peel it off, put it in a pile for the laundry. After my shower, I can't find the bath towels, so I wipe Patrick Bloom's skinny hand towel and tiny square of a face towel all over my body. I feel like a cat rubbing itself on things to leave its mark.

I bring my laptop to the patio. I'm supposed to take notes on an episode of a podcast for my radio class. My whole body hurts from the lack of sleep and, though the podcast is supposed to be some great feat of audio editing, it can't hold my attention. My head keeps drooping.

When my laptop dies, I realize I forgot to bring a charger. Of course.

Biking all the way home for a stupid charger sounds awful. I could go upstairs to Patrick Bloom's study. He might have a charger there. But I already bled all over his cutting board; I don't need to make things worse by breaking into his study. I'd inevitably fuck something up. Accidentally set off an alarm or knock over some priceless heirloom—I don't know what kind of delicate, precious things someone like Patrick Bloom would have in there.

Forget the computer, I'm only here for two more days. I'll consider it a digital detox.

I want to be having more fun in Patrick Bloom's home than I am. I get the joint I brought and take it outside to smoke on the deck. I hope his neighbors don't complain about the smell. No one cares about pot in Berkeley, but I don't know if the rules are different in the hills. These are the hippies who sold out, not the hippies who became crackheads and now line the streets just a few miles away.

I take a long rip.

I was thirteen when I first smoked. We lived in a two-bedroom apartment by then—my mother and I still shared a room, which we split down the middle with a folding wooden divider. Jack had his own room, barely bigger than a closet. It was so small that when he and I sat on the carpet beside his bed, leaning against the comforter that smelled like Old Spice and boy body, the toes of my checkered Vans touched the door.

"I want you to smoke with me," he said. I snorted like it was a joke, but he looked me square in the eyes. "I don't want you doing it for the first time with some randos."

I watched how the light flickered off his face as he took the first hit. I tried to match his stoicism, the length of his inhale, the way his finger flickered over the carb. My throat screamed, but I didn't dare cough.

When the bowl was cashed, Jack put a mixed CD in his Discman and leaned close to share his headphones. His blood-shot eyes half-closed. He tongued his lip piercing, wheeling that little metal hoop around and around. I wanted to be closer to him. I wanted, I thought with a flash that scared me, to lick the curve of skin just above the chain he wore around his neck.

A song came on and Jack pulled the jewel case from under his bed. The track names were handwritten in Sharpie. The one we were listening to was called "Sister Jack."

"It's you," he said with a stoner's laugh. He patted my knee and the inside of my leg went electric.

I grip the banister of Patrick Bloom's patio until the worn wood starts to splinter. I blow a cloud of smoke and imagine it conjuring Jack. Why do I still think of him as part of my life? He's nothing more than a shadow.

The weed has hit me and I'm starving. I go back to the garden and snap off a head of corn. A grub pokes out from the folds of husk. I pluck it out and stomp it underfoot. Inside, I sauté the corn in a thick pat of butter.

I've smoked enough to tranquilize a horse, but the second my head touches Patrick Bloom's pillow, I find that, once again, I cannot sleep.

If I move around, maybe my exhaustion will catch up with me.

I put on my sneakers and leave the house for a walk through the neighborhood. My heart races faster as I make my way up and down the lurching hills. The dark-windowed houses loom overhead and the quiet is punctuated by bursts of sound. A dog barking as I pass, a motorcycle backfiring somewhere high on the twisted roads. I wonder what I'd look like to someone watching from inside one of these beautiful houses. A hoodlum from the flatlands, no doubt.

I turn onto a road where the sidewalk narrows to a sliver. I hear an engine rumble and then a car careens around a blind curve, flying toward me so quickly that I think I'm going to die. The car jerks to swerve around me, the side-view mirror close enough that I could reach out and touch it. I forget to breathe until the streak of rear lights disappears into the night.

It's my last day. I need to keep it together.

I try working on a hard-copy editing test in the garden under the slanted shade of the house, but my brain is out to sea. Flies dive-bomb the caverns of my ears. I swat them away and one of them tumbles into the mug of expensive coffee I made in Patrick Bloom's kitchen. I could fish it out but, instead, I watch it struggle at the surface until its last twitch.

I need to go inside, it's too hot. Might as well grab something to eat first.

I think of Eloise as I go to the carrot bed and try gently tugging on one of the tops. The ground looks soft, but the carrot doesn't budge. I reach my hand into the dirt and feel around for something firm. When I do, I grab it. As I pull my hand up, the soil spews worms with translucent skin. I can see the blackness of their guts.

I yank my hand away. It's crawling with bugs. I drop the carrot, leap back, and beat the insects from my arm. Ants are trapped in the beads of my sweat, their little legs flailing. One fat-bodied ant digs its mouth into the not-yet-healed cut on my index finger, its mandible pinching into my raw flesh so firmly that its whole body stands on end. I squash it with my thumb.

The carrot I picked is short and fat. It looks too pale. I've lost my appetite for it anyhow. I shove it back in the ground, even though I'm sure I've killed it.

I go inside and shower in water so hot that I leave more sweaty than clean.

I'm walking upstairs when I see the study. I think of finding a charger. Using my laptop would help pass the time. I could get work done. Or just bum around on Facebook.

The study is locked, though that doesn't necessarily mean I can't get in.

I shouldn't go in.

I want to, though. I really, really want to. It is, in fact, the only thing that I want to do. My laptop is part of it but, to be honest, I mostly want to know what it's like in there.

Isn't that a perk of house-sitting? Peeking into someone's life?

I run my hands over the smooth wood and examine the lock. Easy. I pull a bobby pin from my hair and wedge it into the keyhole. A trick Jack showed me when we were kids. I wriggle it around until I feel a click, a give, and the lock comes undone.

Sun streams through the windows, illuminating two tall file cabinets. A towering desktop computer sits alongside a bundle of extra laptop chargers. I set my computer on the desk and plug it in.

It'll take awhile to reboot. I figure it's okay to look around in the meantime.

Stacks of books border his desk, which is littered with pens. I come upon a pile of papers. Printouts from Eloise. There's a sticky note on top. *Hope this helps*, it reads. It's meant for Patrick Bloom but it feels like it's for me—if there's a chance I'll become this guy's assistant next year, I should see what I'd actually have to do.

It looks like original writing, not articles or studies. Printed in Times New Roman, twelve-point font with a smattering of grammatical errors.

Something like an essay.

It's . . . an assignment? A class assignment?

It's a chapter.

That can't be right. Patrick Bloom would never have a *grad student* write something for him. I must be mistaken. I open a file cabinet. There are entire drawers dedicated to different books. First, *Man Eat Food*. A bunch of papers have headers that say, *Winnie Ford*. I pull out my phone and look her up on LinkedIn. Berkeley Graduate School of Journalism, class of 2002. Currently a senior editor for the lifestyle magazine that did the shoot of Patrick Bloom's home.

I look through *Microgreen*.

Gardening in Eden.

Truth, Lies, and Celery.

WalkFit.

All of them have traces of the assistants who ghostwrote them. Cover pages with their names. Hand-scrawled marginalia. Last-minute swipes of Wite-Out.

I brace myself and then look through the one for *Mother,*

Wife, Mine, Gone. It takes me an hour of searching through every paper in that pile, but I find it. My favorite line rendered in a student's handwriting: *She took her last breath, jagged and true. She was there. And then she was gone.*

He even had them write the book about his dead wife.

I manage to put the papers back in the files, the files in the cabinet, and I lock the door from the inside on my way out.

I need to go to sleep. Now. That is the only way I'll get through my last evening in this house. I head downstairs to hunt for something that will seriously fuck me up. I haul myself onto the kitchen counter and search through the highest shelf to find what I'm looking for. A bottle of gin. I take it down, fill a cup, and top off the bottle with tap water.

I plunk a handful of ice cubes into my glass and drink it like it's medicine. I'm out of weed, but this guy has to have *something* fun. I rifle through the bathroom. Ibuprofen, acid reflux meds, a box of Tums. Aha, there it is. A prescription bottle with the label torn off. The pills inside are white and round. They look like Ativan, though I'm not totally sure. Fuck it, let's find out. I down two with a gulp of gin.

I put on sweatpants, take off my bra, lie down in Patrick Bloom's bed, and wait for this shit to kick in. I don't even care that my sweat is soaking into his beautiful, expensive comforter.

My body starts to feel heavy, yet floaty. This is good. I release a big sigh. My phone is resting on the bed next to me. I pick it up. My fingers tingle as I dial Jack. It goes to a generic voice mail. I call once more, twice, three times.

I laugh. Jack is not going to pick up. He's never going to pick up.

I remember being sixteen. Lying on my bed, my presence cloaked by the wooden divider in the room, reading a book for class. I knew from the heavy footsteps that Jack had come home. When he came in and slid my mom's drawers open, I peered around the screen to see what he was doing.

Jack was adept at plowing through my mom's things. I knew that she hid cash in her sock drawer because I'd gone looking once and pocketed twenty bucks. But Jack wasn't looking *for* something, he was looking to *hide* something. Something wrapped in a deconstructed brown grocery bag, bound in tape, and tucked under his arm.

"What are you doing?" I asked. Jack jumped. I'd never startled him before.

"Mari, if you don't tell anyone, we can pretend you didn't see anything."

I didn't need to know what was in that package to know that my mom would kick him out if she found it. The idea of that happening was more than I could bear.

I couldn't tell Jack no. Yet he saw my hesitation and knew his secret wasn't safe. His face warped with disgust. He stormed out, shoved the package into his backpack, and left. He didn't come home until the next day.

Jack gave me the silent treatment after that and lived with us for only a few more weeks before disappearing again. That time we didn't find him, not in a strawberry field, not anywhere.

Once in a while, I'd plug his name into Google, but it was like he had never existed at all.

Why did he give my mom his number if he didn't plan on picking up his stupid phone?

Fucker.

I keep calling.

Finally, the ringtone starts ending sooner. He's actively silencing my calls. He's seeing them come through. Jack is out there.

Or maybe his phone is just blocking me.

My vision gets fuzzy.

I blink, slowly. My eyes close. Sleep cradles me.

Is someone knocking on the front door? I prop myself up. My drool has soaked Patrick Bloom's pillow. I look at my phone. It's three a.m.; I've been unconscious for nine hours. The drugs are wearing thin, but I'm still stoned.

I hear two more loud pounds and the chime of the doorbell.

I stumble downstairs and see the silhouette of a man in the front window. Tall, lanky. I know exactly who it is.

I open the door. Jack is wearing a black T-shirt and has a short, tidy beard. He looks older than his thirty-two years. Time and sun have etched lines into his skin. I want to run to him, but he's practically a stranger. I remember that I'm not wearing a bra and cross my arms over my chest.

"Mari, I need your help," he says. Panic thrums behind his eyes. He turns to walk to the street and I follow him, a little sister's instinct. My head is drowning in Ativan and my tongue feels like it's filled with wet sand.

"How'd you find me?" I manage to slur.

"You texted me the address."

"Oh." Right. Of course.

"No one can track it," he says. "You have my burner number."

Why does my brother have a burner phone? And why is that the number I have for him?

He takes me to his car, opens the door, and gestures for me to look in the backseat. There's a thick plastic bag. It's misshapen, but I suspect from its size and heft what it is. Shock rushes through my system, but I'm not as terrified as I know I should be. Thank god I'm on drugs.

"Who was it?"

"It's not part of the job to know that." He emphasizes the word *job* as if this is like any other job he's had. Like pulling beer cans out of bushes on Frat Row or clearing out an anthropology professor's drainpipe or picking strawberries in Gilroy or dealing drugs.

"Where did you . . . ?" I don't have to finish the sentence. *Chop up the body.*

"It doesn't matter."

I wish I hadn't seen it. That he'd dumped the body in the bay or kept driving past Patrick Bloom's house to Tilden and found somewhere to leave it among the rotting eucalyptus trees. But the fact is that I'm standing there looking at it and now I cannot unsee it. I reach in and touch the bag. I feel a jumble of body parts. The knob of an elbow. Stiff flesh, like an unripe tomato.

"The owner's coming back tomorrow," I say.

"He won't know."

It is late, so late that all the lights in all of the houses on the street are off. No one sees us as we pull the bag from the car and carry it to the side plot where nothing grows but weeds. After that, it is Jack's work to bury the body, not mine. He hands me a shopping bag containing khaki shorts, sneakers, boxers, and a short-sleeved plaid button-up. I wince when I feel where the bloodstained patches of fabric have gone cold, but I try not to think about it. I nod off as I wash the man's clothes in the laundry machine. When I'm done, I go into the basement and stuff them in the bottom of a box labeled, *Goodwill.*

For the rest of the night my consciousness ebbs and flows. Eventually I am in bed, though I do not know how I got upstairs. The last thing I remember is Jack whispering that he hadn't planned this. His voice shimmers like the lights of the city twinkling in the distance. He tells me that, sometimes, the impulsive plan is the best plan, the hardest one to track. And when I sent him the image of the garden, and when I said that I was alone house-sitting, and when I kept calling and calling, well, it seemed a little like fate.

I should be worried, but I'm not. We are far away, Jack and I. Above the world in our cave. Everything below us is a blanket of stars. And when I sleep, I dream of falling headlong into Jack's wide-open eyes.

I wake to the sound of the front door opening.

I think I imagined all of this. Then I feel a weight in the bed next to me. Bile lurches at the back of my throat.

Jack stretches his arms overhead, yawning. His white teeth glisten. At some point he shaved, and now I can see the little scar where his lip piercing used to be. He's not wearing a shirt. His body is a tight braid of muscle and there's a tattoo etched onto his chest that I've never seen—an eagle, screaming, its talons outstretched, like it's about to snatch up his nipple. It's not something I would have ever pictured on Jack's skin, but then again, I don't really know Jack anymore, do I?

When his eyes find mine, I give him a look to ask, *Is it done?* and he nods. I slide out of bed and go downstairs.

In the kitchen, Patrick Bloom straightens up from where he was crouched over the zucchini that remained on the table, wilting.

"Sorry, I overslept," I say.

Patrick Bloom's eyes land on something behind me. Jack has followed me. Patrick Bloom gives Jack a smirk, like he is pleased for him. He assumes that we fucked.

"I'm Phil," Jack says, reaching out for a shake. Dread sinks in, heavy as a stone. I don't know if he's lying to save himself or to create a convincing story, but if the body is discovered, I will be the only identifiable person.

Patrick Bloom is the kind of guy who takes a hand that's offered to him. He tells us he has to hop in the shower. He has a conference in downtown Berkeley that afternoon.

Jack curls a finger around the hair that falls between my shoulder blades. It's the touch of someone playing at lover; I have to force myself not to flinch.

I wait for Patrick Bloom to finish talking before I rush to collect my things. When I go to wash my dishes, Patrick Bloom tells me not to bother. The housekeeper will be by later today.

He hands me two crisp hundred-dollar bills and thanks me. I sling my duffel bag over my shoulder, unlock my bike, walk Jack to the car he parked down the street. We do not say anything. He just gives me a half hug, gets in his car, and then he's gone.

It's much easier to bike home now that I'm heading downhill.

Months pass and I keep expecting something to happen. For Patrick Bloom to tell me that he found something in the dirt, worms coiled among bones. For the cops to bang down my door. For my life to be destroyed. But nothing does. Jack disappears again. For good, I think. I try calling, but his line has been disconnected. Eloise must have heard about my supposed boyfriend showing up at Patrick Bloom's house, because she picks another student to be her successor and every time she sees me on campus, she glares. I finish my first year of grad school. I return to New York City over the summer for an internship. I don't come back.

THE TANGY BRINE OF DARK NIGHT

BY LUCY JANE BLEDSOE

Berkeley Marina

Kaylie's grandma weighed only ninety pounds by now, and so carrying her out to the car wasn't too difficult. She cradled the old woman, one arm under her knees and the other under her shoulders, and gently placed her, lying down, along the bench of the backseat. She saw that she'd left her grandma's sneakers untied, so she made secure knots in the laces and then straightened the purple windbreaker, which had bunched up around her bony hips. Kaylie gently shut the door.

Would the trunk be better? Just the thought sent a prickling uneasiness down the backs of Kaylie's arms. She would not put her grandma in the trunk. Period. Besides, she'd need to put the kayak in there. She pointed the remote at the garage door, afraid that it wouldn't open—her grandma hadn't taken the car out in months—but it did. The old white Pontiac started too, and Kaylie backed into the street, carefully straightened the wheels, and put the automatic transmission in park.

This whole plan was fucking crazy. So much so that, if she got caught, she could probably plead insanity. Which was worse, the psych ward or prison? She tried to think of a way out of the course she'd started down, but none came to mind, and so she quietly exited the car and walked over to her neighbor's side yard where they left the kayak, which hadn't been used in so long that lichen crusted its hull. She'd return it before they even realized it was gone. Luckily it was a short boat, with an open deck, none of those scary little hatches to get stuck inside, but it was heavy. Kaylie ended up having to drag it to the car, the pavement grating the plastic, as loud as a cement mixer. If any neighbors looked out their windows, who knew what they'd surmise. Thankfully the Pontiac's trunk was the size of a small room, and she managed to stuff about half of the kayak in, bow first. She put a hand on the stern and pressed down. It didn't wiggle. Not much. It was only a mile or two to the pier—and downhill. Gravity ought to keep the kayak in place.

Kaylie jumped into the driver's seat and began the short journey. As she turned left on San Pablo Avenue, panic fluttered in her chest. The stern end of the kayak angled out of the trunk like an erection. She should have attached a red flag. She should have secured a seat belt around Grandma.

Never mind. She was almost there, and no place calmed her frayed nerves more than the Berkeley Pier, the way that long wooden structure stretched far out into the bay, a lovely straight line conveying people into the world of fish and salt water and sky. Grandma and she had spent their happiest hours sitting in their short chairs, sipping iced tea, Grandma smoking Chesterfields, hands cradling the grips of their fishing rods, gazing at the most profound intersection on earth, the one between sky and sea. They rarely talked while fishing, not to each other, anyway. They didn't have to. Water, fish, air, time. What else did a person need?

Kaylie had almost relaxed, at least she'd regained that gathering of resolve right behind her breastbone, the knowledge of doing right, when that damn Jimi Hendrix guitar riff vibrated in her pocket. Her sister Savannah had been calling repeatedly all day, at first once an hour, and recently about every twenty minutes, as if by calling multiple times today she could make up for the weeks and months she hadn't called. When they *had* talked, the times when Kaylie thought Savannah would want to know about developments in their grandma's condition, Savannah liked to cite her three children, making it crystal clear that Kaylie's childlessness put her in a complete fog of ignorance about what real life entailed. "Three children," Savannah would practically shout, as if parenthood was on par with being the CEO of a prison. She'd also note her "handful" husband. Or her "high-maintenance" husband, if she was irritated with him. Or her "demanding" husband, if she was outright angry with the man, which she often was. And yet all of these adjectives were spoken with pride, emphasizing the heft of her family responsibility load, how full her life was with this man—all to communicate that helping with Grandma was inconsequential compared to what she had on her plate. A man. A family.

Kaylie had tried to keep her resentment, her anger, in check: she too might have had someone "on her plate," had she not spent the last few years caring for Grandma. *Don't mind that ragged cough in the next room, that's just my grandma dying of emphysema.* Very romantic.

Kaylie let the repetitive Jimi Hendrix phrase play out and then tried to return to her memories of hot summer nights, much like this one, on the pier with Grandma. But a siren, just a few streets away, pierced her thoughts. Even the sound of the Pontiac's big rubber tires peeling along the still-sizzling pavement unnerved her. Noises tonight were too loud, as if the god she didn't believe in had turned up the volume. Kaylie twisted on the radio and almost laughed at the sound of

Frank Sinatra's voice. Her grandma's favorite. But of course Savannah wouldn't allow a moment of respite—oh no, the woman could be fucking telepathic when it came to moments of joy that needed to be destroyed. Jimi Hendrix began playing his bit, yet again, and Kaylie couldn't help it, she pulled her phone out of her pocket and looked, hoping it might be someone benign, like the woman she'd met at a conference in Dallas a couple of weeks ago, but no, of course it was Savannah. Again. She should have turned off her ringer, but somehow her sister's angsty presence was almost a comfort. At least it was familiar. And the only family she had left. She tapped *Ignore* and kept driving.

Stopping at the intersection of University and San Pablo, Kaylie put her head out the window and breathed deeply, hoping for a hint of that fishy rotten-wood smell of the pier. Of course she was still a half mile away, but knowing that it was just there, in front of her, another couple of minutes, relieved her. She knew she was doing not just the right thing, but the exact perfect thing. Savannah could go to hell.

A pulsing red light swarmed into the Pontiac. Kaylie was riding the crest of her confidence, and she felt sorry for the poor sop getting pulled over. She strained her eyes toward the dark horizon, toward the bay, pretended she could maybe see, if she looked hard enough, the Golden Gate. That put her in mind of the future, *her* future, and the possibility that, at long last, she'd be free to pursue a life. A real life. Maybe she'd take a trip to Dallas. She and that woman had had a lovely one-night stand, and it'd felt authentic, not like a quickie, more like a glint of possibility. Kaylie had told Grandma all about it when she got home and Grandma had said, yanking off the tubes running to her oxygen tank so she could speak as forcefully as she wanted to speak, "For fuck's sake, get on a goddamn plane for Dallas. I got a few months at best. Pull my damn plug and go get that woman."

Kaylie had laughed and lied, saying, "Nah. She wasn't my type. Besides, I'm not going anywhere."

"You can sell my house when I'm gone. That'll be a nice grubstake for you."

"I'll retire," Kaylie said, lying again. Her grandma's termite-infested house needed a new roof, a few coats of paint, and probably a new foundation. She wouldn't be leaving her job or chasing some woman in Dallas, at least not for a couple of decades.

The pulsing red light, as viscous and deeply colored as cough syrup, kept flooding the interior of the Pontiac. Of course Kaylie was that poor sop getting pulled over.

Breathe, she counseled herself. *Just breathe through this.* Make sure the cop doesn't try to wake up Grandma, that was key. For all Kaylie knew, the Pontiac's registration hadn't been renewed in years. She drove through the intersection, hands at two o'clock and ten o'clock on the steering wheel, and carefully pulled into the Blick Art Materials parking lot. The patrol car followed. The wait, both of them in their cars, felt interminable. Kaylie carefully took her driver's license out of her wallet, and actually found a paid, up-to-date registration in the glove compartment. The uniform finally approached, coming from the rear with a hand on the grip of her gun. Kaylie thanked all the deities for the pale shade of her skin, her fucking whiteness, an accident of fate that would increase her chances of finessing her way through the encounter.

The cop hefted a huge flashlight to shoulder height, as if it were a spiked javelin. She blinded Kaylie by shining it right in her face. Kaylie fumbled her license and registration out the car window as fast as she could. She might have white skin, but other variables in this situation—the contents of the backseat, the kayak in the trunk, and the ancient Pontiac itself—were not going to be helpful. As the cop turned the flashlight's beam on the documents, Kaylie tried to memorize the information on her badge. Officer Marta Ramirez was pretty, even with her hair pulled back in a tight bun, and wore no makeup—a hopeful sign—and carried a nice solid build. She might have been family, but Kaylie knew flirting would not be a good idea in this situation. Still, she might be able to signal sisterhood. *Uh, did you go to Pride this year?* Or, *How does your wife like your uniform?*

Of course that could backfire if she was in fact straight. Or even if she wasn't. Kaylie kept her mouth shut.

Marta (and why not be on a first-name basis in the privacy of Kaylie's own mind?) shined her light into the backseat. "Who's this?"

"That's my grandma."

"Why is she—"

"She's ninety-three. Full-on Alzheimer's. Sleeping is so difficult for her. You've heard of sundown syndrome?"

The cop's whole body loosened, slumped a little. Her eyes softened. "Oh, yeah. My grandma too."

"Really? I'm sorry to hear that. Anyway, Grandma's like a baby who can only fall asleep in a moving car. So I take her out at night sometimes, just drive her around so she can sleep." Kaylie was pleased with her quick thinking, and as she spoke, she tried to come up with as good of an explanation for the kayak.

"You should put the seat belt on her."

"I know! I usually do. I was just realizing that when you pulled me over."

"I pulled you over because the kayak is improperly secured." The cop shot the beam of her massive flashlight at the erect kayak stern. "That's a real hazard. It doesn't look like you've tied it at all. If it slides out, someone could get killed."

"God, I'm sorry. Stupid of me. Yeah, I borrowed the kayak from a friend this past weekend. I figured if I was going to drive Grandma around tonight, I might as well use the opportunity to return the kayak. I mean, she won't wake up when I get to my friend's house. I just have to slide the kayak out and drag it to her side yard."

Just shut the fuck up. Less is more, idiot. Stop talking.

The cop paused for far too long. Kaylie could see all the questions flashing through her mind. The woman took a deep breath of assessment.

"I'm sorry," Kaylie repeated, with lots of feeling.

Officer Marta Ramirez (Kaylie returned, in her mind, to the more respectful full title and name) began a slow circumnavigation of the Pontiac, using her flashlight to examine all four tires, and even look under the carriage. She shined her light into the passenger-side back window and gazed at Kaylie's grandma for a long time. A very long time. Long enough for Kaylie to wonder if prison was really like *Orange Is the New Black*, long enough for her to consider the possibility that behind bars she might actually, at long last, find a girlfriend. She wouldn't have to worry about fixing up or selling the house. She wouldn't have to lift anyone in and out of a bathtub, clean sheets soaked with piss or streaked with shit, listen to the painful sounds of someone she loved trying to breathe. That part was all over now—it was as if she realized this for the first time, just now as the cop stared at her grandma in the backseat—whether she went to prison or not.

When Officer Ramirez circled back to the driver's window, she pressed her lips together and made eye contact. "Okay. I'm not going to write you a ticket."

Wait. Kaylie had almost begun looking forward to prison. To not having a single job other than surviving. If she'd been given another few moments, she might have started fantasizing about prison sex. Maybe instead she should start fantasizing policewoman sex, gratitude sex.

"I really, really, really appreciate that," Kaylie said. "Thank you."

"Get Grandma home. And get a rack for that kayak."

"I will! Tomorrow. I mean, I'll get Grandma home right now, and a rack for the kayak tomorrow. I mean, for next time I borrow it."

Now that their official interaction was over, could Kaylie ask Marta Ramirez for her phone number? She imagined cracking that joke, if it was one, for Grandma, and Grandma's loud honking laugh. *Do it!* the ghost of Grandma shouted. *Do it!*

"Hey," Kaylie said as the cop started walking away. "I mean, I don't know if you're married or not. But I wondered if maybe some time you'd like—"

The woman spun around on the soles of her shiny black practical tie-up shoes. "Really?" she responded. "I just let you off. I mean, *I just let you off*, and—"

"And I said thank you. Good night." Kaylie rolled up her window and started the engine, the car lurched forward, and she almost hit a parked car as she tried to turn the huge tank around. Marta Ramirez was busy getting into her own vehicle and didn't bother to look up again.

Five minutes later, Kaylie parked the car in one of the spots along the Berkeley waterfront, on the east side of the pier. She rolled down her window and sat listening to the wavelets lapping against the giant stones which formed the barrier between the bay and the parking spaces. It was high tide, and the water splashed within feet of her car. At last she could fill her nostrils with the salty wet smell of the bay.

Twisting around in her seat, she couldn't see much of Grandma in the dark, but Kaylie knew exactly what she looked like: the sparse pale smoke hair, the tissuey skin with deep laugh lines, her thin frail limbs, knobby with arthritis.

"We're here, Grandma," she whispered, and a wave of grief rolled through her.

Only to be interrupted by Jimi Hendrix.

Savannah lived an hour away, in Vacaville, but Kaylie could count on the fingers of one hand the times her sister had been over to help with Grandma in the past six months. Oh, but she'd had plenty of advice. She'd done *research*. She'd suggested herbal remedies. New doctors. Just last month she proposed a trip to the Mayo Clinic. As if there were a cure for advanced emphysema.

When Kaylie let her know a few weeks ago that the end was near, and wanted to keep her in the loop about their options, Savannah had responded with outrage. She thought Kaylie's "predictions" were "premature." She specifically said that using the words "dying" and "hospice" were manipulative on Kaylie's part. As if she were maliciously trying to pry Savannah away from her blue-ribbon children and husband. At the end of her rant, Savannah announced that she'd "look into the situation," and hung up.

Late this afternoon, as Grandma had struggled to draw air into her lungs, her whole body racked with pain, Kaylie spooned doses of morphine into her mouth. One after another. Once Grandma lost consciousness, it was nearly impossible to get her to swallow more, but the other options for killing her were horrifying, and so Kaylie cradled her ancient skull in the crook of her elbow, wrapping her arm around so she could use her hand to hold Grandma's jaw open. She continued dripping morphine onto her tongue, sometimes massaging her throat to ease it down, until she finished her off at eight fifteen p.m., just as dusk softened the harsh light of day.

Kaylie knew, without a shred of doubt, that Grandma would want exactly that—to have Kaylie be the one—and exactly this, what she was about to do next.

But now that they'd at long last arrived at the pier, *back* at the pier, Kaylie's will began collapsing. Not her resolve. She knew this was right. But the physical energy necessary to carry it out went missing. She realized that she hadn't eaten anything all day, not even a bowl of cereal. She briefly considered stopping in at Skates Restaurant, just on the other side of the pier, for some sustaining nutrients, but the idea of sitting at a table clad with a starched white cloth and shiny cutlery, surrounded by the sounds of clinking cocktails, digging into sole meunière, while her grandma waited unguarded in the backseat of the Pontiac, just wasn't right.

Kaylie stalled by listening to her phone messages. In the first one, from midmorning, Savannah simply asked, "So how is she?" This one was followed by a couple of insistent demands of, "Why aren't you calling me back?" In the next, Savannah announced that she was coming to Berkeley, that she'd leave right after she put the kids to bed. Kaylie should expect her by nine o'clock.

She must have just missed her. By now Savannah had probably parked her Lexus in front of Grandma's house, keyed her way in the front door, and found the empty bed. Kaylie had made sure to bring the bottles, eyedropper, and even the spoon with her, to not leave anything sketchy at the bedside, but now she wished she'd stopped on her way to the marina to drop them in a garbage bin far from home, and also far from the marina. She should chuck them now, in any case. If Savannah called the police, and that would definitely be her style, then Kaylie needed to be free of evidence.

She grabbed the plastic bag into which she'd stuffed all the paraphernalia and got out of the car, locking Grandma in, as if that would be necessary. Walking at the pace Savannah used for exercise—she called it *pep-stepping*—Kaylie hustled along the harbor until she came to one of the public bathrooms. Perfect. Her bagful of gear looked like it belonged to any addict, and she stuffed it deep into the garbage bin, shoving it under some McDonald's bags. Then she crouched down by water's edge and washed her hands, the rank iciness triggering so many memories, though she refused to cry. She had to finish what she'd begun, and she had to do it quickly.

And yet, walking back to the car she couldn't resist stopping at the entrance to the pier, long fenced off due to structural issues too expensive for the city to fix. One of her most painful regrets was how, in the past few years during Grandma's illness, she hadn't been able to bring her to the pier. They'd come a few times to the water's edge, where the Pontiac was now parked, and even tried fishing from the rocky barrier, but it wasn't the same, not even close. Navigating a catch across those sharp, massive rocks was nearly impossible. Anyway, all their friends were gone.

Kaylie put a sneaker toe through one of the diamond-shaped openings of the chain-link fence barring admittance to the pier. It was an easy climb—only a few feet high, and no barbed wire—and a moment later she leaped down on the other side. Oh, how good it felt to walk that length, smell the barnacles clinging to rotting wood, the soft breeze a balm against the inland heat, its touch as intimate as a lover's. And beyond, the lights of San Francisco, blinking their friendly message of hope in a ravaged country. Best of all, though, was the splash of the bay, slurping and wallowing, concealing all its bounty, so much life swimming right below her feet, the perch, bass, crabs, halibut, and stingrays. Once they'd caught a small shark.

Duong and Tham Nguyen had helped them land the shark and that night Grandma invited their family over to dinner. It was one of the best nights ever. They brought a bunch of crazy Vietnamese dishes, and she and Grandma made potato salad and green Jell-O with canned tangerine slices. The adults drank a lot of beer and smoked lots of cigarettes. They all shouted jokes into the night.

Kaylie was fifteen that year. Savannah had long since disowned her sister and grandma. She hated that they ate fish they caught themselves, hated that Grandma chain-smoked, hated even her array of friends from the pier, claimed that they were just a bunch of homeless people. "Maybe," Grandma had answered the first time Savannah shouted that assessment, but actually they weren't. Duong and Tham Nguyen ran a framing business in Berkeley. Pamela Roberts, an ancient black woman who fished every single day, even well into her dementia, and who everyone watched out for, had had a union job at the Ford auto assembly plant in Richmond until she retired. Shelly, a young black woman, was a public librarian in Oakland, and always fished with her two terriers as companions. James and Frank, a couple of Irish brothers, who staged loud, funny arguments as they fished, mostly for the entertainment of others, worked construction when they could get it. Everyone shared food and drinks and stories, when they felt like it, and also respected a person's desire for solitude and quiet. Kaylie and her grandma knew everyone *and* their stories. Who'd recently arrived in the Bay Area, or even in the country. Who'd been left by a partner. Who was struggling to make rent. One white guy, probably around sixty, was reportedly a billionaire, and yet every Sunday he sat with his feet up on the railing, a fishing line draped into the bay, never talked to anyone, but never bothered anyone, either. Fishing was a community, and Grandma had been at its heart.

Once over the chain-link fence, Kaylie walked quickly to avoid being spotted by anyone on shore. The pier was no longer lit, and soon the tangy brine of dark night encompassed her stride. She didn't think Savannah would look for them here. Would she? It certainly made the most sense—that they'd come here—but it was a completely different kind of sense than the kind her sister possessed. If Savannah *did* call the police, it was possible that Officer Marta Ramirez had filed some sort of event report, even if she hadn't written a ticket, and they could be tracked pretty quickly. Kaylie shouldn't dally. Because once her sister decided on a course of action, good luck trying to divert her. At the age of twelve, Savannah had talked her way into a scholarship at a private school in Berkeley. Her biggest fear was that her classmates would so much as glimpse their grandma, with her wispy hair, the scalp showing through even when she was young, and her smoky breath and exuberant manner of talking, her loud honking laugh. Savannah moved out when she was seventeen and worked at Nordstrom to put herself through community college. She won sales awards with big bonuses. She now sold high-end furniture. She'd already said, well before it was an appropriate concession, that Kaylie could have the house. Now wasn't that generous, inasmuch as the house needed more work than its value.

Kaylie heard voices. The dark lumps at the end of the pier were people. Quietly, she started backing up. She'd heard of rogue youths robbing people out here. One time armed teens forced a couple to jump into the bay where the water is so cold, hypothermia claims a body in about ten minutes. Even if you're a good swimmer, you don't have a chance.

Unfortunately, that's when her phone rang again, Jimi Hendrix joyously making love to his guitar, loud and encompassing, as if he were playing the very night air.

"What the fuck?" a voice at the end of the pier said.

"Shit," said another. "We got company."

She heard the crinkle of cellophane bags, the clunk of dropped half-full aluminum cans. A second later, three youths sprinted past her, their bare chests—two white and one brown—skinny as hope. They passed so quickly she didn't even have time to be scared. She listened to their sneakered feet pound all the way to the end of the pier. She heard the faint clinking of the chain-link fence as they heaved themselves over it. Then she cracked up, laughed out loud: those boys were afraid of *her*.

Kaylie's laughter morphed into tears, and she collapsed onto the wooden planks of the pier, stretching out on her back and looking up through the blur of her tears at the few pale stars, the ones bright enough to shine through the city haze of artificial light. She wished she'd brought a fishing rod, longed for the feel of its grip in her hand, the jiggle of a bite, the tug at the beginning of the fish's resistance, and then the gentle, steady, focused reeling in. No one could clean a fish as expertly as Grandma, slicing through the fish belly with her boning knife, scraping out the guts. Of course the best part was eating the fried fish, usually with a side of chips or nothing else at all. Every single time, after cleaning her plate, Grandma would say the exact same words: "Nothing better than eating fish you caught yourself." Then she'd grin ear to ear as if it were an original comment or the first time she'd said it. Often after a good fish fry, they went to the grocery store for ice cream, which they brought home and ate straight from the carton. Once Savannah had made one of her rare visits as they were scraping the bottom of a tub of double-fudge caramel swirl, and she'd literally groaned out loud in disgust.

Kaylie wiped her wet face with the bottom of her T-shirt, got to her feet, and walked to the end of the pier. The kids had left half-drunk beers and half-eaten bags of chips. She was sorry she'd scared them away. Stupid kids trying to enjoy a summer night. Kaylie climbed up on the thick railroad tie that formed the bottom of the blockade at the pier's end. She peered through the vertical pilings at the long stretch of black water. A breeze ruffled the surface.

No, not a breeze. Something was there, in the water. A hard shiver shot through to Kaylie's core. Yes, it was a body, dark and wet, and apparently alive, as it slithered out of the water and then sank again. Someone was drowning. She grabbed her phone at the same time as she looked down the pier, trying to see if the kids were still nearby. She could call the police with one tap, but despite earlier fantasies, she didn't actually want to go to prison. The police were much more likely to book her than the kids, since she was here and they were gone, not to mention the dead body in the Pontiac. Anyway, the dark night, the teeming bay, the decaying wood, her jagged hunger, her grief, the crazy tsunamis of grief—these all converged to destroy any brain function she had left. She at least knew enough to not trust her perceptions anymore.

Kaylie pushed her face back through the pilings and studied the surface of the bay. Had she imagined the body? She reached into the bag of Doritos, tossed a handful onto the water, and then screamed as something surged to the surface, opened its whiskered jaws, and swallowed the chips. She tossed in another handful, and the beast was joined by two more, writhing, diving, snorting.

The fright manufactured by her traumatized imagination prevented Kaylie from actually laughing, but she might have at another time. Just sea lions. The fishing community hated them. Their ranks were growing, and they ate more than their share of the bay fish. Also, they'd become bold. Sometimes people fed them scraps, after cleaning their catch, teaching them that people meant food. Recently a sea lion literally boarded a docked fishing boat and bit a woman's leg. Another had lunged so forcefully out of the water that it had nearly inhaled a guy's arm as he tried to toss fish heads in the water. A swimmer had been attacked by a sea lion just last year. Kaylie threw them the rest of the chips, and then, what the hell, poured them what was left of the beers too.

Walking back down the pier, she figured she'd better call her sister. She should have much earlier, to ward off the search. To give Kaylie a bit more time.

"Where *are* you?" Savannah screeched. "I'm at Grandma's. She's not here."

Savannah had always had a sixth sense, maybe full-on telepathy, born of her desperation to ward off the dangers she saw and felt and heard at every turn. Especially the dangers of Kaylie and Grandma and their embarrassing presences in her life. Of course Savannah couldn't know that Kaylie—and Grandma—were at the Berkeley Pier. And yet, it was very hard for Kaylie to not believe that she *did* know.

"Answer me, Kaylie. Answer me now. Is Grandma okay?"

"Of course Grandma's okay. Why wouldn't she be?"

"Uh, maybe because she has emphysema?"

"I think she said she's having dinner at the Garcias' house tonight. Did you try there?"

"Of course I didn't try there. I have no idea who the Garcias are."

"Yellow house on the corner."

"I'm supposed to just go knock on their door?"

"If you want to see Grandma."

"It's after ten. She wouldn't still be there. Plus, she hasn't been out of bed in days."

"Can't help you." Kaylie tapped off her phone. Naturally, it rang again immediately. She debated the pros and cons of answering, and was not able to conjure logic about either choice, so she went with the pull of a ringing phone and answered.

"I'm calling the police," Savannah said. "Grandma better not be with you, because if she is, they'll find you. I can give them your phone number and they can track you."

"You're sounding crazy, Van," Kaylie said, using the nickname she knew her sister hated.

Even now, even with the prospect of their grandma being missing, her sister took the time to correct: "*Sa-van-nah.*"

Kaylie tapped out of the call again and vowed to not answer until she'd finished. How long until Savannah checked the garage and discovered that the Pontiac was missing?

Back at the car, she realized that getting the kayak and her grandma over the giant craggy boulders would be next to impossible, so she drove quickly to the boat ramp on the other side of the marina. There, it was easy to slide the boat into the water. She gently hefted Grandma out of the backseat and placed her in the front of the kayak. She couldn't cry now. She just couldn't.

She dropped into the back of the kayak, placing a leg on

either side of Grandma, and used the blade of the paddle to shove off the floor of the cement ramp, and just like that, they were adrift in the harbor. She paddled hard, and damned if a half-moon didn't rise over the hills just as she cleared the breakwater. It'd been plenty bright even without the moonlight, but now she could see perfectly well, maybe too well, because others might be able to spot them from shore too. But there was no turning back. She couldn't quite predict what her sister would do. She'd be crazy irate, and so it was possible she'd go full bore for a murder charge. But no, she definitely wouldn't want that publicity. One way or another, though, somehow someone would have to account for the missing person. Then again, maybe not. People died all the time and folks didn't ask for specifics on body disposal. The neighbors would just express their condolences.

The strong bay currents carried the kayak with its two passengers, the dead one resting against the stomach and chest of the living one, swiftly away from shore. The moonlight sparkled on the crests of the wavelets as a fresh breeze whipped up. Kaylie tugged the blade through the thick black water, but with the wind and the currents, her efforts seemed to have no effect at all. She looked over her shoulder at the Golden Gate where even stronger currents swept out to the Pacific Ocean.

She'd hoped to get under the pier, where she'd gently ease her grandma into a beloved last resting place. She'd imagined a quiet decorous ritual, a peaceful slip into the salty depths. But she didn't have the strength to fight the forces of nature, these strong bay currents. So she rested the paddle across her thighs and allowed the westward drift.

The Jimi Hendrix riff danced against her breast where she'd shoved her phone into her jacket's inside pocket. She reached in, grabbed the phone, and threw it as far as she could, the splash much too tiny to feel satisfying. Maybe they'd think she drowned. She could move to another part of the country, somewhere entirely unexpected, like North Dakota, and become a different person altogether.

The idea of disappearing, of faking her own death, reminded Kaylie that she did in fact have a life, a fairly nice one—sure, no girlfriend yet, but a decent job, a place to live. Funny how a person can keep functioning even when they think they can't. Life goes on. Hers would anyway. With its devastating disappointments. Its small joys. The occasional ecstasy. She didn't want to move to North Dakota. She wanted to stay here. Her grandma's death felt like obliteration, like suffocation, like too deep a hole to ever emerge from, but she would emerge. Kaylie knew that.

When a dark shape, like a colossal slug, surfaced alongside the kayak, Kaylie startled. The wet mammal was joined by another, and then another. Kaylie's brain quivered like a jellyfish, the fear squishing thought, until, all at once, she realized how much Grandma would love this. How somehow, in the midst of her confusion and grief, she'd taken all the exact right actions. There was only one left, and it would be brutal, clumsy, horrific. But she had no choice at all, and even if she did have a choice, this would be the one she'd make. She imagined Grandma's grin if she could see herself now, dead in the front of a small plastic kayak, cruising along a speedy San Francisco Bay current at night, a pod of sea lions swimming alongside, their snorts prehistoric, their smell as rank as rotten oysters, as they chaperoned her into the next life.

For courage, Kaylie gazed out at the Berkeley Pier, a thin black line in the distance, a horizon itself, splitting the moon-sparkled water from the pale gray sky. Then she laid the paddle along the length of the kayak; it wouldn't do to lose it now. Nor would flipping the entire boat be a good idea. She'd have to muster superhuman strength, and also be swift.

Kaylie shoved her arms under her grandma's shoulders and clasped her ribs. One, two, three, *heave.*

The kayak rocked to the side, nearly capsizing, but the body remained on board. Already Kaylie was sweating.

Ambulating on her hands and feet, she crawled over Grandma's body to the other end of the kayak, again nearly capsizing. Once there, she rested a moment, steadying her heart and mind, and then swung her grandma's stiffening legs into the water.

That's when the head of one sea lion rose up, the beast making eye contact with Kaylie. Maybe it smiled. Maybe its yellow teeth and deep maw gave Kaylie a shot of adrenaline. She pitched her grandma's body into the water with a single shove. The splash was modest, and the old woman sank instantly. Several dark hides mounded out of the water before diving after the body.

Kaylie paddled away with all her might, hoping for a tide change that would sweep her toward shore, toward her house and modest life, her decent job and the possibility of a girlfriend one day, maybe even Officer Marta Ramirez. You never knew. What she did know was that she wanted to live awhile longer. She wanted to be around when the pier reopened, if it ever did, and wondered if Duong and Tham Nguyen, Pamela Roberts, Shelly the librarian, James and Frank, the lone rich dude, all their friends, whether they'd come back, or if there'd be a whole new crowd. Maybe they'd gentrify the pier, bring in food trucks and artists tables. Kaylie didn't know. But she paddled as if her life depended on it, which it did.

TWIN FLAMES

BY MARA FAYE LETHEM

Southside

Final interview with Núria Callas Perales, September 12 and 13, 2018, Barcelona, Spain. Transcribed and edited by Montse Àrcadia Sala, amanuensis of the Gumshoe Division of the Church of Núria, Berkeley, California. Translated by Mara Faye Lethem.

DAY I

"You want to know the difference between good and evil?" Dramatic pause. "Tea is good, and coffee is evil." It's one of those jokes that depends a lot on the delivery. And who's doing the delivering. Louise was the only person I could imagine ever really pulling it off. I'm sure you've read that I was "in her orbit" or "under her spell" or whatever. I just wanted to get close to her. From the very first day I met her, at that highly unorthodox job interview, when she told me she was hoping to find someone who could "continue her work." Maybe it's because English is my third language, but I never thought that could mean what the tabloid press said it meant.

I could describe Louise Slade in many ways. The term "force of nature" comes to mind. She was a little, shining nugget of a woman, in a purple silk shirt, her white hair whisked up into a thin bun, with a lovely sheen of high-SPF sunscreen and nice, bony fingers. A mix of noblesse oblige and ecclesiastical shabby chic. I've always had a thing for older women. Be careful what you wish for, they say. I did get close to her.

And, yeah, she did, somehow, get under my skin.

I was never really in favor of the defense that I was under her spell or, as your lawyers worked up, "temporary insanity due to soul transference," but I have to admit there are parts of it that make sense. I mean, in the context of the episodes of lost time and mental disorientation associated with walk-ins. That said, I do remember a lot of details, although I'm aware that there are those who believe they form part of a shift in memories, or a link via the silver cord. Louise often spoke wistfully of her identical sister Cordelia, and their days as cheesecake reporters after graduating with twin master's degrees from Yale at the age of seventeen. "We had the first painted toenails in Atlanta," I recall. "Bloodred." Louise had a number of stock rhetorical questions, one that haunts me is: "What's a spinster . . . ? A woman who spins. A woman with a job."

It was that job that kept me in the Bay Area, when I thought I was just passing through. Your lawyers keep writing to me, they say I was searching for my path, following the angel number, and eventually experiencing an incompatibility between the upper and lower chakras. I can't really corroborate that. At first, I really liked the Mission—it had the best weather—but something drew me to Berkeley. In college towns you're less likely to have to explain what being a Catalan is. Not that I bothered anymore by that point. I just said I was from Barcelona; most everybody had heard of that, even back then.

We're talking 1991, my salad days. Before the dot-com boom and all, when Berkeley was slightly more convincing as a hippie town. Now that I've become associated with it as the most famous walk-in since Anwar Sadat, despite my geographical distance I have a front-row seat to some of the city's more deeply weird elements. No offense. There's even a whole publishing house that came up around all the theories, but I don't need to tell you that. My version is that I was fleeing a hairy divorce, ironically from an American named Bob. I was also fleeing Catalonia, in some ways I guess how everybody flees their home, or at least considers doing, at some point. The lawyers call it "overwhelming evidence you were no longer yourself" and the seekers see it as "new approaches to solving unsolvable problems."

There were things about Bob—being American, from Berkeley, in fact—that made me see my city, Barcelona on the eve of the Olympics, in a different light. And my quick once-around with civil matrimony left me feeling that everyone was thinking, *I told you so.* Your lawyers still write to explain how I was experiencing an unhealthy soul tie, and should have been wearing hats to protect my crown chakra.

Me, Barcelona, Berkeley, we're all so different now. I'll never live down the dramatic reenactments on that episode of *Unsolved Mysteries.* I came to wish the looks I saw on people's faces were only saying, *I told you so.* They should've had that actress made up with bruises on her arms and all over her psyche. Because that was how I arrived in Berkeley, back in 1991. A Berkeley that seemed to be still living off the fumes of the late sixties, which were fumes so strong you might just want to breathe them in all your life, especially when you had a car and a redwood hot tub. I didn't have my own hot tub, of course, but I had a working code for the secret backyard one on Essex, and that made me feel lucky enough. I didn't have a car, either, but the BART dropped me off on 16th and Mission where I could get burritos as big as a *braç de gitano** and Salvadorean chicken soup, and back in Berkeley I could binge on

---

* Translator's note: Google it.

new flavors of Vietnamese and Thai, all cheap and nourishing to my little prematurely divorced Catalan soul. The lawyers who want to vindicate me consider this sudden shift in my tastes "consistent, further proof."

It was definitely true that I'd been having a lot of strange new feelings in America. I chalked it up to a struggle with the identity codes and political correctness. You know, Indigenous Peoples' Day and all that. I found some of it exhausting, like the effort of speaking English all the time, and there was also a feeling of relief, since I didn't seem to fit into any of the identity parameters. My Catalan accent was rarely recognized. But Louise noticed it, right away. Her shorthand for Catalan was "someone with a love of language." Hers was a very sophisticated reductionism, that made me feel I could never surprise her.

At the time I recall feeling I was escaping, getting away both from and with something, hiding in plain sight. The California sun felt familiar, since Berkeley and Barcelona had similar climates for eight months out of the year. And I loved being Cal-adjacent. Near as I could be to the university without being enrolled. I would spend hours on Friday nights at Moe's Books, up on the third floor where no one would bother me. I know some Núrites feel that space is a portal. I can't speak to that. I can say that books both saved my life and scared me to death. I wanted to be surrounded by all those books, but I was afraid to open many of them, and indifferent to others. I liked their smell, and the pure abundance of them. And I liked to see Moe at the helm, when I came in during the day, in his hexagonal playpen of piled-up stacks that needed pricing. It was at Moe's that I first saw the volume *Welcome to Planet Earth*. I hated everything about that book, mostly the cover because that was as far as I got. I don't know how much more respectful I can be about this shit, really. That's why I'm taking the time to explain this, as best I can. I'm hoping you will bring this message back to Berkeley and get them all to just leave me the fuck alone. I do not have the answers you seek.

In those days I would go to the secret hot tub at least once every few weeks. Sometimes alone, sometimes with a friend, a guy who made sets for a Chicano theater company, who also liked weed and acid and was a little bit in love with me so he would listen to me go on about, well, about pretty much whatever I felt like going on about. Not at the Essex Hot Tub, though. The sign clearly read: *SILENCE, NO TALKING.* Maybe that was what I liked best about it. In the throes of those salad days, I was seeking both quiet and conversation. And sex, of course. I was twenty-one years old.

Núrites describe that period of my life as a major neurological rewiring, in which Louise's soul was studying my Akashic records and behaviors to master my physical body. I've always been honest with anyone who's come to me, like you have, with these questions. After what I'd been through with Bob, I was just looking for a good time, the very earthbound pleasures of the flesh.

I always made sure to read the *Daily Cal* classifieds, and consider all the possibilities located therein. That was where I came across Louise's ad. For someone who spoke Spanish and English, and could use a computer. Definitely did not say *starseed with a mission.* I forget the exact wording because she always referred to me, once I got the job, as her amanuensis. Which sounded better than secretary, or dictation-taker. It at least sounded like I took dictation in a medieval cloister. I took dictation in her apartment. You know the place, on Spruce Street, in Normandy Village. I remember when I showed up for the interview, thinking it looked like a reproduction of something an adventurous, fabulously wealthy young heir would have had brought back from his travels, piece by piece, and reconstructed. But more modest. Like maybe a groundskeeper's hut on the Hearst Castle grounds.

Just off campus, Normandy Village was strangely out of time, with whitewashed walls and a cock painted on the front. I had to walk into the courtyard and then up narrow steps that wrapped around a turret to reach her wooden door with its rounded top, and the inscription, *You know how little while we have to stay / And, once departed may return no more*, from the third verse of the *Rubáiyát of Omar Khayyám*. And open the door she did, into an irregularly shaped space, half cozy and half witch's oven. It was oddly meta to be fleeing Europe and harrowing memories of a guy named Bob into some Californian architect's fantasy of a French village, but I got used to it soon enough. The entryway led into a sort of railroad kitchen, which in turn led into the room where we worked, her pages piled up among early American furniture and Oriental rugs that had arrived there on the SS *Virginia* via the Oakland dock.

Louise's sleeping berth overlooked the desk she stood in front of to give dictation and the wooden card table where her little cubical Apple computer she liked to address as "Mac" sat. She never touched Mac. Some evenings she would type up pages on her Smith Corona, and then cut and straight-pin passages in edited order so I could transfer them to digital format the next day. Yes, I am aware of the metaphorical readings some Núrites give to these tasks but, really, it was just my job.

Most days she would dictate to me, like a classically trained thespian improvising. We were writing a biography of Joan Miró, a man she admired for his ability to stay in touch with his poetic soul and be nourished by nature, like a pagan (she was highly ecumenical, though *not* into New Age). She also saw his life as a parallel to the twentieth century itself, the century of modernity, the century where we recognized evil and yet were still unable to avoid it. In that way it some-how came to represent the culmination of her life's work as a "ghost" writer, Louise's secret autobiography.

I was more interested in her than in Joan Miró, and when I could get her talking about her own life, I was happy. A good biography, Louise would tell me, should read like a detective story. I could tell she was more comfortable with Miró's chaste *terroir* flavor than a lot of the detective stories that had been written since she'd stopped reading detective stories. She told me that she'd hoped to become a priest, although the way she said it, it seemed more like an answer to an interview question than a burning ambition. She always came across as feisty and brilliant and adorable in interviews. "I see no reason to marry and have children—Cordelia did that for me" was another of her stock quotes. I guess at eighty-six you are lucky to still be able to perform the greatest-hits version of your life for an im-pressionable young woman, even if she is often vaguely hung over. I enjoyed my role in the daily matinee show.

"Good morning!" she'd chirp each weekday when I called her, first thing. Every day my response, which I believe she scripted, was, "What's good about it?" The lawyers call this grooming. There *was* a lot of repetition. One of Louise's bits of advice I'm still mulling over was this: "When you are read-ing your colleagues' books, make a list of all the mistakes you find. And when you've finished, throw away the list." At the time it made me wonder about my failed marriage, about the lists of peeves and scars we all compile, and that are so hard to release. But then maybe divorce is just a form of throwing away the list. I guess murder is another.

DAY II

Behind me, when I sat in front of Mac, was the fireplace hearth. Sometimes Louise would have me pick up a Dura-flame log on my way over to Spruce Street, and we would burn it over the course of the morning. Sometimes she would invite me to a thimbleful of sherry. It was on a day when those two things combined that she told me the story I will now relate to you, to the best of my memory. Her tone was prophetic. Her drawn-on eyebrows were well arched. The dim light given off by the various lamps and the log made her eyes gleam. It was a damp day, and she was obviously in one of the rare moods where I could artfully pry some details about her life from her.

It's been more than two decades since that day by the Du-raflame when Louise briefly stepped out of character. Mostly, when we weren't drinking tea—"so strong it could walk!"—or making our lunch of chicken soup—"Do you know why Chinese food tastes so good . . . ? It's cut up into little pieces!"—she was all work. Her conversational gambits were efforts that seemed directed at convincing me to take up the task of con-tinuing on in her irreplaceable place. But on that damp day, she opened up a little more to me. She was likely feeling the weight of outliving so many people, including, just the year before, her twin sister Cordelia. "We used to be identical," Louise would say, "but we lived such different lives that the point came when no one would ever confuse us again." Cor-delia had married a Paraguayan and had three children, and painted her eyebrows on in more of a parabola. When she'd died, Louise said she knew what death was like.

On that day, the fire was reflecting in her cornflower-blue eyes. She stared into it and sighed. Usually she would intel-lectualize her emotions, convert them somehow into a pithy fortune-cookie aphorism. But instead of that sigh being a segue into an interfaith interpretation of *vishwaprana*, the cosmic breath, she inhaled deeply through her nose and blinked as she looked into the log, which was like some flambé version of a large Tootsie Roll, a California architect's description of the primeval campfire around which humans have always told stories.

The soundtrack in my mind to this scene is "In Your Eyes" from Peter Gabriel's *So* album. As I believe I mentioned, I have a soft spot for little old ladies. I just want to help them across the street, if you know what I mean. But really, what I saw in her eyes wasn't a flicker of crypto-lesbic romance. What I saw in her eyes instead was pain, tempered by the years. "Times aren't what they used to be. And they never were." I could tell that Louise was done. Done playing it safe, done being a vessel for other people's mistakes. Louise had lived a little bit in Cordelia's shadow, like she had to toe the line, not have her own problems, not add to her mother's concern.

It turns out those pat interview answers of hers are much easier to quote as the years pass, but I'm going to do my best here. In the hope that this will be the last time. Louise began by describing, as she had conveyed to me before, the holy trinity that was her relationship with Cordelia and their mother, also named Cordelia. Their itinerant lives as journalists, memorably in Mexico City in the early thirties where they were able to watch Diego Rivera and Orozco simultaneously at work on their murals on opposite walls of the Palacio de Bellas Artes, "a nonexistent competition between a millionaire communist who stood talking in front of his neat geometrical lines, and a stocky, unattractive one-armed man bending forward on the solitude of his scaffolding to paint his soul in living fire." She did have a way with words.

"Oh, Louise," I interjected, in my best jaded American accent, "what broke up your triumvirate?" My English is very good, but marked by Latinisms. I could see she liked my usage of the word *triumvirate*. I knew the twins had had a very intimate upbringing à trois. Their mother Cordelia Slade was a writer too. And had lived with Louise in that very same storybook apartment until her death. But the younger Cordelia Slade became Cordelia Zenarrutza, when she married a Paraguayan military man from an old family, who was twenty-two years her senior. Of course, Louise informed me, the midthirties was not a great time to be from Paraguay. At the time I'd barely even heard mention of the Chaco War, and certainly never heard it referred to by its nickname: the Green Hell. When Cordelia Zenarrutza, Mrs. José Félix Zenarrutza-Sánchez, set sail for the Southern Cone, Louise and Cordelia Slade Senior would have to wait at least ten days for an airmail update. The Chaco was sparsely inhabited, a vast region of virgin jungles and deserted plains burning under the tropical sun, with rumors of oil wealth, and access to the Paraguay River, something the landlocked countries of Bolivia and Paraguay both very much wanted to control.

José Félix's military victories in the conflict would later buoy him to the presidency. Six months later, he dissolved the legislature and suspended the constitution to write his own, granting himself sweeping powers. Six months after that, almost to the day, he perished in a plane crash en route to his summer residence. José Félix's constitution remained in effect until 1971. But this wasn't the story Louise told me that day as she stared into the fire. No, the story she told me was a story of Green Hell. The price Cordelia Zenarrutza paid to become First Lady of Paraguay, however briefly.

"Cordelia never wrote to us about her time in Boquerón.

She didn't put it into words for me until after she and my niece and nephews were back in California." That was when Louise looked away from the flames briefly and straight at me. "But she didn't have to. Those weeks she spent in Boquerón, I didn't sleep well at all. Every night I was visited by demons. They pinned me down and ripped at my sweaty nightgown. Mother was shocked at the noises I made beside her in our twin beds, and at how much water I drank. I was insatiably thirsty."

I noticed a cataract in Louise's eye, like a passing altostratus cloud.

"I'll never understand how José Félix could bring his young bride there, to that Green Hell . . . When Cordelia came back to us and described it, I already knew what it looked like. The thatched roof on the Boquerón outpost, the tall, tall pole with the Paraguayan flag, the only water source a well miles away at Isla Poí. With decomposing bodies floating in it." Louise moved her gaze back onto the composite log. "We were the only women there . . . I've never killed anyone. But I know what it's like. My sister did it for me."

That night was the last time I ever went to the Essex Hot Tub. I tried a few times after that, but my code no longer worked. I remember the heady scent of blossoming trees as I walked down Stuart. It's common knowledge what happened at the hot tub that night. And I told you already, I don't want to talk about Bob. It's like the punch line to that joke: *What do you call a guy with no arms and no legs floating in a pool?*

How could I have ever thought that I could get away from my ex-husband by fleeing to his hometown? It turned out Bob was within the radius of six degrees of separation from me all that time. And in the center, dead in the center, was the Essex Hot Tub. Did we have the same entrance code?

The Church of Núria, now located in Normandy Village, is just batshit. As wrongheaded as a cargo cult. Sure, there've been moments where I enjoyed the attention, especially from that sweet soul-integration teacher, Penny. I will say this, though: I'm done. You're the last pilgrim I will entertain. I don't know why babies shit so much. Or little dogs. Or men. I don't know why women are expected to clean that shit up. I can't explain these things for you. Please, stop asking for the answers to your questions. I don't know why marriage is rape and why war is rape and why rape is rape and why tea is good and coffee is evil.

All I know is that Cordelia Zenarrutza took her three children to Pasadena, put the Green Hell and the Palacio de los López behind her, and didn't remarry. Louise and I never finished that book on Miró, on the twentieth century, and on the difference between good and evil. And despite what you've read in the papers, and the attempts at extradition, for many years I wasn't sure whether I'd actually killed Bob, or whether I'd just added him to the list of mistakes. And then thrown it away.

"LUCKY DAY"

BY THOMAS BURCHFIELD
Berkeley Public Library

T he rule was simple: no patrons were to be admitted to the library before it opened, no matter how hard they knocked on the big glass doors. The staff wouldn't even bother with eye contact. Patrons could knock till their knuckles broke and complain till their voices cracked, but they weren't getting in.

Mason, a cautious man who'd been working at the Berkeley Public Library as an aide for only three weeks (sneaking back into Berkeley after four years away, following his mother's death and his family's turbulent dissolution), understood this immediately.

He'd arrived at nine a.m. that morning with the manager of the day, Slim, an enormous languid fellow with spiky yellow hair and a wart on his nose that turned red during heavy rain, such as had been whipping the Bay Area the last three days with frenzied enthusiasm. BART service was sputtering even more than usual and ACT busses were detouring around flooded areas. Most everyone else would be late.

Except for Mason who, for his own reasons, left his closet-sized studio apartment near the Ashby Street BART extra early and took carefully planned detours.

Once Slim had punched the alarm codes to the Bancroft Street employee entrance and let Mason in, he apologized profusely. The new library director was arriving today, first day on the job, loose ends with the catering for the welcome reception. Slim would only be a few minutes. Would Mason mind being left alone, just for a while? Then he dashed back out into the rain.

Too new to object, Mason got right to work, opening the sorting room, checking the phone messages—sure enough, even Cleve, his manager, was mired in traffic. (Oh well. It was three hours until opening.) Mason next pinned the daily assignment sheet to the bulletin board. His first-hour duty: clean up and straighten the new bookshelves on the first floor, the first thing patrons saw as they entered from the sunken plaza.

The task was mundane to anyone but Mason, who sank into happy reverie: this was the best time to be in the library, alone, before anyone else arrived, among all the minds great and small, talented and not, that could fit on the shelves. As always, he found some of these minds had fallen or slumped over since yesterday; others had been picked up and abandoned far from home and now lay rejected, lost, and unloved. Mason took them all home. He'd edge the rows of books until the spines were perfectly snug (except for books by his favorite authors—those he brought forward out of line just a fraction). Then he'd run his fingertips over the rows of Mylar mirrors, each spine labeled *NEW* in red block letters, shining with promise.

Deep in his fun, he only heard the pounding on the glass door as a murmur from far above. When it finally penetrated, desperate and persistent, he swam awake like a drowsy fish. Then his irritated glance turned into a double take.

It was Sharpie banging at the door. He was a regular patron, one of the two kinds of characters who made the library a second home. The first were those who had someone to take care of them; the second, the majority, were those who had no one—the homeless.

Sharpie was among the latter. He was still very young, his fuzzy face not yet cured red by exposure; friendly, boyishly handsome, but clearly hapless. He wore the same tracksuit every day, black nylon with yellow stripes, and grimy black-and-yellow cross-trainers with loose heels that slapped against his bare feet as he walked. Extremely claustrophobic, his usual spot was the first-floor reading room, by the romance novels, an enormous greasy backpack, swollen with his material life, by his side. He'd spend most of his day reading the romance novels, or seeming to. It was strange, Mason's fellow staffers remarked—a young man reading romance novels, a *homeless* young man.

It was Mason who said, "I bet that's where he finds love." Then, blushing, he added, "I mean, he's not finding much of it anywhere else, is he?"

And now here he was, over two hours early, without his backpack, clutching his left side with one hand, thumping on the glass with the other, smearing it with reddish-brown paste, while outside the three-day storm was whipping into day four.

"Help me!" Sharpie cried, a sad voice under the hard rain. "Help me, man! I'm hurtin'!"

Rising to face a real emergency, Mason's conscience brushed the rule off the table.

He let Sharpie in.

The plan, a quick gel in Mason's mind, was to sit him down, then thumb 911. But as he took Sharpie by his cold, wet nylon arm, bony and trembling, and started to guide him between the new fiction shelves to a nearby bench, the door banged again, so violently it shook. This time, someone was calling—no, barking—Mason's name, like the knuckles on glass. As Mason turned to look, Sharpie slipped out of his grasp.

Mason grew sick as his vision shook, spun, and tilted. He'd been dreading this moment ever since he'd snuck back into Berkeley—his big brother Harry, long lost and best forgotten; Harry pounding on the blood-smeared door as he shouted Mason's name. His fevered face and rusty-gray beard ran and dripped with rain. As the brothers faced each other through the glass, Mason's reflection stared back out, a homely big-eared ghost under his brother's brilliant sharp bones. A memory of their mother's face briefly joined them and Mason once again heard her last words, from years ago, and a promise he'd made.

"Hey! *Ma-son!*" Harry banged again on the door, his cracked grinning face still handsome as a god, though one left out in the weather for too long. No matter what happened, Harry's corpse would be a beautiful ruin, handsomer dead than Mason alive.

Mason crept toward the door, drawing out his wallet, fumbling out a tenner. He opened the door just enough to insert his face: *Hi, Harry, gee, what d'ya know! Uh, I'm busy, nice to see you; sorry, Harry, the library doesn't open till noon; here, ten bucks, take it, Harry; get outta the rain, buy a sandwich at the E-Z Stop Deli.*

But, like a big camel, once Harry got his nose in, he took the whole tent. He slapped the door open and passed through Mason as though he were mist. "My brain's so big," Mason remembered him saying, "I don't see the world. It's just some shit to play with."

Nope, no telling Harry what to do when or when to do what.

Mason turned to follow him, but Harry suddenly spun about and pulled him into a rib-bending embrace.

"Bro! Awwww, my little broaaaa! Where ya been, Big Ears!?" Mason's feet left the floor as Harry spun him around like a dance partner. Close up, his face looked flayed and pitted by the weather, his pupils widening, turning his eyes into black pits. A wet bouquet of the street steamed from the fake-fur collar of his thick coat. His breath was a cloud of stale tobacco and dead animal.

Harry set Mason down hard enough to bend his knees. Mason, now facing the door again, tried to glance behind him. *Where'd Sharpie—*

Harry punched his arm, that familiar hard-knuckle jab: "Wake up, Mase, y'twerp! You ain't seen me in more years than I got fingers left." His mutilated right hand stole back into its stinky coat slot, where he preferred to keep it. "So, how's it goin', buddy?"

"Um, all right. Harry—"

His brother blew right past him: "Never mind. You don't give a shit. I don't give a shit."

Mason stood staring for a few seconds out at a small crowd that was filling the sunken plaza in the dismal downpour. Someone held up a smartphone. A young girl was now banging at the door—young and fresh (but not for long), shabby in a strangely boutique manner, *homeless du jour.* But Mason's mind was a frozen swamp of panic, so there'd be no more early entries. He turned to find his brother had passed through the security gate and was now pretending to marvel at the blond-wood bookshelves on wheels.

"Wow! Workin' the library! Mighta known you'd be workin' for The Man! Good hustle there, bro! Are these all the pwecious tomeths?"

"Just the new ones. Got 'em on the back wall, there too. And the DV—look, Harry—"

"Whoa, lovely beautiful building, man." He gazed around with his wide black eyes. "Love those green art deco walls outside." He shoved one of the shelves so it moved. "But here you got these dumbass shelves on wheels." He rolled his eyes. "*Cheap, cheap, cheap*," he sang. "You're so brilliant, you work in a library that uses Ikea shelves." Then he sneered. "Of course, you can *read*. You're dyslexia *freeee*, y'stuck-up little shit."

"You're not supposed to be in here, Harry," Mason dropped his voice and tried to enunciate like Harry, each word a hammer tap. "We don't o-pen un-til noon—"

"*You're not supposed to be in here, Harry*," the big man mimicked, a skill that once rolled waves of laughter across a room. He jabbed a finger right at his little brother: "*You* just let some other asshole in, Mase." His voice scraped like a file, his eyes two black marbles. "*I saw you*." He splayed his good left hand over his chest, nodding. "And I—me—I'm your lonnnng-lost *bro-ther*." Harry's lips curled and split apart to show his brown teeth, a bad omen. "How long you been back in town? You been avoidin' me since you got this job. I seen you, man. I seen you peekin' up over the BART steps, like a little prairie dog! Too chickenshit to go outside!"

Mason's eyes skittered about. He was still all alone in the building. The manager hadn't returned. Maybe an assistant had arrived, or another aide, better that, they'd be more likely to help him cover his mistake—no, mistakes. He'd made two of them—no, that was one mistake, twice in a row. He needed assistance, but by no means wanted it. Better, much better, if he could shovel this mess out the door all by himself, so no one would ever go *What the fuck?* and—what—what about—

The new library director! Ohhh, fuck me! New boss, first day on the job, maniacs crawling the floor before the doors even—

"Whoa! What's this!?" Harry fixed his bullet stare on the floor at his feet, right by the "Lucky Day" shelves, which housed especially popular books.

"Blood!" He fully bared his big brown crumbling teeth, the gums shrunk to the roots. He marched deeper into the library, toward the circulation desk, following the blood spatters.

"Wellll, what the fuck we got here? Trail of blood! Ooo! That could be the title of your next shitty screenplay, Mase! I'd say someone's hurt! What d'ya say we go help him!?" He stopped and turned to Mason, his face aghast, slapped his good hand over his mouth. "Oops! I forgot! Ssshhh in the library!" Then he pointed the finger, whispering, "And you'd better hush too, lil' bro." He turned back to the hunt. "Fuck libraries, man," he whispered loudly. "Can't read, can't talk like I like to. Can't be my*self*." He swayed as he followed the trail of little red splashes, dissolved from rainwater, toward the first-floor reading room.

"Harry . . ." Mason maintained his library voice, compressed and quiet, sitting on the dreary apprehension that he and his brother were rebooting the same goddamn movie.

Harry spun around again, pointing, suddenly growing larger and larger, until Mason began to feel neck strain.

"Mase, mind your own fuckin' business for once, will ya? Three, four years and I'm *still* findin' you under my feet!" His finger was shaking. It was a familiar pattern. The angrier he got, the more his brain, sloshing with chemical imbalances and bad wiring, would misfire. "All the times I kicked you and . . . y'just didn't *learn* . . ."

As Harry ranted away, Sharpie slipped out of the reading room behind him and up the old main staircase, still clutching his side. Harry must have seen Mason's eyes shift, because he turned back toward the reading room in time to see the tail of

Sharpie's shadow paint the steps. He turned on Mason again, his fist raised. Mason flinched and ducked. Harry laughed. He laughed harder as Mason feebly patted at his pants pocket, where he kept his cell phone.

"Playin' with yourself in public again!" Harry teased. "Never could keep your hands off your pecker!" Then his face darkened further. "Or is that a gun you got there? Better not be. 'Cause I got . . . *this!*"

Harry yanked a little pistol out of his pocket. It was a .22, dull black, brown taped handle. It was much too small for his huge hands and with two fingers of his gun hand missing— ring finger and pinky, blown off while juggling a lit cherry bomb—Harry's grip on it was clumsy at best. But even a bad shot can wound or kill.

"Harry! Harry, what're you doing?" Mason cried as his brother started up the steps.

Harry stopped to stare down, offended: "What am I doin'? I'm killin' the little fuck I caught screwin' my girlfriend in my tent! Do you know what that does to a man!? No, ya don't. 'Cause you've never been a man. Now you stay down here like a good boy, or I'll shoot your funny ears off!"

Then he stomped on up the stairs. "Sharpie, you fuck!" he called, hissing like a rattlesnake. "I'm comin' for ya! Fuckin' better run, Sharpie, 'cause I'm the fuckin' Term-in-a-tor! I'm gonna shoot your dick off and stuff it in your mouth!"

Then he tripped and the pistol fell from his hand, clattered on the landing. He picked it up with his left hand, his not-gun hand.

Mason ran to the bottom of the stairs. "Listen, Harry—"

Harry spun around on the landing, pointing the pistol: "No, *you* listen. You promised Mother you'd look after me. And you *didn't.* See what happens when you don't keep a promise, Mason? You pay! Now you stay there, got me? This ain't none of your business."

That's not what she said, Mason wanted to argue, but arguing would have been madness. Instead, as Mason dashed up the stairs after Harry, he did what he should have done the second he saw Sharpie at the door: he pulled out his cell phone. He fat-fingered the keypad as he tripped up the steps: 011, 912, 921, finally: "Berkeley Police Department Emergency Services . . . Slow down, sir . . . What's the address again? . . . Is this a medical or police emergency? . . . How many intruders, sir? . . . One of them is armed? Your name again, please—"

BATTERY LOW, the little screen broke in. And then it closed its eye with perfect timing as a gunshot cracked from the reading room, echoing through the whole building. Mason jumped and so did his phone, right out of his hand.

He now stood in the grand old former lobby. He turned to the high-ceilinged reading room to see Sharpie dashing out from the Japanese-Spanish section, clutching his side as he scurried behind the double row of long reading tables. He ran into the far corner, into the modern world and US history section. Harry came out from between the Chinese DVDs and nonfiction, awkwardly clutching the little gun in his big hands. His fingers would barely fit in the trigger guard. No wonder Sharpie was still alive.

"Oopsie! Sorry, Mase!" Harry waved the .22 in the air. "I forgot my silencer! Next time!" Then he disappeared behind the first row of the 910s, the travel books: "Sharpie, you little shit!"

He moved in on Sharpie, winding from shelf row to shelf row. He fired again, then again, aiming through gaps in the shelves. The first bullet banged off metal. The second bullet, fired from the 920s, the biographies, broke the spine of

Deirdre Bair's Al Capone biography. As the book shuddered and slumped over, the bullet ripped out the other side and sent a Gandhi biography sprawling to the floor.

Sharpie scurried back and forth crying and whimpering at the far end. Harry seemed to take a teasing pleasure in the hunt. As he drew closer, he swept row after row of books to the floor, as though that would give him better aim; books that Mason had spent a good part of yesterday reshelving, straightening, until they were lined up like the proudest soldiers in the best army on parade. All that work . . . all the care Mason took . . . now *this*!

Mason followed, staying back a couple rows. The pattern was clear now. Harry was losing the point of his anger, which was congealing into a ball of rage firing in all directions. This was Harry all over: he'd never be happy until everyone else was drowning in the same lake of misery.

Mason had no plan either, only a dismal fear and a deeper despair. He'd lost his job now. What else was left to lose? At that moment another emotion appeared—spontaneously, it seemed.

"Harry!" Mason suddenly shouted. "Harry, stop it!"

His own voice scared him. It startled Harry too, because he spun around and stared back at Mason through a gap in the shelves. He put a finger to his lips and took aim right at Mason.

"I told you to shush!"

Crack! went the pistol. *Zip!* went the bullet as it split the pinna of Mason's ear. Warm liquid ran between his fingers and down his arm.

"Awwww! I shot Mason's poor widdle ear! Keep it up and you're gonna say goodbye to the other one!"

But as Harry spun back to his quarry, he fumbled his gun

again and accidentally kicked it out from the shelves into the middle of the room. As he stepped out and kneeled to retrieve it, Sharpie made a break. But he'd lost a lot of blood and as he crossed the reading room back the way he came, he slipped on it, fell hard on his wounded side, with a sad cry.

Now Harry rose to his full height. He marched down on Sharpie with high stalking steps, as though stepping over trip wires. Sharpie was going nowhere. And weak little Mason, what would *he* do? What he always did. Shake like a leaf.

But, as he had been about so much else, Harry was wrong. Mason was staring at his bloody hand, watching it turn into a bloody fist as he fully remembered their mother's last words.

And they weren't "Take care of Harry."

They were "Have Harry put away."

That was the promise Mason had failed to keep. His fear and confusion turned inside out like a sock, into purpose and rage. Even though he was already as good as fired, he'd defend Sharpie and this library, this island in the world for both of them, to the last. He was nowhere near Harry's size, but he had an idea to make himself look bigger.

As Harry reached the far end of the first row of reading tables, Mason jumped from floor to chair to tabletop. He dashed and leaped over the tabletops, avoiding the fixed study lamps, heading right for Harry, who stood a few steps from where Sharpie lay helpless and bleeding.

Swaying about, Harry took aim with both hands: "Fuck my girl, will ya—"

"Harry!" Mason shouted.

Harry spun around as Mason sprang off the table through the air. The pistol cracked again as Mason slammed down onto his brother and they crashed together into a bare wall. Mason took a hard punch in the shoulder. His ears exploded, a jolt shook his whole body. The air sputtering out in a rosy mist from his right lung choked off his scream as he hit the floor.

Mason opened his eyes as Harry slammed down flat and hard inches away. A tooth flew out when his face bounced on the floor. He'd been tackled, knocked flat, by a someone Mason had never seen before, a stoutly built woman with bushy hair. She'd hit Harry like a falling bookshelf.

"What's going on here? Are you all right?"

Harry tried to get up, but she cracked him a good one with a hammy forearm. "Oof!" His head bounced on the floor again.

"Stay put!"

But he wouldn't listen, so she thumped him once more. Harry surrendered in blubbering tears.

Good hit, Mason wanted to say. Anxious cries swirled in with galloping footsteps. He also wanted to ask if Sharpie was all right, but by then he was shutting down as Harry sputtered in fury, his face reflected in the sheet of blood spreading between them.

"Fuck!" Harry spat out another bloody tooth. "How come this shit always happens to me?"

Mason awoke thinking he was lying at the bottom of an aquarium. He was tightly wrapped and braced, a rubber mask glued to his face, his ears still ringing. As he rattled in place in his cocoon, the ceiling, seen through watery light, slid overhead. Blurred faces swam by, then swam away. But for a ball of pain in his shoulder, he felt serene, detached.

Voices whispered behind the ringing and clamor. One was Sharpie's: "Can I check out a book . . . so I got something to read in the hospital?"

Harry's voice was there too, barking and spitting, but it mattered nothing to Mason. The last time it had taken four cops to subdue him. *Probably take a thousand this time*, Mason drowsily thought.

Among those two voices, there came a third. It was the woman who'd finally brought Harry down: "It's been a hell of a first day on the job . . ."

Mason floated down the stairs to the first floor and out through the security gates. He heard smatterings of applause. So, they'd opened at last. "Go, Mason!" someone cried.

Then the daily greeting rumbled out through the PA system: "*Good afternoon! Welcome to the Berkeley Public Library! We apologize for the late opening after our little kerfuffle. The second-floor reading room will remain closed for the time being! Our Tai-chi-for-Lunch class at one p.m. is canceled for today. Again, we apologize! However, our three o'clock Super Cinema program in the Community Meeting Room will continue with O Brother, Where Art Thou? The temperature outside is forty-five degrees, but it looks like we're getting a break from all the bad weather! Again, welcome . . . and have a great day!*"

Indeed it was looking to be a fine day, as bits of blue sky showed through the gray ceiling.

"Make way for the hero!" someone cried.

"What's so funny?" the EMT asked as they loaded Mason into the ambulance. But with that mask fastened over his mouth and nose, Mason couldn't tell him.

BARROOM BUTTERFLY

BY BARRY GIFFORD

Central Berkeley

Roy's grandfather subscribed to several magazines, among them *Time*, *Field & Stream*, *Sport*, and *Reader's Digest*, but the one that interested Roy most was *San Francisco Bay Crime Monthly*. One afternoon Roy came home from school and found his grandfather reading a new issue.

"Hi, Pops. Anything good in there?"

"Hello, boy. Yes, I've just started an intriguing story."

Roy sat down on the floor next to his grandfather's chair. "Can you read it to me?"

"How old are you now, Roy?"

"Ten."

"I don't know everything that's in this one yet. I wouldn't want your mother to get mad at me if there's something she doesn't want you to hear."

"She's not home. Anyway, I've heard everything."

"You have, huh? All right, but I might have to leave out some gruesome details, if there are any."

"Those are the best parts, Pops. I won't tell Mom. Start at the beginning."

Barroom Butterfly
by Willy V. Reese

Elmer Mooney, a plumber walking to work at seven a.m. last

Wednesday morning, noticed a body wedged into a crevice between two apartment buildings on the 800 block of Gilman Street in West Berkeley's Little Chicago neighborhood. He telephoned police as soon as he arrived at Kosztolanski Plumbing and Pipeworks, his place of employment, and told them of his discovery.

The dead body was identified as that of Roland Diamond, thirty-four years old, a well-known Bay Area art dealer and lecturer at the University of California who resided on Indian Rock Road in Berkeley. He was unmarried and according to acquaintances had a reputation as a playboy who had once been engaged to the Nob Hill society heiress Olivia Demaris Swan.

Detectives learned that Diamond had been seen on the evening prior to the discovery of his corpse in the company of Miss Jewel Cortez, twenty-one, at the bar of the Hotel Madagascar on San Pablo Avenue, where Miss Cortez was staying. When questioned, Miss Cortez, who gave her profession as "chanteuse," a French word for singer, told authorities she had "a couple of cocktails" with Diamond, with whom she said she had only a passing acquaintance, after which, at approximately nine p.m., he accompanied her to her room, where he attempted by force to have sex with her.

"He was drunk," Cortez told police. "I didn't invite him in, he insisted on walking me to my door. I pushed him out of my room into the hallway but he wouldn't let go of me. We struggled and he fell down the stairs leading to the landing below. He hit his head on the wall and lay still. I returned to my room, packed my suitcase, and left the hotel without speaking to anyone."

Jewel Cortez confessed that before leaving the hotel she removed Roland Diamond's car keys from his coat pocket and drove in his car, a 1954 Packard Caribbean, to Los Angeles, where, two days later, she was apprehended while driving the vehicle in that city's Echo Park area. Miss Cortez was taken into custody on suspicion of car theft. Upon interrogation by the Los Angeles police, she claimed not to know that Diamond was dead, that he had loaned her his car so that she could visit friends in LA, where she had resided before moving to Berkeley. Miss Cortez also said she had no idea how his body had wound up in the Little Chicago neighborhood. When informed that examination of Diamond's corpse revealed a bullet wound in his heart, Cortez professed ignorance of the shooting and declared that she had never even handled a gun, let alone fired one, in her whole life.

Betty Corley, a resident of the Hotel Madagascar, described Jewel Cortez as "a barroom butterfly." When asked by Detective Sergeant Gus Argo what she meant by that, Miss Corley said, "You know, she got around." Then added, "Men never know what a spooked woman will do, do they?"

Berkeley, California, May 4, 1955

"What does she mean by *spooked*?" Roy asked. "Frightened?"

"Yes, but her point is that women can be unpredictable."

"Is my mother unpredictable?"

Pops laughed. "Your mother is only thirty-two years old and she's already been married three times. What do you think?"

PART II

DIRECTLY ACROSS FROM THE GOLDEN GATE

EAT YOUR PHEASANT, DRINK YOUR WINE

BY SHANTHI SEKARAN

Kensington

Henry Wheeler walks into the Inn Kensington looking for all the world like a man who's just gotten
laid. He wears a humid sort of smile and his arms
dangle from his shoulders like sausage ropes. With him is a
woman: younger, her long dark hair parted in the middle, her
mouth set straight and firm. She leads him by the hand like a
mother. He bumps into a square table, holds his hand up, and
mumbles something, still smiling, still wrapped in the good
love or slow sex or whatever has tugged him into this Friday
morning. Shaila has spotted him, I can tell. Her chest tenses.
Dread and longing course by on opposite tracks as our man
Henry scoots into a booth, flips his hair back, squints, grins,
and examines the hot sauce before him.

He takes a few seconds to spot us. His smile drops. The
woman is talking and he tries to look at her, but his eyes dart
back, again and again, to Shaila. At last, he gets up.

"Fuck," Shaila whispers. "Fuck fuck." He walks to the
bathroom and Shaila gets up and follows.

They speak all at once. They stop. I can feel the pump of
Shaila's heart, the heat rising up her neck. They stand and
look at each other, waiting.

"What are you doing here?" she finally asks.

"I need to come clean, Shaila."

"Henry."

"I need to."

"No."

"I won't tell anyone you were involved—"

"No. You *promised*."

"Cynthia says it's breaking me. She said I need to get this off my conscience."

"Cynthia."

He points weakly to the booth.

Shaila shakes her head, faster and faster.

"Cynthia said if I just go to the police and tell them about the—"

"*Cynthia*," she hisses. "*Cynthia*."

"You'll be fine, Shaila—"

"They'll *know*, Henry! They'll know I was there!"

Diners begin to turn to the noise. A manager stomps toward us. That's when I leap from her pocket and run. They see me. They all see me. A lady screams. Feet everywhere, scraping chairs, mayhem. I escape through the door and scoot behind a telephone poll, my chest pounding.

Shaila finds me. The street is quiet again, but for a man standing in the café doorway, growling and cursing. "What were you doing?" she asks me.

"Creating a diversion."

"You could have been killed!"

A rat's heart, on average, beats four hundred times a minute. This sort of excitement is no good for me. My heart isn't used to such things.

Henry Wheeler came into our lives the night Shaila found some chickens in a supermarket dumpster. On Telegraph Avenue, the surge of feet had calmed for the night. Only the odd clutch of sneakers passed by, all of them talking at once, none bothering to look down, none willing to part with a dollar bill or food still warm in restaurant doggie bags. I was fine. There's always food for a rat on Telegraph. But from inside her jacket pocket, I could hear Shaila's belly rumble.

I poked my head out. "Let's find you something to eat," I said. She looked down at me, her brown eyes glazed with hunger. The neon lights of the smoke shop lit her skin a pale blue. I tugged at her pocket. She rose on unsteady knees. If I could have carried her myself, I would have. If I could have brought her a feast, I would have. The best I could do was keep her moving.

The supermarket on Shattuck threw out its fresh food at ten p.m., and she'd learned to dive in, sift through the salad-bar detritus, and find the packaged foods. I had only to skim the surface of the trash heap to find a good plump tomato, a heel of stale bread, a few cheese cubes. She sifted and sighed and I nibbled. She gagged and cursed and I swallowed. Finally, she struck gold. "Look at this!" she called.

She held aloft a black plastic container. "Roasted chicken!" She pried open the lid, stood right in the dumpster, and tore at the meat with her nails. She held out a morsel for me, salty and fatty with some kind of red peppery paste rubbed into the skin.

"Look!" Shaila pointed. In the dumpster behind her sat four more packaged chickens.

She returned to Telegraph triumphant, a tower of chickens tucked into her elbow: "Motherfuckers! I bring you chickens!" A few men sat in a tight clutch and passed something around. You'd think they'd have jumped up for the food, but no one budged. It wasn't food they were looking for.

One man did get up. I hadn't seen him before. The shop

lights gleamed off his hair as he lit a cigarette. He nodded at Shaila, plucked a chicken from her stack, and sank to the curb.

Never have I seen a human eat so fast. One minute the chicken was there, whole and plump and orange brown. The next, she was nothing but rib cage and ankles.

He looked at Shaila and she stared back. "Are you not hungry?" he asked.

"Who are you?" she replied.

He tore off the wishbone and held it out to her. "Henry Wheeler."

She snatched it. "Why're you out here?" she asked.

He blinked. "I don't understand the question."

The man was well dressed in a thick turtleneck and denim jacket. He had the sort of strong jaw and square chin that humans are known for. I don't trust a strong jaw. I don't trust a square chin.

From his belt he unhooked a metallic mug. "You want to know why I'm on the street?"

"Yeah."

"Why are *you* out here?"

"Stepdad."

He nodded. "I hear that a lot. Out here."

"Oh yeah? You talk to a lot of people? Out here?"

He picked at his front teeth.

"Who are you really?" she asked.

"What do you mean?"

"I mean I've never seen you before, but you roll up today in your nice jeans and your jacket looking all clean, and you talk like you know what it's like to be out here, but you don't *look* like you know what it's like. You *look* like you took a shower this morning."

"Fucking stepdads," was all he said. He reached up. She held out the wishbone. They both pulled. Shaila won.

He lit a fresh cigarette and we watched the ash grow until it dropped and scattered in a gray shower. "You sleeping out tonight?" he asked.

"Yes."

"It's gonna be a cold one."

"Do you have a better idea?"

He smiled and leaned back on his elbows. "Yeah."

Shaila jumped to her feet and nearly sent me flying. She backed away and I could smell her alarm. "It's making sense now," she whispered. And yes, all at once, it was. The clothes, the shave, the jaw line. Henry Wheeler stood up.

She took her knife from her back pocket and held it out. "You're a pimp." He walked toward her. "Get the fuck *away*." She jabbed her knife at the air. He stopped, raised both hands.

"I'm not a pimp," he said. His hands dropped to his sides. "Do I look like a pimp?"

She kept her knife raised. "I'm not going anywhere with you until you tell me what the fuck you're doing here."

He raised his arms to the sky again. "I'm a grad student. Okay? I'm a grad student."

"Fuck you," she said, and we meant it.

Henry the grad student took us back to his apartment that night. We walked from Telegraph up through campus, its buildings lit from the ground like old monuments. We walked past the big clocktower as it chimed midnight. We got on a bus that took us high up into the hills, to a neighborhood of steeply sloped driveways and houses with fairy-tale turrets. I watched Shaila strip off her clothes and get in the shower. "Oh my god," she said, letting the hot water flatten her hair to her shoulders in great black sheets. I scooted into an open cabinet and relieved myself. Henry lived in what he called an in-law. A house in which humans keep their elders.

What kept Shaila from running? Back to the group, back to what she knew? I'd like to say it was intuition—I know my own had settled. I didn't like the man, but he didn't have the predator in him. Most likely, it was the thought of one more night on Telegraph, waking at every footfall, fingers wrapped around her knife. She might have gone anywhere that night. She might have trusted anyone.

Out of the shower, Shaila stood before the mirror, gazing into it as the steam cleared. Droplets of water poured from her hair down her naked legs. I'm not sure what she was looking for when she slid a finger over her clavicle, traced circles over the round knob of her shoulder. I'd started to fall asleep in the warm womb of that room when we heard a knock on the door.

"Hey." The grad student. "You all right in there?" A pause. "No drugs. Okay?"

Shaila did not answer. Slowly, she put on her old dirty clothes, covering that hot, clean skin with the filth of Telegraph Avenue.

When she opened the bathroom door again, Henry had gone. On the floor were a pair of soft gray pants and a plaid shirt, neatly folded. Shaila tore her old clothes off for the new. She scooped me up and placed me in her flannel chest pocket. Through its cloth I could feel the shower's residual warmth, the small mountain of her nipple.

I stuck my head out. Henry had a real kitchen with a microwave and a bowl of apples on the counter. He had a kitchen table overtaken by a computer and stacks of paper. We sat on the sofa and watched him type frantically, as if he'd forgotten

Shaila was there. A bus passed. Its headlights flashed through the window.

"Where are we?" she asked. He looked up, dazed. "What part of Berkeley is this?"

"Kensington. North. Way up." He picked up a metal mug and sipped from it.

"What's with you and that mug?" she asked.

He looked at it, shrugged. "It's my travel mug. It's no-spill. Insulated. It's extremely expensive."

Shaila scoffed.

He stood up then, but didn't move from the table. "You won't steal anything, will you?"

"If I wanted to steal something, I'd steal it."

He stood by his computer, processing this.

"I won't steal anything," she said. "Asshole."

He straightened some papers on his desk, tapped them, looked out the window, at this moonless void called Kensington. He was much less sure of himself, now that she was actually in his house.

He disappeared into a back room and came out with a stack of blankets. "The sofa's yours."

"Where's your roommate?"

"I don't have one."

She looked at the bay window, the spacious living room, the hardwood floors.

"Rent control," he said.

She peered out the window. "The main house? Is that rented out too?"

"The owner lives there. Skye."

She considered this. "I wonder when she bought the place. It's probably worth about a million now. Do you think she has a mortgage?"

"You ask a lot of questions about real estate."

She shrugged. "Bay Area kid."

Shaila made a bed on the sofa and turned to him. "Thank you," she said. "You didn't have to do this."

"I know. You're welcome." He smiled. "Good night."

"Good night."

"Sleep well." He turned and left.

"Wait!" she called.

"Yeah?"

"I have a knife. Touch me and I'll kill you."

"Okay." His bedroom door clicked shut.

Shaila pulled open her pocket.

"Hey you," she said.

"Hello."

"You'd better stay hidden, my friend. Grad student doesn't know about you."

"I realize that."

She stood up and searched the corners, tiptoed into the kitchen, and opened, silently, a cupboard under the sink. "What do you think?" I hopped from her pocket and poked my head into the cupboard. I could hear the scratch and scuttle of rodent life. Mice. I could smell them.

She sighed. "I know. It's small. I'm sorry."

"It seems cold," I said. "I'm not sure."

"Okay. One night. In my pocket. And you'll get up before sunrise and get into this cupboard before anyone sees you. Okay?"

"Yes. Yes."

"You can get up that early?"

"Absolutely."

I didn't know how tired I was until Shaila lay down, grew

still, and I could finally snuggle into the curve of her breast. Fatigue heaved me over its shoulder and I sank down and down, until it seemed I was upside down, eyes shut, the night somersaulting around me.

I first met Shaila at the Lothlorien co-op on the south side of campus. It had been a week since I'd left my home high in the rafters of a church. So far, no one had noticed me. You have to look down if you're going to see me, and not a lot of people look down. I would have stayed there a good long while, I think, if I hadn't met Shaila.

That particular afternoon, I had climbed atop the fridge. I hate heights. No. Hate is the wrong word. High places invoke nausea, dizziness, the hot breath of my own demise. But someone had left a cinnamon bun up there. I will do almost anything for a cinnamon bun.

I'd eaten my fill of the pastry, my gut wailing against its seams, when I heard Shaila enter. I glanced down and nearly fainted from the vertigo. I must have made a sound because she looked straight at me. She didn't scream or whack at me with a broom. She gazed up for a very long time, her eyes squinting, nose twitching high in the air. Then she dragged a chair over, climbed onto it, and lifted me into her palm.

"Hi," was all she said.

"Hi," I answered.

"What're you doing up there?" And I liked that she didn't call me *little buddy* or *little fella*. She spoke to me like she respected me. "Are you a rat or a mouse?"

"I'm a rat."

She nodded. "Not a bad place for a rat." She stroked my head with one finger, just between my ears, and I fell relentlessly in love.

Shaila was brown like me but browner, human brown and so much bigger, with long black hair, tied that day into a swirl resembling the crown of a cinnamon bun. She slipped me into the front breast pocket of her jacket, a soft and dark home, redolent of rosemary. Eventually, I would chew a small slit in the fabric, a porthole to the world.

"I'm not supposed to be here either," she whispered. She opened the fridge and from the blast of cold she grabbed a plastic container. As an afterthought, she leaped up and grabbed for the bun.

"Please don't jump like that," I called. "It's very jarring for me."

"I got you a little something too, Lothlorien."

And now you know my name.

It was almost morning when I woke. Out on Telegraph, this was always the safest hour, when the street slept and cars were rare. In an hour or two, storefront grates would rattle open. Trucks would make their deliveries. Street vendors would set up card tables stacked with beaded necklaces and T-shirts.

Outside the window: a leafy vine, a lavender sky. Across the courtyard stood the main house, ivory-walled with a tiled roof, a majestic aloe plant beside its door. The fog had stayed away that morning, and the house bathed in sunlight.

I crawled from Shaila's pocket to the kitchen. No feet to be seen. No grad student. In the living room, I found a small hole and slipped into it. I could see from there, at least. I would not spend this life in a cupboard.

Soon after, Henry shuffled into the kitchen and brewed some coffee. The smell did not wake Shaila. She'd learned on the street to sleep hard when she could. He poured his coffee into his metallic mug, gazed at Shaila's sleeping form, and left.

She and I would spend that day indoors, watching television and eating toast. The house was heat and light. I would never again feel her so at peace.

Henry came home in the late afternoon. At the sound of his key in the door, Shaila hissed and I ran for my hole. He bounded in, smiling wide, a stack of paper in his arms.

"Hey, honey," she said flatly. "How was your day?"

He spread his papers over the dining table. "Decent. How was yours?"

They made dinner together, chatting easily, like roommates. I'd never seen Shaila like this: stepping lightly in bare feet, laughing and kicking him gently in the shins. Henry poured her a glass of wine, but stopped before he handed it over. "How old are you?"

"Nineteen."

"Old enough," he said, and poured himself a glass.

They had finished dinner, two heaping plates of pasta with red sauce and meatballs, when Henry asked, "Can I interview you? Would you mind?" He flicked his hair from his eyes and grabbed a pencil and notebook. "I'd love a woman's perspective."

Shaila sat down at the kitchen table. She tucked a strand of hair behind her ear. Softly, she spoke of leaving home, of finding her way from a town called Larkspur to her perch on Telegraph Avenue. She talked about the thrill of those first days that stretched as long and warm as a South Berkeley sidewalk—finding herself among people who sought no one's approval but their own, who could live without the material frippery of the life she'd come from. She spoke of the Telegraph sidewalk and Telegraph sleeping bags, the Telegraph men and the Telegraph feet endlessly tromping by. At a certain point, Henry stopped writing and simply watched her. When a strand of hair fell to her face, he reached out and slid it back behind her ear. She stopped talking. His hand stayed there, cradling the high curve of her neck. Her mouth opened slightly, silently. He kissed her.

They stood and he led her to his bedroom. The house smelled of something new, at once animal and familiar and deeply unsettling. I hopped onto the table, my stomach pumping, my head in a frenzy. I climbed atop a stack of paper and read. A title: "Anarchist Movements Among Northern Californian Homeless Populations." I hunkered down and relieved myself. A trail of piss, a scatter of pellets. *Eat your pheasant, drink your wine. Your days are numbered, bourgeois swine.*

What is it to watch someone you love fall in love with someone else? I bore no illusions about Shaila. I knew who I was. I knew who she was. And yet, to watch her watch him. Her hand on his shoulder. To watch her lie, for hours sometimes, in a nest of blankets, her eyes locked on his, those turbulent pools fallen still, her tight stony shoulders grown soft. *Run, Lothlorien*, I told myself. *Leave her here. She's happy now. She doesn't need you anymore.*

But I couldn't. I did find a tunnel from the in-law to the back garden, where I could sneak into the main house for bread and cookies and fruit. It was risky, moving out in the open like that, but I had little left to lose.

A few weeks later: a knock at the door. Henry emerged from his room in a kimono. I hadn't seen Shaila for hours and hours. On the porch stood an old woman, her mop of hair, glasses. She held up a brown paper bag.

"Little fuckers!" she said. "I have a rat. Do you have a rat? I have a rat. I was putting away an old coat yesterday when I opened the door to a closet full of turds. Did you know about this?"

"Yeah. I found some droppings too." Henry pressed the sleep from his eyes, ruffled his hair, and yawned.

She looked him up and down. "So you know that if you got one rat, you've got a colony. That's what they say. One moves in and the rest follow." She pointed to the ceiling. "Ever hear their little feet on the roof? Scraping sounds? That's them. Little toenails." She thrust the bag at him. "I brought you some poison and a trap."

Shaila emerged from the bedroom wearing nothing but Henry's shirt. She stood behind him. The old woman's eyebrows jumped.

"Skye, this is Shaila. My girlfriend."

Shaila raised a hand in a shy wave.

"Uh-huh," Skye muttered. "Well, I'll leave you to it. Get that trap set, hear? PayDay bars. That's what they say." The woman left.

"Was that her?" Shaila asked.

"Yes, indeed," Henry said, pulling a trap out of the bag. "Skye Wasserman. Ex-hippie. Beloved companion to Janis Joplin. Debtless owner of a million-dollar home." He held the trap up. It was gray, with a thick metal U-bar. He reached into the bag again and pulled out a plastic parcel. "Rat poison," he said, peering at the package. "Strychnine. Wow. How old is this stuff?"

"I doubt it's legal," Shaila said.

"Strychnine could kill a human."

"Well, only a human dumb enough to eat strychnine." She grinned. "Darwinism. Right?"

But Henry didn't respond. He was staring through her, past her, into a flicker of possibility.

* * *

After we see Henry at the Inn Kensington, he won't leave Shaila alone. His name flashes on her phone three, four times a day. Each time it does, I tell her not to answer. And each time, she answers. She picks up where she leaves off. Yelling. Crying. Pleading.

Here's what Henry and Shaila were fighting about that morning in the diner. Here's what could bring her world crashing down:

When Skye left, Henry set the trap and placed it in the corner of the living room. He didn't have a PayDay bar, so he smeared some almond butter on the little tray. If he thought I'd fall for that nonsense, he was sorely mistaken. A rat doesn't die in a trap unless he wants to.

Shaila ran a hand down Henry's arm. She scanned the room for me, but I'd hidden myself well. She kissed his shoulder, pressed her face into his chest, and I knew. I was losing her completely.

Skye Wasserman came back the next afternoon. "Any luck with the trap?"

Henry opened the door wide. "Come in!" he said. "No luck yet. It should take a day or two." He led Skye into the living room.

Shaila was there, wearing real clothes this time. "Can I offer you some tea?" Good Indian girl. She made her way to the kitchen before Skye could answer. "We only have green, I'm afraid," she called.

"Green's good," Skye said, then turned to Henry. "She's not living here, is she?"

"No, no." They sat on the sofa. "Just . . . you know." He grinned.

"Young love," Skye said.

Henry's laugh brought my vertigo back.

"How's the dissertation coming along?"

Shaila emerged with a steaming mug. She sat next to Henry, wove her fingers through his. The two of them watched Skye Wasserman, millionaire hippie landlord, take her first sip of tea.

Skye slurped the last of her tea and slapped her knees. "Time for this old hag to shove off," she said. "Leave you young lovers to it."

"Let me walk you back, Skye," Henry said. His hands shook as he stood.

I looked at Shaila, whose eyes darted from Henry to Skye, Skye to Henry.

"Well," Skye said, placing a hand on Henry's arm, "aren't you a gentleman. Normally I'd say no, but today . . ." She held her hand up, turned it from side to side. "I'm not quite myself today."

"Let's get you to bed, Skye," Henry said, his voice silken. "It's probably something seasonal."

Thirty minutes later, Henry returned. He stepped through the door, collapsed to his knees, and rolled into a ball.

Quietly, Shaila kneeled beside him. "You did it."

He nodded into his knees and let out a moan.

"How did you do it?" she asked.

For the first time, I felt for him. He lay there for a long while, Shaila rubbing his back. He didn't move. Shaila sat beside him with her hands on her knees. Minutes passed, Shaila on all fours now, her head hanging, her impatience flooding the room.

Finally, she reached out and grabbed him by the square chin. "Tell me how you did it, Henry."

So Henry told her. Skye Wasserman had started fainting, collapsing, by the time they reached her living room. The poison was working, but he wanted to be sure. He said it three times. *I just wanted to be sure, Shaila. We needed to be sure.* So he took a throw pillow and pressed it to the old lady's face until she stopped breathing, until her poisoned limbs stopped jerking, until her smothered screams fell silent.

"What do we do now?" Shaila asked. Henry looked up, eyes red and hollow. He wiped his nose with his sleeve.

Reader, they threw her in the bay.

Skye Wasserman had no children, no family. Henry had made sure of this. She'd fully paid off her home. She had no job, no one who would miss her. Hers was the classic tale of the wealthy old spinster, poisoned and smothered by a graduate student, his homeless girlfriend, and her undercover pet rat.

Shaila and Henry moved into the main house a few days later. They didn't move any of their furniture. Even Henry's clothes stayed in his closet. "We don't want to raise suspicions," he said. "Neighbors notice the strangest things."

So Henry and Shaila played house. Shaila cooked dinners on a six-burner stove and Henry cleared up, loading the dishwasher, wiping down the granite countertops, sweeping a broom over Spanish tiles. Henry made coffee in the mornings—never tea. In the in-law, the rat trap with its almond butter grew dusty. I could hear mice in the walls still, and now and then I thought of joining them. But, well, me and high places.

I made myself comfortable in the in-law. Shaila got a job at Pegasus Books. "It feels good to be making my own money," she said to me one day. "I'm doing it, Lothlorien. I can finally afford the Bay Area." She smiled wide and real, like she believed what she was saying.

For a few months, we lived a good life. I'd spend the days roaming the Kensington hills, thick with succulents, with overhanging oaks and redwoods. I'd nestle into rocks that drank in the day's warmth. In the evenings, I'd return to the in-law, watching the main house through my window. Some nights Shaila would stop in and see me. Some nights she would not. But soon—humans are such predictable creatures—the fighting began. Shaila's cries drifted across the yard. Henry's shouts were hard and cold as iron beams. Often he'd push her out their front door, Shaila reeling backward, catching herself on the patio railing.

When I think back, it's hard to pinpoint when exactly the changes began. I can't help but think it started a few weeks after the big move. (This is what Shaila called it, whenever she referred to the terrible death of Skye Wasserman. *The big move*.) Here was the first sign: I was alone one night in the in-law unit, asleep on the sofa. Through the silence of my midnight kitchen, I heard a scraping. And then a thunderous snap. It echoed through the empty house.

"It's the trap," I said aloud, to no one. I ran to the corner of the house and stopped. A screech, unmistakable.

A shift in the moonlight and there she was, a female mouse the color of dryer lint. Her head sat centimeters from the curl of almond butter, her neck nearly flattened beneath the U-bar. I hadn't thought about the trap in months. The almond butter had fogged over with dust and I couldn't have imagined another creature finding it. This one did. She was small. Her eyes, solid black, bulged from their sockets. The bar was supposed to flip and kill instantly, Henry had said. That's what made the trap humane.

The mouse struggled, managed to drag the trap a few inches along the hardwood floor. And then she stopped. With each panting breath, her small body swelled and receded. At last, she sighed. Her eyes rolled up to look into mine.

"I'm sorry," I said. "I'm sorry."

The mouse grew still, released a stream of urine. The yellow liquid trailed to the edge of a floorboard and ran in a rivulet along its seam.

Shaila came to me later that evening, her body shaking even before she saw the mouse. When she did see her, she cried out, picked me up, and held me to her cheek, where I could taste saltwater trails. "Lothlorien," she whispered.

Henry burst through the door and I scurried into her pocket. "Fuck," he said, crouching by the trap. "Well. Let's get rid of it." He turned to Shaila. "What's the matter with you?"

From her pocket, I watched him fiddle with the U-bar, curse quietly, then pick up the trap, the mouse's body drooping off its edge. At the outside garbage can, he threw them both in, trap and body together.

Shaila stayed in the in-law with me that evening. "I'm sorry you had to see that," she said.

"Thank you for staying with me."

She ran a finger between my ears. "I don't know where he's gone. He's gone all the time now. I think he's seeing someone else." I rested a paw on her finger. "He can see whoever he wants," she sighed. "I'm not going anywhere. I'm not letting him go."

I won't ever understand humans.

A week later, Henry pushed Shaila out their door again. This time, he threw after her an assortment of her belongings—a few shirts she'd managed to buy over the months, a pair of jeans, a phone.

Shaila found me in the in-law. She cried in great racking sobs, on her knees, holding her stomach. She cried until she could barely breathe, and all I could do was watch, my paw on her foot.

Dusk turned to night. "Can we leave now?" I asked.

She picked up her phone and dialed. "Papa," she said, "come get me? I want to come home."

It's been a year since we left Henry's house. A good year. Shaila's at Berkeley City College now. She wants to finish in three years and go for an MBA. She's been back home, living with her parents. There was no stepdad. Only Mummy and Papa, mild-mannered doctors, bewildered and terrified by her absence, ecstatic to have her home. Mummy would quite happily send me to the sewers, but Shaila keeps me safe in a cage in her bedroom, slips me into her pocket whenever she leaves the house. I've been auditing her classes on the sly, absorbing what I can of macroeconomics and Tolstoy.

It's a late Saturday afternoon. The mist has not burned off, but hangs low and heavy over the hills. Shaila and I are on a bus, winding up those old familiar streets. In the in-law, Henry waits.

"Hi!" He's breathless and bright-eyed when he opens the door. I search behind him for the willowy form of the new woman, but she is nowhere. "We're alone," he says.

I can feel the sad heave of Shaila's chest, the thump of her battered heart. Henry places a hand on her chin, lifts it, and they kiss.

But it's only a kiss, as they say, and a few minutes later, Henry's in the kitchen, filling the water kettle. I jump from Shaila's pocket. "Lothlorien!" she hisses. I find my old hiding spot. In the distance, the kettle rumbles to a boil.

Henry is still determined to talk about the murder, at least with his therapist, and Shaila pleads for his silence. He's already told his acupuncturist, he says, and Shaila shrieks and shoves him in the chest. With a single hand, he shoves her back and sends her tumbling off the sofa.

Then he gets up, moves to the kitchen, and fills Shaila's mug with water and a tea bag. He pulls his own Extremely Expensive Travel Mug out of the cupboard, and fills that up as well.

"I plan to head to the police station today," he says. "If I have to serve time, I'm okay with that. If they trace things back to you, well, I'm sorry. I'm sorry for that."

Shaila's head sinks into her hands. She sits there, silent. I want to be with her.

Sometimes, an old rat gets a new idea. It seems, initially, like a very good idea, and eventually, like the only possible idea. As the tea steeps and the argument continues, this old rat climbs atop the fridge—the height is staggering, but I close my eyes and smell for what I need. And there it is. Still there, that old bag of poison.

Thank goodness for the precious materialism of the bourgeoisie. I rustle a strychnine pellet from the bag and drop it in his Extremely Expensive Travel Mug. He will die today, this man so adept at throwing away the bodies of women, this man so ready to ruin Shaila's life.

I watch from my high perch, my nerves writhing. Henry takes the two mugs back to the sofa, and it occurs to me that he just might give Shaila his travel mug. The thought sends me squealing. He looks up, suddenly alert. Shaila pulls at his hand.

"Hey," she says.

"I thought I heard something." He takes her hand. "The thing is, Shaila, I've learned a lot about accountability.

Cynthia—she's taught me a lot. We're in therapy together—"

"You're in therapy? Together? You've been together how long?"

"Our relationship has been fast, yes. It's been very intense. But it feels right." His eyes shine with certainty as he picks up—I shudder with gratitude—his very own travel mug.

He drinks the tea down in a long, glorious slurp.

"Does she know about me?" Shaila asks.

"She does not."

She should be relieved but instead she looks hurt.

"But she'll stay with me if they put me away. She's promised." That's when he peers into the mug. "Holy shit," he says. He gasps and gags.

Shaila watches him. She doesn't know.

"You put something in here," he says. "What did you do?" He bends over and tries to vomit but can't.

"What are you talking about?"

"You did this!" He lunges at her now, grabs her by the throat. I leap from the fridge, shrieking. Shaila lifts a boot and kicks him in the chest. He falls to the ground.

I run at him. I will tear him apart. He looks down, sees me, and squeals. He leaps onto the couch and scurries behind Shaila, who is holding her throat, gagging for air. "Run," she croaks. And I do.

I am nowhere now. And everywhere. Isn't that the rodent's way?

"Look," she says, her voice hoarse. I can no longer see her. "Give me your mug. I'll drink it myself. There's nothing in there." I know the sound of Shaila sipping. That's how well I know her. I hear that sound.

"Shaila," Henry says. Rats know the rasp of death. We know it in our bones.

I step out of my hiding place and watch Henry, who looks so very sorry now.

"Shaila," he says again, and collapses to the floor. Shaila gapes at him, picks up the travel mug, and drops it like it's scalded her.

When she sees me, she knows. "You. What did you do?" Her eyes grow wide.

I must hurry now. I run to the fridge, leap to the top, not even noticing the height, and I push the bag of strychnine to its edge.

She looks at it, looks at me, then holds her throat. "Oh god," she says. She runs from the house.

"Wait!" I run out after her.

The ambulance finds Shaila rolled into a ball on the sidewalk. She's managed to stumble half a block before falling to her knees. They load her onto a stretcher. They do not see me. "Lothlorien," she gasps as they lift her aboard. But I'm too slow. The ambulance doors slam shut, and I have to let her go. It's for the best, I think. A hospital is no place for a rat.

Eventually, they find Henry, dead on the floor of the in-law. A quiet graduate student, clothes in his closet, a typically bare fridge, an unfinished thesis, a clear suicide. Both houses are empty now. Even the mice are gone. Shaila will know to find me here, and so I wait among my hardwood floors, my Spanish tiles, my granite countertops.

But a rat needs a home. My homing instinct is strong, though I won't go back to my family. Mine didn't even bother naming me. I was standard issue *Rattus norvegicus* until the day I met Shaila. I left home because my family lived high up in the rafters of the church and I, with my vertigo, couldn't move or think or breathe up there. It's a wonder I managed to leave at all. It was my sister who led me, eyes closed, mouth clamped around her tail, from our rafter down a drainage pipe and onto safe ground. On the ground, I felt like myself, for maybe the first time. On the ground, I could move, I could run, I could leave.

Why do people leave the homes they know? Sometimes, simply to live.

Shaila is my home now. Without her, I am a refugee. Four hundred beats a minute, and I count every one. In the main house, I find a hole so dark and tight a human wouldn't know it existed. It is my own penitential cave, in which I wait for her, in which I repeat to myself the only thought possible: *She is alive.* It was only a sip. Shaila will be back for me soon.

EVERY MAN AND EVERY WOMAN IS A STAR

by Nick Mamatas

Ho Chi Minh Park

My stalkers come in two flavors—communists and occultists. The former, despite the millions dead at their feet, are gormless fetishists. The latter, though theurgy is nothing but applied dishonesty, they are the dangerous ones. I know; in my time I was both a revolutionary socialist and a ritual magician. Then, after my mentor was murdered, I had to kill a few people, my own father included, in self-defense. I went to prison. I had some time to think. Some crackpot wrote a true crime book about me, entitled, *Love Is the Law: Patricide, Power, and Perversion on Long Island*. It was a best seller for a season, and well-creased mass market paperbacks can still be found in Moe's, Pegasus, and the shadier sort of used bookstores beloved by the creeps who like to follow me around. There used to be some fan websites about me, on Geocities and Angelfire, with black backgrounds and fonts that dripped red. But I got old, moved to California, had a kid, and started a new life. Now only the hard-core remain.

I've found that the best defense is a good offense. I teach yoga, in the park. The aging Reds of Berkeley still call it Ho Chi Minh Park, but the occultists, who are middle-class squares and generally out-of-towners as well, know it as Willard. I lead a group through four basic asanas as described in "Liber E vel Exercitiorum." If you threw a stick in this town and managed to miss a frozen yogurt shop, you'd hit a yoga studio, and one staffed by young lithe blondes with serious ponytails and welcoming smiles. There are only three reasons to come to my class instead—that it's free, and it's me, are the exoteric reasons.

One of my students attends faithfully, for the esoteric reason. She sweats, she grinds her teeth, every morning. *Tense every muscle and be still.* She gets off on that. When I finally asked her for her name—Lindsey—she nearly orgasmed on the spot, her white-girl dreadlocks shivering, thanks to the sheer attention I paid her.

It was just me and her the morning of the Hayward quake. Even the big redwoods in the northeast corner of the park started to sway, and the chain-link fences of the nearby tennis courts sang. Lindsey opened her eyes, let an undisciplined gasp escape. I glared at her. *Stay still.* A car roared up Hillegass Avenue, swaying more wildly than it needed to; the driver honked the horn as a telephone wire snapped and whipped the asphalt. The lawn chairs we used for our first asana, The God, tipped over as well.

"How long . . . ?" Lindsey asked through gritted teeth. I found myself focusing on my Muladhara chakra, and imagined my coccyx sinking into the earth, a bone drill in black dirt. Lindsey couldn't hold her posture anymore and fell over. A moment later, the quake subsided. Nothing but the sound of flapping wings, and then the creak and roar of falling branches, of people opening doors and shouting into the streets, and of sirens. The air smelled like ozone and sweat.

"Next position is—" I started to say, but a male-seeming groan stopped me. I didn't turn my head, but Lindsey could see him.

"That guy was behind a tree . . ." she said. In Berkeley,

in general, it is not at all unusual for some mentally marginal individual to spend all day hanging out in a copse of trees, but I already knew who he was. "We have to help him."

"Is that our will?" I asked Lindsey. "Or just *your* will? Or is it *his* will that you end our session prematurely?"

"I also need to walk it off," she replied, gingerly picking herself up.

"I *do* need help!" Heinrich said, a pile on the ground, pinned under a heavy-seeming branch. "I think my leg is broken!"

"A lot of people are going to need help," I said as I assumed the thunderbolt position, left heel under my ass, arms over the knees. "Why chose the one who's closest?"

Heinrich was one of Berkeley's freelance revolutionaries. He was in his late forties, born too late for campus riots and the Free Speech Movement, but right on time for ninety-second punk rock songs about Reagan nuking the world and polyamorous tangles with patchouli-drenched sex-positive sex bunnies and occasionally their mothers. He was microfamous for a series of pamphlets attempting to rehabilitate Bukharin as an anarchist, but every four years he blinked and voted for the Democratic candidate for president. Heinrich was, of course, in love with me.

"Can you walk?" Lindsey asked him. Yoga had made her strong. She lifted the branch off Heinrich's leg; he grunted hard, slid out from under it, and picked himself up. "I can," he said. "I can stand anyway."

"Walk yourself to Alta Bates before the ER fills up," I said. "Maybe you have internal bleeding, or a concussion."

"Don't say that!" he hissed at me. I smiled. He was superstitious, or at least worried about the possibility that what I articulate in words might soon manifest in reality. I don't believe in making things *too* easy for my stalkers.

"You're a little old to be climbing trees, or playing the Peeping Tom," Lindsey said. She moved away from Heinrich to reclaim her spot on the grass near me. Heinrich limped after her and announced that he was going to join the class, then tried to twist himself into the asana. It's a difficult posture when one is in the best of health, and he'd clearly banged himself up.

"What do you want?" I asked him.

"Why . . . there was an earthquake just a minute ago? Don't you want to go to your home and check for damage?" Heinrich asked.

"Don't you?" Lindsey asked.

"He's homeless," I said. "Sheltered, probably with a storage unit, but homeless, probably for economic reasons that he recasts as political to his friends when he takes advantage of their showers and electrical outlets." I pushed myself back into my position, mouth sealed shut, nostrils pulling air into me, then expelling it.

"Maybe it doesn't matter anymore . . ." said Heinrich. "But I heard something the other night that I thought you'd want to know." I didn't move. One shouldn't even speak while holding an asana. Heinrich had already shattered Lindsey's concentration. "It's about Riley."

Riley was his sole name, because he considered it more efficient to become world famous and win the Google Awareness Lottery than it was to keep his surname. Riley doesn't need an introduction. What does need an introduction is why Heinrich would bring him up to me—Riley and my father had gone to college together, and there both of them got involved with magick. Riley became a millionaire, and my father became a drug addict who tried to kill—no, *sacrifice*—me to the spirit of capitalism. That was in 1989, just as the Berlin Wall crumbled. Now Riley's a billionaire, and my father's in the grave I put him in. Do you have one of those vocal-activated Internet of Things Assistants in your home? That's thanks to Riley. He clearly conceptualized of the service as a type of familiar, but Alexa or some other disembodied voice that does your bidding isn't *your* familiar, it is his. You just invited it into your home.

I still didn't move. *Let there be a void*, I thought, *and let Heinrich fill it with his voice.*

"He's building something in the hills," he said. He gestured broadly to the west, toward the end of Derby Street and the beginning of the Claremont Canyon Regional Preserve. Another silence, another void.

Lindsey, the good girl, said, "He's not building anything. He owns a company. Someone else is doing the actual work." She looked to me for a nod of approval, but I didn't grant her one.

"People have seen him out there," Heinrich said.

Finally, I was driven to speak. "Have none of your friends anything better to do than follow around people more notorious than you are." I stood up out of my stance. "Class is over. Do what thou wilt, comrades." Then to Heinrich I added, "If you try to follow me, I'll stab you."

Heinrich smiled. Stalkers know their prey—he got me.

Home was a 1981 Dodge Sportsman RV I usually kept somewhere close to the park. The plates were fake. I had no license, registration, or insurance. Our toilet had long since given up the ghost, but the old Willard Pool building opens the showers twice a week, and the park itself has public restrooms. The public library—where my kid Pan did his schoolwork online under a false name—and the downtown YMCA supply the rest, so long as we stay healthy and climate change doesn't bring snow to the Bay Area. We owned so little that there was nothing in the few cabinets to spill out onto the floor.

Like a lot of people around here, I'm off the grid. I'm also offline—no e-mail address, burner phones, no social media, no bank account. No health insurance or food stamps either. I'm just extremely lucky when it comes to, for example, scratch-off lottery tickets, and in attracting yoga students who insist on pressing money and prepaid gift cards into my hands. None of this is political; I'm no lifestyle anarchist or chemtrail-and-powerline kook.

I kept a low profile to stay off Riley's radar. He was the one stalker I didn't dare make it easy for.

"Hi, Dawn," Pan said when I walked in. He was stretched out on the bench behind the table, his nose stuck in a volume of Lovecraft stories. A pimply little tween, with knobby knees and wrists, and everything he touched he smeared with a fine layer of grease. Sure, I love him. For a while there, I even loved his father, a Greek guy who flew me to Europe and hid me on his yiayia's goat farm after I got out of prison. Pan was born on a kitchen table. We're both used to cramped quarters.

"Panagiotis, let's get the map and the pendulum. We're moving."

That brought him out of his book. "Where?"

"That's what the pendulum is for."

"What about . . . Will?"

I ignored that and got the full-page highway map of the United States and pendulum myself. I nudged his feet off the bench with my hip and took a seat, then spread the map across the table.

"Will this bucket of bolts even survive the freeways?" Pan

asked. "How much gas money do we have? I have three books out from the library that I haven't finished yet."

"Berkeley does have an excellent library system," I said. "Be quiet."

I swung the pendulum over the map, muttering certain words and trying to clear my mind. Pan's words—"The truck isn't prepped for cold weather, or hot weather, or, or, or"—intruded, and interfered with the results. The pendulum settled over Berkeley, and when I tried again, it settled over the same spot, as if there were a magnet nailed to the underside of the table. "I suppose a move away from the Hayward Fault is in order . . ." Pan started to say, but then he just said, "Oh," and looked at the dark shadow the pendulum cast upon the map.

We were staying here. I should have sent Pan with a few dollars to the CVS or something while I refocused and tried again, but I was nervous to let him out of my sight. Riley hadn't attempted to contact me during the years I was in prison, or since my release, though I always expected he might reach out. There's something about being unfathomably rich, so wealthy that "one-percenter" doesn't cover it, that makes someone a very confident communicator. Not a week goes by in the Bay Area without some billionaire announcing that he wants to write the name of his app across the surface of the moon with a laser, or fund an endowed art history chair to generate new -isms to invest in, or give his favorite thoroughbred mare surgery sufficient to make her bipedal and thus more fuckable. And all this I heard about from people muttering at the supermarket, or glances at the headlines of discarded newspapers.

I had avoided the Internet since I got out of prison in 2004, to obscure myself from Riley, but he simply snuck up on my blind spot and took over. For a week, all the social conversation turned to Riley, and his project up in Claremont

Canyon right above my neighborhood. At the Peace and Freedom meetings at Niebyl-Proctor, his name was a rare curse. Usually I stood in the back, by the door, my arms crossed, silent, and let the social democrats (old, white, eager to run for office) and the Maoists (younger than me, people of color, hoping we would finally just vote to arm ourselves and storm up Telegraph Avenue) argue it out. *It* being anything from whom to support in Syria—surely our good thoughts would tip the scales in the left direction—to the question of whether shopping at Amazon.com was ethical. It's not.

Riley confused everyone. His companies had never had a profitable quarter, yet he was one of the ten richest men in the world. He marketed Rcoins, his own cryptocurrency, but human beings weren't allowed to use them; the artificial intelligences he installed in homes instead traded them among themselves on virtual marketplaces. He was a capitalist who accumulated neither capital nor profits. He had no employees, but instead simply announced some idea or tweeted out some flowcharts, and other companies turned their efforts into realizing his fancies. Whatever Riley was doing, it wasn't anything Marx had ever predicted would come to pass, not even in his weird and speculative *Grundrisse* notebooks. And thus, he was the topic of the next meeting.

That night, I was finally driven to speak. Pan, normally as bored as a kid in church at these meetings, whipped his head around and gaped at me. "It's magic," I said. Because I'd been silent for years, because I was white, because I have resting rage face, I wasn't interrupted or scolded. Into the void, I spoke again. "Real magic." I was tempted to roll up my sleeves and show off the unicursal hexagrams tattooed on my forearms, but I had their attention sufficiently already. "Applied psychology, heavy on symbolism, designed to alter our brain chemistries and social relationships. There's a specter haunting capitalism, and it's him. The question remains the same as it's been since 1903—what is to be done?"

It takes a lot in Berkeley to be looked upon as some sort of kook, and with this crowd it's even more of a challenge, but somehow I was managing it. I soldiered on: "We all talk about social systems and how they overdeteremine society, and reality. That's why nobody here has ever driven up to Seattle and fricked Jeff Bezos." Someone giggled. "As in Alexander Berkman assassinating Henry Clay Frick," I explained.

A general murmur of disagreement rose. I was losing them.

I spread my arms and bellowed, "Quiet!" The effect was like a prison guard turning off a television in the common area. A roomful of sullen, burning stares.

"Riley is having something built up in the hills," I said, calm again. "That's the rumor anyway."

"Where did you hear this rumor!" an older woman snapped.

"Scuttlebutt," I said. "Maybe it's nothing. But we know we're all discussing him because supposedly he has his thumb in some local pies."

"I heard it caused the earthquake the other week," the woman said. "Whatever he's doing up there." Now *she* was the one who lost the audience. *There are earthquakes all the time . . . We're due for an even bigger one . . .* came the mutters. *No, she might be right, I saw on YouTube . . .*

"I propose comrades who enjoy hiking make a concerted effort to find out what, if anything, might be under construction up there," I said.

Heinrich, who had been facilitating the meeting, smiled widely enough that I could see his tobacco road teeth from across the room. "Of course you realize, comrade," he said to me, gleefully, "that generally speaking, anyone who volunteers an idea also volunteers her labor to organize the intervention. Do you enjoy hiking? You've been attending our meetings for months, and your child has probably eaten his weight in cookies from the refreshment table during that time, but in truth we know very little about you." He was just excited to talk down to me, to lord his tiny influence over me.

"Some of you do," I said. A few men, only men of course, glanced at the floor or became suddenly interested in the paperbacks on the shelf closest to their seats. "But no, I'm from *Lawn Guyland*," I amped up my old accent. "I'm not much for hiking. But if there is something in the hills, and if our class enemy is involved, and if we *can* do something, we *should* do something. Someone has to do something. Praxis, not just theory."

"There you have it then," said Heinrich. "Not much for hiking." The conversation resumed without me, and Riley was just another abstraction for leftists to tinker with. I waved for Pan and we slid out the door. Someone snorted the word "praxis" as we left.

In the morning, when I awoke, Pan was gone. I went to the park to teach my class and told Lindsey that my son had vanished in the night. She was distraught on my behalf, and peppered me with questions. Had he been bullied at school or seemed worried? What happened last night? When had I last seen him? I made her be silent and put her through the asanas, willing her to focus and tense with a glare and serene quiet.

We attracted a crowd again. Heinrich and several of the hangers-on from the previous night's meeting. Now they were ready to help. Not the best start, but a start. I created a void, and they filled it. Lindsey broke down and told them what had happened. They decided to ask me for a picture of Pan, and to leaflet the area. If there's one thing leftists are still good at it, its wheatpasting flyers onto lampposts. I let them think it was their idea, and I let them stew while I performed my four asanas.

The reality is that Crowley had poisoned these asanas. Traditionally, seated yoga is meant to be performed with a certain lightness. The stretches are slow, tantalizing. The practitioner is to be comfortable, to let the muscles settle upon the bones. Crowley practiced maximum tension, absolute silence, the cultivation of pain. And he practiced in the nude, of course, as did his acolytes. Perhaps he just got off on watching men and women grimace and sweat on his command, or maybe his kink was the pain he forced *himself* to endure.

I was ready for the pain too. It took less than a day for the narrative to unfurl as I'd wanted it to. I was offline, but Pan had an official identity for his online school, and he had a library card. One of the books he'd checked out recently was *Love Is the Law*, and from there it was easy enough to determine that I was Dawn Seliger, the third most famous criminal from Long Island after Amy Fischer and Ricky Kasso. I told the police everything I knew—that after we had attended a political meeting where I recommended a search of the Berkeley Hills to settle some local rumors, we went to the RV where we sleep. I even let them inside, so they could see two beds made up. The loft bed was for me, the couch for Panagiotis.

"He must have left during the night," I explained. They didn't bother to run my plates, because I filled the voids of their minds with my narrative. An excitable boy, lost in the woods. That's the important thing. Find the boy, save the boy, be good men, be heroes for a change, not just the armed servants of the bourgeois state.

One benefit of an RV was that I was able to evade most news media just by driving to another neighborhood. The police, of course, could track me easily and impound my home, so I drove south, into Oakland's Temescal neighborhood. The OPD and BPD tend to cooperate when their own asses are on the line—protests and riots—but when it's just some missing kid, or another piece-of-shit mobile home parked under an overpass, Oakland will let Berkeley hang 100 percent of the time.

I moved my class to the little greenway behind the Claremont DMV and practiced alone for one morning and afternoon, squeezing out sweat and anxiety. Then I headed back to Berkeley. All of Telegraph Avenue was flyered, and the storefronts along College Avenue, which were usually far too tony to allow a mere missing child to interfere with trade, featured Pan's face. It just made sense—an impressionable kid deciding to do what his neglectful mother wanted him to do, so long as it sounded like an adventure.

That night, the moon was new and I walked back into Berkeley, and saw dozens of small lights dotting the dark hills. Real flashlights, lanterns, and of course, given the town, endless numbers of lights from smartphones. They were looking for him, ten thousand twinkling fireflies. No, fireflies are a Long Island thing—there hasn't been one in Berkeley for forty million years. They were all tiny stars.

Lindsey found me on the third day, and joined class in silence, as she had been trained to. But perhaps I wasn't so good a yogi after all, because when we stood upon one leg in the third posture, the ibis, she started talking.

"Your forefinger is supposed to be on your lips," I said. "To remind you."

"I just feel so bad about your kid, up there, alone. Pan-pan-panna . . ." she said.

"Panagiotis," I responded. "But people call him Pan for the obvious reason."

"What does it mean?"

If I didn't talk, she would think something was seriously wrong with me, and perhaps even go to the police. I kept my position, and spoke though my finger was pressed to my lips. "Panagiotis means all-sainted. Having to do with Mary, the Mother of God. And Pan, well Pan is the goat god. The lord of wild spaces, cliffs, and, you know, panic. The name suggests companionship."

"Huh." Lindsey wobbled on the one leg on which she was standing.

"Pan was the only god who died," I told her.

Then she was quiet, as she was supposed to be.

"A sailor, passing the island of Paxoi, heard a voice calling out to him, that said, *When you reach Palodes, take care to proclaim that the great god Pan is dead.*"

She was silent still, and quivering.

"Palodes cannot be found on any map," I continued. "Probably it has since been consumed by the sea. But the sailor arrived there, and the port city fell to grief. The old gods were dying, a new one was born. It was terrifying, worse than any panic the goat man had stirred up when he yet lived." Another temblor passed under us, an aftershock from the quake of earlier in the week, but we stayed erect, one foot up, for a long time, and our muscles burned. Without her even knowing it, Lindsey got what she wanted—an example of real magic.

Finally, I had earned Riley's attention. Sending Pan to search the hills alone, and having him "get lost," did it. A black

Mercedes had parked itself behind my RV, and I do mean parked itself, as it was a self-driving car, with the legally mandated warning stripes and signage across the doors and bumpers. The doors were unlocked, so I slipped inside and waited. I hadn't really driven more than a few blocks since Long Island. Prison, a few weeks begging for couch space, then a couple years in Greece, then California, staying on the couches or in the beds of comrades with a squalling infant. The windows were tinted, the trip fairly long, and the radio disabled, but the car still the nicest *thing* I'd been in for a very long time.

We stopped at what I guessed was either a quickly purchased or a quickly *built* home—it was all windows, and jutted out of the side of the hill on stilts—north of Berkeley, near Tilden Park. The car must have made some lazy spiral through town, or had sketched a magic circle with its route, or perhaps Riley's techno-familiars weren't as good as all that after all. He was waiting for me at the end of a long driveway, and greeted me with a smile and a wave, as if I had his dinner order in my lap.

Riley didn't say hello to me, but instead shared one of his bromides: "There are no political solutions, only technological ones. All the rest is propaganda."

"Solutions to what?" I asked.

"Come inside," he said.

Riley was an old man now. I guess my father would have been nearly eighty as well. Riley had managed to stay slim, and held himself with the casually erect posture of a tai chi master. His right arm, which had been struck by a car right after my last conversation with him in 1989, was still withered and bent. Despite the weather, he wore a turtleneck. I'd marked his neck during that same conversation, with a punch from my trusty punk rock–girl spiked ring. In the popular imagination,

Riley's interest in voice-commanded objects and household artificial intelligence had stemmed from his disability, but I knew that wasn't the case.

In the kitchen, the refrigerator crushed some fruit and poured a pair of drinks, but we had to fetch the glasses ourselves and bring them to the table.

"I found your son," he said.

"What's your big project?" I asked.

"Don't you care about your son?"

"Of course I do."

"Don't you care whether he's alive?" Riley said. It wasn't really a question. "Did prison harden you, or were you always truly the psychopath that hack author of *Love Is the Law* made you out to be?"

"Pan's alive," I said. "I would know if he wasn't. Did *he* find *you*?"

"Yes . . ." Riley's lips tried to twist into a snicker, but he straightened them. "He found the project anyway, and the crew."

"He's a good boy," I said. "He knows every inch of those hiking trails, and isn't afraid to leave them. He's half mountain goat, I swear. What are you doing up there?"

"It's a solution to the Bay Area's housing crisis," Riley answered.

I laughed. "What, an earthquake machine atop the Hayward Fault or something? The first house that would collapse would be *this* one!" I stomped on the floor for emphasis. The place really had been slapped together out of ticky-tacky, like the old song says.

Riley just peered at me. His eyes were . . . friendly. "Your son is alive, but he's not well."

"You hurt him." That wasn't a question.

"I wasn't even there," Riley said. "He got injured. My contractors found him. He had a certain book with him, and the on-site medic got his blood type, so I got a call. I'm a libertarian. I don't believe in aggression. No force, no fraud. I would never personally hurt a child."

"You're building an earthquake machine, so spare me the rhetoric about who you'd hurt," I said. "Where is Pan?"

"It's not an earthquake machine." Riley's voice was tinted with sudden impatience. "It's an earthquake *futures* machine."

"You're going to predict earthquakes, months in advance."

"In order to make strategic real estate purchases, and investments in publicly held insurance companies, yes," Riley said. "Once we solve this problem, we can broadcast the real risks of continuing to live in the Bay Area, and that should bring down prices, except for black-swan events—quakes eight and over, which of course will reduce supply and thus raise the prices. But now we'll be able to predict such events far in advance. Real estate can be a hedge, not a speculative investment."

I sipped my drink. My throat was suddenly very dry. "That sounds like the sort of technology people would want to seize for the greater good. Nationalize it, make the code open source. We'll build in the safest places, firm up the buildings and infrastructure in the vulnerable areas, make sure everyone is protected."

Riley laughed. "You think the government wants such a thing? Think of all the money it would cost them to make the Bay Area, or any place, safe from quakes. The government can't even handle hurricanes, and those roll up out of the Gulf of Mexico like clockwork. We need a free-market solution."

"I don't mean the *bourgeois* government, Riley, Jesus Christ. Where's Panagiotis?"

"The car will take you to him, if you want."

"Why are you doing all this?" I asked. "Why did you bring me here, why are we even having this conversation?"

"I always wanted to thank you for killing your father," Riley said. His tone was bland. "I've wanted to thank you for a long time." He held out his arms, like he wanted a hug. "Golden Dawn Seliger!"

"Well rehearsed," I said. "How do I know you're not going to send the car off a cliff if I get into it, or just have it run over Pan with me in it, to frame me?"

"I don't believe in—"

"Force or fraud, yeah yeah."

"What I mean is that there's no need for me to do any such thing, as I've already won. Thanks to you, really. Once your father was out of the way, I was able to truly cultivate an understanding of magick. It made me what I am. Your example made me what I am. Every man and every woman is a star, and you've been my guiding light for a long time."

"Ever since I managed to get away from you." I looked pointedly at his arm, at his turtleneck.

"Yes, but now there's no reason to chase you. I'm everywhere. Even if you don't own a cell phone, everyone you encounter does, and if you talk to them, I hear it. You ever step in front of a security camera, or enter someone's house, or pass through an automatic door, I'm there with you. I told you, I've won. Take the car, collect your son. If you're smart, you'll send him to school and he can make something of himself. That's better than whatever you were planning to make of him."

"A god," I said. "Thanks for the juice, Riley."

"It's matched to your metabolism. Yoga suits you. You've slimmed down. Looks good. Are you the local occult MILF?"

"Don't neg me, bro," I said, and he laughed.

In the car, I slid into the driver's seat. The mechanisms were strong; you weren't supposed to be able to wrestle the steering wheel away from the AI, or press the pedals against the will of the machine. But I had spent years practicing my asanas, tensing and flexing my muscles, exercising my tendons. It's isometrics, powered by will. I sank into the seat, lowered my chakra, put my hands on the wheel, and gripped with all my strength.

Driving the car was like trying to navigate the RV with the emergency brake on, but I did it. I could feel where the car wanted to turn, and assert my will. It was a long crawl through winding hills, but at least there was no chance of coincidentally-on-purpose heading off a cliff. Of course, Riley was actively monitoring my route; he knew everything about me, like a proper stalker, except for my thoughts.

I was telling the truth when I said to Riley that I'd know if Pan were dead. My lie was one of omission—I *knew* Pan was dead. I felt it when I'd told Lindsey the story from Plutarch. I hadn't even meant to; it had just come out of me. My True Will.

I let the car leave the road and take a recently carved dirt path into the hills. The Mercedes had been modified for rugged terrain, and I let it do most of the work. The car took the long way around, down through Siesta Valley, then back north on a route parallel to Grizzly Peak Boulevard, until I was back in South Berkeley, and Claremont Canyon. In the woods I could see the search parties at it again, those little lights, but they were unnecessary.

The car's headlamps illuminated Pan's body. He was laid out on a blue tarp, his flesh white as bone, horse flies and night birds evacuating in the glare. There was a neat hole in the middle of his forehead, an open third eye. The engine idled, the passenger-side door unlocked, and I had to scooch across both seats to step outside.

My poor son.

My poor dead god. A sacrifice I made, of a god, not *to* a god.

Of course Riley didn't do it. He just hired someone and gave him the order to shoot whoever came close. Property rights. That it was a child, *my* child, was just one of those coincidences that any occultist will tell you do not exist. There are no coincidences. And I was there now, to be found by the search parties and their smartphones, the insane and abusive mother who killed her own child. And they'd only be half wrong. There was probably a gun nearby, with my fingerprints lifted from my old arrest records, artfully decorating the grip.

The machine stood next to Pan's body, like an obelisk. It was a bit like a cell phone tower in appearance, definitely a sensor of some sort, and not an "earthquake machine."

I, however, *was* an earthquake machine. And after long practice, I was immune to pain. I kneeled before my son, and sat into the thunderbolt asana. I tensed every muscle in my body, forced my Muladhara chakra down into my coccyx and deep into the hill, deeper than Riley's futures machine had been sunk, and focused my will, calling out to the restive Hayward Fault.

And O, she answered me.

STILL LIFE, REVIVING

BY KIMN NEILSON

Ocean View

I have loved leaving things behind: lovers, cities, jobs. Leaving before the end of things, the nasty part, the annoying part. I just bought a computer, my first. You tap the track pad with two fingers and a little box comes up. You can tap "back" with one finger and it returns to the previous page. Back, back, back, though what I liked to do was skip forward, forward, forward.

But then something lies in wait for you, doesn't it? Life itself taps back, back, back; time itself wheels around and bites you.

Hired for a weird job, that's how I met you.

I came into town too broke for a room so I slept behind a building on the campus that first night. Next night I was drinking one long beer at a place called Marvell's, sitting at the bar reading—it was *Giles Goat-Boy*—and you spilled my beer and apologized a little too much and bought me another and then two more and at the end of the night I was in your bed in a rooming house down the street and had a particularly unspecific bit of work for the next day.

In the morning you bought me eggs and toast at the Cecil— it just closed only last month—and we drank lattes and I began to feel situated. I relaxed a little. There you go. See? I go back, back, back, and I can trace exactly where it went the wrong way, where it went, as they say, down.

We walked around the corner and got into your beat-up truck with a Six-Pac on the back. I noticed the gun rack sans guns running behind our heads. The truck was old but the interior was clean—no wrappers, old coffee cups, not even dust or dirt. I felt even more keenly how stinky I must be getting—well, that night I'd have money for a laundromat.

The work was at the marina, you said, simple stuff. Shifting boxes, cleaning. Ever work around boats? I'd done a little trawling in Alaska, like everybody, and before that stewarded on a cruise ship, but that was like waiting tables. Besides, I got fired and put off at the next port, hence Alaska, hence the trawler.

You listened and nodded and turned on the radio. We rolled down University Avenue and onto the road leading past boatyards and bait shops, then fancy restaurants at the end of the pier. It was your basic winter morning, nothing spectacular, but even so, the water glittered as the sun rose, the air smelled different, the wind was sharper, all giving me the feeling things were shifting forward, forward, forward . . .

You told me to stay in the truck while you opened the gate and checked the boat. Coming back a few minutes later you said that the owner's selling and needs to move his stuff off and clean the boat. That's it. But really clean—I thought you meant oil the woodwork, polish the chrome, but you brought out disinfectant, rubber gloves, scrubbers.

The hold was jammed with boxes. We began by pulling some out, then you were down in there handing them to me. These weren't boxes picked up behind the liquor store. Not large, maybe a foot square of super-sturdy cardboard and all about equal weight. When they were all out on deck the boat looked like a sandcastle moving gently with the tide. You went to the truck and brought back a dolly; as I stacked the boxes on the dock you ran them back to the truck. It probably wasn't two hours gone when we were done.

You handed me a hundred dollars in twenties and told me to start scrubbing—every inch. The boat needed to be pristine for the new owners. You'd be back in a few hours with another hundred but if I finished before you were back just lock up the boat—it was a simple Yale lock on an iron bar— and meet back at the rooming house.

A kiss and you were gone.

I should have been a scholar, that's what my folks thought. For the only child of two professors, it was obviously the path for me. I did seem to drift into university towns a lot. I understood how they operated, always cheap food joints, cheap beer, places to hang out, places to wash up, plenty of books, bookstores, cafés. I no longer really looked like a student, but I looked exactly like those people who had graduated and never moved on. Why leave when everything that made life easy was all around you?

My life wasn't exactly easy but it seemed to be the way I needed it to be. My parents died in their sixties, a few years apart. After that, feeling no ties to our hometown, I never went back. I wasn't happy but I wasn't particularly unhappy either and I'll tell you, I think that's how a lot of people feel and it's probably enough. I would have been happy/unhappy enough to just keep riding around America but you arranged for me to get nailed down pretty permanently here in good old Berkeley.

I'm a good worker, in a shallow, time-sensitive sort of way. A few days, clear instructions, decent money—no problem. I can do stupid work well for a short period of time. The longest I stayed on a job was also one of the filthiest—digging worms in a bank of a river in Kansas. On yet another college campus, I was sitting on some steps in their main plaza when I saw a young woman carrying a stack of buckets, just a few buckets too high for her to manage. I caught them on the way down and helped her into the biology building with them, after which she asked me if I needed work and how did I feel about mud and bugs?

The pay wasn't that good but I liked her and she respected me and didn't pry. We dug worms, she sorted out the ones she needed for her study, and we put the rest back. We did this for a month. Then her funds ran out, we shook hands, and I headed west.

I spent the next few hours scrubbing that boat down and the whole time it nagged at me that I was waiting for you to come back. It would have been fine for you to give me the whole two hundred dollars and say see you in a few days, but here's what I hate: feeling stuck somewhere while waiting on someone else's plans. I was going to do the work then leave, as you'd said, whether you showed up or not, and I told myself to let go of worrying about the money, let go of meeting up again with you, and yet, it hovered—the money, you—as I moved from cabin to deck, a little sick from the constant smell of the disinfectant, only a little better on deck, but definitely feeling worse and worse about being trapped into this day on the boat, even though I had right at the beginning, as always, decided not to allow myself to be trapped.

So there I was, in my innocent state, worrying about an illusory entrapment. By then it was close to noon. A late-middle-aged man in tennies and a polo shirt let himself through the dock gate and as he walked by he said hi and asked if that was my boat. I told him I was just cleaning it for the owner and he nodded and kept going, boarding a boat near the end of the dock. I heard him say something—maybe there'd been some-one on his boat waiting?—but ten minutes later it was cop cars and sirens coming down that road and I didn't wait to see but dropped the scrubber, grabbed my coat and pack, and ran. I'd seen a scrabbly park just a little south of the restaurants and I headed there.

I noticed I still had the rubber gloves on. I pulled them off still running and dropped them in a trash can at the back of the last restaurant. Once in the bushes I changed from my sky-blue T-shirt into one that was a washed-out gray, and I put on my sunglasses and a baseball cap. The shore curved a little and I could see cops spilling out of their cars and onto the dock and talking with the man in the polo shirt, who was pointing at the boat I'd been on, and right then the coroner's van pulled up and I was off, coming finally to a frontage road and then San Pablo Avenue where I caught a bus to down-town Oakland, knowing that somewhere down there was a Greyhound bus station. I had a hundred dollars in my pocket and I knew how to get out of town.

I hadn't realized how 1984 things were already getting. I mean now, apparently, you can't go a block without CCTV grabbing a shot of you. Back then it was much spottier, but not spotty enough: dockside, first restaurant, second restaurant, liquor store where I got on the crosstown bus—all had me on their radar. I was sitting in the Greyhound station when they arrested me.

I was left to stew in a decrepit interview room. Boredom and tension fought over me. After a few hours there was a scram-bling in the hall outside the door and two big detectives burst in and deposited themselves opposite me. They introduced themselves as Doran and Peake, and Doran, the bigger of the two, started in. You know we have the gloves, right? With perfect prints on the *inside*, you know? We have all kinds of pictures of you. So you might want to tell us exactly what happened and maybe we can work something out with the DA . . .

So I told them. I didn't protect you and it didn't help me one bit. Something (someone) had blocked off the camera for a couple of hours that morning on the dock, so all they had was me and Polo Shirt, who turned out to be a retired judge. They had witnesses for you and me at the bar, but we didn't see anyone at your rooming house and you'd paid them in cash up front and left with no forwarding address. They got prints from your room—of dozens of people. It seems they didn't waste much time and money trying to track those people down and none of the prints matched up with the few they had from the boat. The part of the boat I hadn't gotten to yet had some brain matter belonging to the body that had worked itself loose from its weights and bobbed up next to the judge's boat. Their only question was what was my connection to the victim and motive for the crime?

Mine too, about you. And I've had fifteen years to think about it. Because I wouldn't tell them what they wanted, I got fifteen years to life; because I was a model prisoner, I got released at the first parole hearing, with the stipulation that I remain in Alameda County and out of trouble and in touch with my parole officer for the next five years.

So here I am, stuck in Berkeley, though it's a wide heaven after prison, and all I want to do is go out looking for you. This is my fantasy: I find you and I go to the police and they still have those fingerprints on file and I let them take it from there. Or, I find you and do the thing I just spent fifteen years paying for.

Or I could let it go. In prison I taught myself to do internally what I'd been doing outside: drop it, move on. Forward, forward, forward. I read a lot of books, I kept to myself. I wrote one letter—to the Kansas grad student studying worms—but it turned out that she and the grad student she'd married— another worm specialist—had been killed in a tornado while on a worm expedition. Her mother was kind enough to write me back.

So I keep to myself, I do stupid jobs well, I live in a rented room. I saved enough money to buy a used computer and pay a guy living here to teach me how to use it, and now, my friend, I'm tracking you down.

SHALLOW AND DEEP
BY JASON S. RIDLER
Downtown Berkeley

NOW

"Worried you were gone, bro."

We'd circled North Berkeley BART once, like friends who didn't want to go home. Because this is what the market wants. Not tomes analyzing the realpolitik in Stalin's Russia. Or the butchery of the Gulag in gold mining. Or anything else from my fields.

"Need fresh shots. Nothing fuzzy. Clear. A hundred. I can make anything work, but a hundred is best. Gives me variety to play with, allows for redundancy. Video good if you can scratch it."

The homeless bundle shook. Slip-on sandals and black-bottomed white socks, it nestled like a dust bunny on the outer rotunda of the station, desiccated mouth twitching beneath a yellow Warriors shirt. We descended the stairs to a parking lot we didn't use, Ford bikes with punctured tires stationed to our left.

"Variety is good. But just the face."

My next class was eight a.m., if Bernie showed.

5Chan snorted, then spat phlegm on the windshield of a red Prius. "The body is useless to the client."

A gaggle of passengers scurried out of the station with intentional steps and a panoply of uniforms: suits, skirts, bike shorts, designer jeans with custom rips, and everyone's perfume and cologne long liquidated.

"Meet in two weeks here on Saturday. Old e-mails are dead. Got it?"

I nodded. 5Chan liked me timid, quiet, and listening. Made him feel in control. And it bought me work and information.

5Chan lit up an immaculately rolled joint and took his time dragging in smoke. Hoodie, limited-edition *Purple Rain* concert shirt before his time by a decade, Chucks, and well-cultivated and shiny beard that smelled of pine. Berkeley trash, but "computers" got him leveled up. He had never offered me a hit.

"Two grand. More coming if you stick. No more vanishing acts. You are my golden egg, Koba. How the fuck do you do it?"

I shrugged, because it was rhetorical.

The smoke flittered out of his mouth as he spoke. "My dad was a grocer. Worked at Andronico's for years. Said that there was only two things that people always need. Bread and caskets. But he was wrong. Lust, bro. That's our bread and casket."

I just wanted the assignment, not a lesson, I had prep. We turned left.

"I saw it coming," His eyes narrowed, an oracle revealing wisdom to a plebe. "People are tired of fake. Silicon tits and Kardashian ass outside their paygrade. They want to fuck their neighbor, their boss, the UCB slut at Trader Joe's who thinks they're a cuck, their mom, their grandma. That's the escape, Koba. Slap the ex-girlfriend's face on a porn star, then watch her gangbanged and double-stuffed until she's sucking come between ten guys' toes and calling them daddy. That's the dream. That's the future, Koba. And we're the kings in Berkeley. Say, you ever want one for yourself, you let me know."

I smiled. "Can't afford our rates."

He wheezed, holding the joint at his lips. "No doubt. No doubt. Okay, back to work."

He gave me the target, then went his own way.

Walking down Delaware, I steadied my breathing while the sun flared my skin.

I knew her. But we hadn't met.

Sonja was a Republican. Former track star who hurt her knee and switched to teaching. She was recently promoted up and into the position of bulldog between teachers and parents. We'd never met face to face, but she'd given a tour around the school's cubicles once. Busty blonde, high voice, pink heels, with a lime sundress and bubbly affect that assured the parents walking the grounds that the teachers here were first-rate. "We even have PhDs in biology, history, and more. So Ainsley is getting the best." The mother mentioned her daughter had an intensive cross-country running schedule. "That's great! Where do you run?"

"My old school, and Aquatic Park."

"Me too! Maybe we can be run buddies."

Aquatic Park. Not far from me. Hell. This was almost too easy.

I pressed the crooked gate to the back entrance of my illegal in-law. My monitor shone blue in the dark, casting shadows from book towers onto the furniture of my old life. Love seat. Futon. Books. Mail about debt.

One job. Two grand. Fifty-Seven Hours of Teaching.

Thucydides warned about immediate and long-term causes for landmark events. Empires don't fall because someone dies. Wars don't start because an emperor is shot while on tour. The Soviet Union didn't crumble because Reagan was chosen by God to defeat the Evil Empire.

Beside my futon was my camera bag.
I checked the BP website.

*Hey, Russel. Wanted to touch base. Bernie's parents have
requested that Bernie find another teacher after the incident you reported. While we understand their desire, I
want you to know that Berkeley Prep is proud to have
you and stands by your assessment. You've done so well
mentoring our most challenged students, and we know
that summer is difficult in terms of hours and you'd like
to maintain more than ten hours a week (believe me, I
know!). I promise that we will fill your roster as soon as
possible. Hold tight, Dr. Walker!*

Sonja K. Tempest, BSc
Director of Student Relations

I checked my student report.

*RUSSEL FIELDS—Student Evaluation. I apologize for
the use of feminine pronouns but in the interest of time I
will use she as Bernie continues to change her mind on
which she prefers. Bernie arrived at class fifteen minutes
late. When asked why she said "bus" even though I saw
her in study hall in the period before class. As I e-mailed
you earlier, the assignment sent via e-mail by Bernie was
only two pages long, not ten. When I asked why it was so
short she said, "I write concisely." I indicated that was no
excuse and the paper was, as it stood, a failure. She said,
"So what?" I said that meant she would have to repeat
the entire class again. When she said, "I don't care," I
informed her that without a proper paper she would fail*

history and not be eligible for graduation and thus could not apply to college.

At this point Bernie stood and swung her fist in front of my face while calling me a liar, someone who talked behind her back, and then called me a "cunt."

An hour after that report, I'd found 5Chan's emergency e-mail. My message? *Can shoot.*

Ducks hustled for an upper-class family's artisanal crumbs from Acme Bread on a patch of exposed pathway that ran beside the lagoon. A chunk of property that was grassy, with a parking lot for early-morning stoners and kayakers. A sax player sat on the only bench, a cut tree stump keeping him shining bright as he ran scales through game-show themes: *Wheel of Fortune, The Price Is Right,* and *Jeopardy!* before he trailed off.

I shuffled in beige, exhausted from another useless night on Indeed. I sat beneath the tree, adjusting the lens of my geriatric Canon, and then assumed the position of a bored thirtysomething taking in nature's splendor because he didn't get laid the night before. Cars rumbled behind me to find empty spots to smoke up. Behind us all, Amtrak blew its way the hell out of Berkeley. My warm-up was shooting the parade of Aquatic Park:

—One unicycle teen with handlebar mustache.

—One forty-year-old white woman in black with full makeup who pushed a five-hundred-dollar covered stroller holding a Chihuahua who eyed all with the indifference of Molotov.

—One black man and a Latina in red exercise gear, weights tied to their ankles, lapping the old man in the gray tracksuit who was almost as overweight as me.

—Gaggle of stoner chicks in black and too much purple eye shadow and band T-shirts, shambling and laughing and speaking like texts.

—A gray homeless fortysomething in long sleeves who smelled like sun-bleached urine, pulling a trolley of corporate beer cans with craft labels and Coke bottles.

Ten burning minutes later, the bouncing blonde emerged from behind the red cabin that rents three-wheeled bikes to the disabled. Sonja: fit but chubby, unable or unwilling to kill her freshman fifteen. A white-and-blue Stanford shirt and pink trunks. No sunglasses (5Chan would be ecstatic).

I focused. Then I shot her face a hundred times, tracking her, then switched from photo to video.

"You."

I released the trigger.

Bernie stood above me. Again. Baggy striped sweater. Elbows angular. Brown trousers and terra-cotta clogs. I kept *his* preferred pronoun in mind.

"Morning."

"What are you doing here?"

"Relaxing. You?"

"I always walk the park. I never see you."

I nodded. "Guess I'm like a ghost outside the school."

Bernie stinkfaced. "You do photography?"

"Sometimes."

Bernie had three emotions: rage, indifference, and excitement if we were talking about the manga and anime that he liked. Bernie's eyes tracked Sonja and *mooned*, countenance starved.

The next move would dictate my future. So I said nothing.

Bernie blinked. "5Chan?"

I exhaled and smiled.

Bernie did not. "No way."

I shrugged. Sonja had already run the exposed patch and into the thicket of shadows made by Aquatic Park's winding corridor of trees.

"You can't tell."

I put my camera down. Still recording.

"You can't say anything. I'll tell them you sent them to me."

Bernie was smart but scared and talking dumb. No one made him spend two grand of his parents' cash for pictures of teachers he wanted to fuck.

I had him. Better than a black eye he refused to give me. I stood. Bernie backed up. Leaves cut shallows of light across his sweating face. "I'm sorry you won't be in my class anymore, Bernie. I was looking forward to your paper on the Pink Triangles as victims of the Holocaust."

"Huh?"

"We made good progress." I took a step back. "Hope you can find a teacher who understands you and your interests, Bernie."

Tiny fists shook so hard I expected them to leak red and white.

"I think that's what I do best. Understand students. Help them get what they want and I get paid for it."

I tapped the camera, next to the red light.

Bernie recoiled, then stopped. "I don't get it."

I hit pause. "I'd love to be a photographer full-time. I'm really good. Especially faces." I sighed. "But not enough money in it, so I have to keep teaching. Wish I had more clients. Until then I may have to keep teaching. Including you."

Bernie's face scrunched.

"Take care, Bernie. Enjoy what you see in the park."

Hey Russel! I'm sorry but I haven't found any new stu-

dents yet, but trust me I am trying! As soon as we have some. And thanks for taking over Camera Club! We've had some new hires and we need photo ID and pictures for the teacher wall. Can you be here at 8:00, Dr. Walker? And thanks for the specs on making it more glamorous! I can't wait. My old one has me looking like a hag! LOL!

S

"Dude, I told you. I fucking told you." Ashby BART was a concrete bunker that could have probably taken a non-nuke ICBM hit. 5Chan and I walked the perimeter, him in the lead, puffing vape in my face. "We're blowing up. I got so many orders I may need to hire more shooters."

I shrugged. "Might increase the risk."

"Shit. You're right. Dude, we are going to clear close to fifty K this quarter if you can do what you do."

I smiled.

"My work is sick and getting sicker. This last one was like sticking your weird lesbian aunt into a slasher flick and vine. I almost kept a copy. Almost."

I nodded.

"Damn, bro. Say something! You're making enough to have one of your own. Hell, I'm feeling magnanimous. I'll do a freebie. Just name it."

Never saw any of the finished work. What 5Chan did with the carousel of other people's fantasies. Bank teller. Bus driver. Clerks in designer women's dress shops. Lots of waitresses, bartenders, and other service personnel. Nurse. Hygenist. Teachers. So many teachers. Weekends in Walnut Creek, Concord, and San Leandro at gyms, outside yoga classes, and in downtown Berkeley near the theaters. And that awful parking lot at Trader Joe's.

"Really?"

5Chan held in his vape stream, then let it out his nose. "Name it."

"The one you made for the client who wanted Sonja Tempest."

He ssssss'd. "Can't do it, bro. That's the 5Chan guarantee: one-of-a-kind work for one-of-a-kind clients."

"You said name it." I shrugged.

He huffed a laugh. "Okay, okay. Just this once. Because we are on the cusp of a renaissance. But don't judge, okay? We're all entitled to our fucked-up shit."

I pushed the USB inside the port. The screen went black before Microsoft Silverlight read the file and readied it. No credits, just a fade.

There was Sonja. Sorta.

Alone on the edge of the bed, legs crossed, arms braced on the black mattress. Dirty-blond now. The outfit was official. Pencil skirt and caramel stockings. Black heels and purple blouse. But fuck if that wasn't Sonja's face.

"Hey there," she said in a voice twenty years and packs of Luckys older. "I know that right now, things are hard." She unbuttoned her blouse. "And it seems like there's no escape. And you're so alone." My gut sank. "You're different. So different there's no one you can talk to." Sonja caressed the space between DD breasts held back by a frayed black bra. "But there is someone who likes you. Who thinks about you all the time." Sonja bit her lip. "So I want you to watch this when you feel like no one notices you. No one cares. No one sees." Sonja pulled her legs open. Her cock was red and throbbing. "But I do. You make me want to touch myself. You make me want you. You make me do this . . . I know this is what you want, and I can't help it. You make me do it! I don't . . . have . . . a choice!"

Hey, Russel. I totally get it. We all need to find ways to make it and I'm sorry your time at BP is now over. I'd just gotten off the phone with Bernie's parents who had reconsidered their decision. So much uncertainty! Thanks so much for helping so many of our students. You'll be missed. ST

BOY TOY

BY JIM NISBET

Yacht Harbor

Captain Ron Tagus was pairing a whiskey with a weather check when his phone rang. He glanced at its display: 2:35 a.m. Blocked. He finished the pour, turned down the VHF, and took the call. "What's up, boss?"

"We're going out."

"Sure." Captain Ron glanced over his shoulder at a calendar tacked to the bulkhead behind him. "What day?" He set down the bottle and drew the flat stub of a carpenter's pencil out of the folded brim of his watch cap.

"Tonight."

He moved the tip of the pencil to a square labeled *Monday*. "What time?"

"What time is it now?"

"Two thirty-six."

"Let's shoot for three fifteen."

The faceted lead of the knife-sharpened pencil hovered above the empty square. "That's not tonight. That's this morning."

"Your circadian hair-splitting is of no interest to me at the moment." That was the boss's carefree vocabulary all right, but the tone was off. Brittle, like.

Ron turned away from the calendar. "Regan—"

"Under sail," the boss added.

Captain Ron glanced at the darkened porthole that

topped the whiskey bottle like the dot on a letter *i*. "There will be a little weather."

"All the better."

Pause. Ron asked her where she was.

"On the bridge."

"How fast are you going?"

"A hundred and three."

He believed her. "Hey."

"Hey *what?*"

"You okay?"

"Just peachy." She hung up.

Before reverting to its matrix of icons, the display informed him that the call from Blocked had lasted fifty-three seconds. Captain Ron dropped the phone into a gimbaled cup holder and chased it with the pencil. On the bulkhead behind the settee on the other side of the chart table hung a handsome analog barometer, an antique with a six-inch bezel of tarnished brass. Its arrow pointed almost straight up, and Captain Ron could easily discern its reading of 29.3 inches of mercury. He slid off the settee to administer the glass two taps of a fingernail, and the needle dropped a single mensuration, to 29.2. It had been falling all day, creeping counterclockwise over the lovely italic script of the word *Change* inked onto the card covering the instrument's face, leaving the telltale behind at 30.1. For a couple of days, Stella, the common name around the waterfront for the female version of NOAA's weather-reading robot, and Stanley, her male counterpart, had been predicting a blow, with winds hooting into the thirties bringing one to two inches of rain. A typical winter storm. The cube of ice capsized in the dram of whiskey. A gust tugged at the trucks. A standing wave rippled through the lengths of the paired staysail halyards, taut along the mizzen, so that they clattered up and down the mast like a little girl running from one end to the other of a hardwood floor in her mother's shoes. The elevating pitch of crescendoing whistles and whirring shrieks, peculiar to a couple of acres of masts and rigging as a rising wind combs through them, virtually encouraged windward vessels to crush their fenders between hull and dock, and the lines of leeward vessels to stretch their snubbers, so that the otherwise deserted marina was phantomic with sound. *We won't even take the cover off the main,* thought Ron, as he took up the glass of whiskey. *Boy Toy* could certainly be sailed under a reefed mainsail; but as she went short sail, being a ketch, she handled much better under a foresail with mizzen and no main at all, a suite commonly known as jib and jigger. *We'll motor out of the harbor, of course, a series of tight zigzags, and once out we'll stay out. After the low pressure has made its way down the coast we'll come home, and not until. It'll remain a little rough in front of the breakwater, shoal as it is there, but we'll be coming back by daylight.* He glanced at a light-blue line that undulated across the calendar week—by daylight and on the flood. Altogether, the makings of an excellent excursion. He downed the whiskey at a go, tossed the ice cube into the sink, parked the empty glass next to it, and set about stowing anything that wasn't nailed down.

If it takes time to rig a sloop, with its single mast, it takes approximately twice as long to rig a ketch, with its two. Tonight the timing would be about the same as the latter because, despite leaving the main furled, he wanted to switch out the jib. After little debate he went with the No. 4, which was 80 percent of the foretriangle, instead of the spitfire, at 35 percent the smallest sail aboard. A spitfire would be flown only in the most extreme conditions, to keep headway on the vessel sufficient to maintain steerage, a situation in which, so long as Captain Ron had been in charge, *Boy Toy* had never found herself. Ron rigged the mizzen first, a simple matter of removing the canvas cover and shackling the halyard to the head of the sail. Dropping the rolled cover down the companionway as he moved to the bow, he unrove the sheets from the clew of the No. 2 jib, moved the sheet leads forward to a mark on each genoa track, and unbent the 125. Despite the rising wind and because of a big motor cruiser called *Pay Dirt*, three stories high and seventy feet long, to windward, whose bulk blanketed the dock between her majesty and *Boy Toy*, he managed to fold the 125 into its bag without spending the rest of the night keeping both on the dock and out of the drink. He was reboarding with the sail bag when a chirp of tires alerted him to a car, and he looked up in time to see a pair of headlights swivel off Spinnaker Way into the parking lot. This would be a Jaguar roadster, green as a pool table, with two leather seats, many horsepower, and, inevitably, its top down. The roadster's brakes locked up and it skidded to a stop in its reserved parking place. Bits of gravel tumbled down the riprap to the water, just in front of the Jaguar's front bumper. A little hasty.

The sky had darkened considerably, leaving no stars visible, and the north wind that had chauffeured the storm down the coast now backed southwest. At perhaps twenty knots the wind made quite a racket as it foraged through the huddled shipping, on the prowl for the unbattened, the unstayed, the carelessly lashed. Even as Ron made this observation, an improperly secured roller furler aboard *Cohiba*, a sixty-five-foot sloop with an eighty-foot mast docked on the other side of the marina, unspooled the better part of its charge in less time than it takes to tell it, leaving a thousand square feet of high-tech fabric thundering to leeward, sheets aflail.

That's an easy ten or twelve grand worth of trouble, thought Ron. *The spreaders will tear that sail to shreds if somebody doesn't soon get it under control; dangerous, too, even in broad daylight.* It's hard to comprehend how much power a big sail like that has until you get launched off a boat by one. Meanwhile, back on *Boy* Toy, there would be no such thing as raising the No. 4 dockside in order to double check the positioning of the sheet leads. Not in this wind. Captain Ron backed down the companionway ladder, dragging the sail bag after him. He gathered up the mizzen cover in passing, and as he backed along the cabin sole with his arms full of textile, he caught a glimpse, through the chart table porthole, of a pair of open-toed stiletto heels, red with a pedicure to match, and heard them overhead as they boarded the boat. When Captain Ron came out of the forward locker bearing the No. 4, Regan Ellis was standing at the chart table, half turned away from him, downing a shot of whiskey, after which she promptly poured another. The neck of the whiskey bottle made a little tintinnabulation against the rim of the glass, for her hands were trembling. Feeling the skipper's presence, however, Regan pulled herself together. But she didn't greet him, nor did she meet his eye. *Okay,* thought Captain Ron, *we've had a rough night at the office. I'll just go about my business.* To get himself and the sail through the narrowest point in the saloon, he backed around her, turning as he went, so that he and the sail bag swiveled from facing forward to facing starboard to facing aft.

Despite his determination to manage otherwise, their eyes met, and Captain Ron could draw only one conclusion: tonight, a woman he knew for her remarkable self-possession was a mess. "What's up?"

No answer.

"You seem . . ." *What's the word? Upset? Pissed off? Disconcerted?*

Regan refocused a thousand-yard stare onto Ron's face, mere inches in front of hers. Her mouth opened, but no sound came out. Her eyes, which were of a green that the roadster could only hope to rival, liquified. She clutched the glass to her sternum. She shook her head.

Captain Ron dropped the sail bag and embraced her. He didn't know what else to do. Her hair smelled of cigarette smoke. The glass smelled of whiskey. A shudder passed through her. Captain Ron realized that, beneath the knee-length faux-ermine coat, his boss might not have any clothes on.

After a full minute she pulled back far enough to place the empty glass against his own sternum, but not so far as to break the embrace. She watched her fingernail, lacquered to match the shoes, trace the rim of the glass. "I'm not going to cry," she told the glass.

"If you can't cry on your own boat," replied Captain Ron, "where can you cry?"

She pursed her lips at the evident truth of this, but made no reply. A gust thrummed the stays. *Boy Toy* rolled to the limit of her snubbers and rebounded.

Captain Ron raised his eyes toward the overhead. "If this keeps up we'll be sailing right here at the dock. We won't have to go—"

"We're going out," she interrupted, still addressing the whiskey glass. "Are you ready?"

Captain Ron nodded toward the sail bag, on the sole abaft him. "Need to bend on the small jib. Then we'll see if we can get out of here without holing somebody's million-dollar yacht."

"I've got insurance," she whispered. And added, "The

bastards." Regan turned out of Ron's arms and finished the drink. She placed the empty glass in the galley sink, and at last she looked at him in the eye. "I'll change clothes, and we'll be off."

That is one good-looking woman, Captain Ron reflected, not for the first time, *who pays me to take her sailing.*

The hint of a smile crept over her lips. "That's right."

"Which part?"

She smiled only a little more.

"All of them."

"Dress for weather." Ron hefted the sail bag and pushed it ahead of him, out the companionway.

The wind brought with it the unmistakable smell of rain as it raked through the harbor in search of mischief, which latter, aboard *Boy Toy*, amounted to having carried over the leeward rail the working or forward ends of both jib sheets, left unattended on deck, along with what standing length could follow until the stopper knots halted the chicanery at the after-cars, just forward of the cockpit, which is why they're called stopper knots. No big deal, although, as Ron soon realized, the ebb, falling strongly under the wind, had carried the lines beneath the boat, port to starboard. He had to walk the cordage forward, then aft and back again, hauling all the while, before he could tease the lines free of some object or other, beneath the rippling opaque brine, and drag them back aboard in a braided tangle, itself remarkable in that a braid is usually accomplished with three or more strands, proving yet again the adage, not confined to matters maritime, that if something can go wrong, it will. Hanging onto the cloth of the No. 4 while he bent its luff to the forestay presented another small challenge. A heavy weather sail is made of stouter stuff, and is respectively stiff, but that doesn't mean it won't blow overboard in a heartbeat of inattention. He used one of the sopping sheets to belay the bulk of the jib to the port bow cleat while he sorted clew from head and tack in the dark, then bent on everything in its proper order, the tack to the foot of the forestay, the head to the halyard's venerable bronze pelican shackle, each with a sennit he'd rove himself, and in between clapped the piston hanks to the forestay, throats port to starboard, in their proper order.

The sail's empty bag he kept aboard by kneeling on it. After a quick trip aft to drop the sail bag down the companionway and retrieve forty feet of half-inch line, back forward he rove a chain knot about jib and forestay, belaying the line to the starboard bow cleat, so the sail wouldn't blow overboard on the way out of the harbor, yet at the proper moment he could raise it out of the slipknots of the chain with a reasonable amount of control. And now, as he deployed a variation on the bowline called a sylvain knot to reave the working ends of both sheets to the clew, an all-too-familiar sound rent the air, and before Captain Ron could so much as bring it to bear, the tip of an upper spreader had speared the big jib aboard *Cohiba* and the sail simultaneously ripped up to its tack and straight down to its boltrope, midway along its foot, opening as it were a vertical geologic fissure with a sound that most closely resembled that of eighty feet of one-hundred-dollar bills glued nose-to-tail being ripped down the middle one end to the other, only louder. The commotion of whipping sheets and streaming Kevlar gave *Cohiba* the appearance of flying to windward, a revenant ship. *Maybe by the time we get back*, Captain Ron reflected, observing Nature's profligate spree, *maybe they'll have that mess under control.*

Regan came topside in full foul-weather regalia—bibbed

Gore-Tex overalls, cuffs velcroed over sea boots, hooded jacket with gasketed sleeves, watch cap, fingerless gloves, a personal flotation device, or pfd, that would inflate at the tug of a lanyard or upon contact with seawater, with a built-in harness, a tether—which reminded Captain Ron that he'd be well-advised to jump below and don similar gear. Engine started, they performed practiced maneuvers to get underway, Regan handling dock lines and fenders with Captain Ron on helm and throttle, for it is not at all uncommon to encounter a capful of wind in this or any other marina on the San Francisco Bay. Blanketed by the considerable mass of *Pay Dirt*, they poked *Boy Toy's* bow into the fairway, got her headed up into the wind, and powered out. The water was very shoal at the entrance, and the chop was considerable, but, decisive on the throttle, they made the two quick turns, one to port, the next to starboard, and cleared the spuming breakwater without incident, leaving the structure's "continuous quick" flashing green light to starboard. The shriek of spars and rigging and the flogging of the ruined jib quickly faded, replaced by the salubrious cough of the diesel, wind in their own rigging, whitecaps slapping and thumping the windward topsides.

After she'd stowed the three fenders, Regan took a seat on the starboard locker, opposite the skipper, just as *Boy Toy* lifted her bow and set it down with a crash. A gout of solid water engulfed the foredeck and streamed aft, port and starboard of house and cockpit, until it sluiced over the after-combing or drained away through the scuppers. Regan closed the companionway hatch and tore free the Velcro collar that covered most of her face. "I feel better already."

"I can't hear you!" Ron shouted above the din.

"I feel better already!" she shouted back.

They motored west, quartering the weather in order to get

some sea room between themselves and the Berkeley Pier, the ruin of which extends west-southwest almost three miles into the bay, coming ashore not three hundred yards south of the marina entrance. With the breeze on port they'd be fine; still, it was dark out there, and rough, and along the entire length of the pier there's but a single light, at its far end, flashing red every four seconds.

After ten minutes, Ron gave the helm to Regan. "Keep her nose into the wind and enough rpms to keep steerage on her. Let the mizzen luff, so she won't start sailing before we're ready."

Regan steered the bow into the wind, the gooseneck over her head rattling as Ron untied and hoisted the sail, its leach clattering. He made fast the halyard, hardened downhaul and outhaul, dropped the sail ties into the starboard locker, and scuttled forward. At the bow, though it was wet work, everything went as planned. Leaving the raised No. 4 with the breeze evenly streaming both sides, Captain Ron collected the forty-foot line and regained the cockpit.

"Okay," he yelled, coiling the length of rope, "let's go sailing!"

One foot on the wheel, Regan hardened the mizzen sheet. Ron took three turns around the starboard winch and hardened the jib sheet. Regan let *Boy Toy* fall off until the boat abruptly heeled as both sails took the wind and fell silent.

"Okay," pronounced Captain Ron, "kill the iron wind."

Regan put the drive in neutral, pulled the choke, and the diesel died with a plaintive tweet. She turned off the key and a silence arose that consisted entirely of the noises made by a wooden boat under sail. Water purled along *Boy Toy's* hull, the odd gout lifted over the port bow, spray descended upon the foul-weather gear worn by the occupants of the cockpit.

Below deck, a chimney in a gimbaled lamp tilted to touch its brass bail, the whiskey glass inched across the stainless-steel basin to the low side of the galley sink, a screwdriver appeared, as if out of nowhere, to roll around on the cabin sole.

On deck, the working sheet creaked on the winch drum as Captain Ron eased it a bit. "Ease the mizzen, please."

Regan made the correction and the starboard rail came up out of the teeming brine.

Satisfied with the state of things, sheets made fast, Captain Ron joined Regan on the port side, their backs to the wind. "Where we going?" he asked, bracing both feet against the mizzen.

"I'm just glad to be going," Regan replied. "I'll leave the details to you."

Ron considered this. "There's four knots of ebb, but with a breeze like this we can go just about anywhere."

"Your call," she reiterated.

"The southwesterly makes for refreshing points of sail," Ron observed, which is true. Prevailing winds on San Francisco Bay blow out of the northwest. "We've got another hour of ebb. Let's reach over to Angel Island, tack, and have another reach behind Alcatraz. Before we get to San Francisco we'll tack again and have a throughly entertaining beat west. Close aboard Fisherman's Wharf or Aquatic Park we'll throw in a northwesterly bias and have ourselves a lovely beam reach toward some point between the middle of the bridge and Point Cavallo." With a glance at the compass he faced the wind, turning his head until the breeze blew evenly over the tips of his ears. "Maybe even a broad reach."

"Either way, it sounds wet," Regan pointed out.

"Wet on deck for sure, salt and fresh water both. By the time we close the bridge the tide will have turned and it'll be blowing like stink and raining too. We'll get as far west and north as we can before we fall off, and then we'll be running dead downwind right up Raccoon Strait. A sleigh ride. If we play our cards right we won't have to touch a string. A little work on the helm, though. With just the two sails we should make six or seven knots over the bottom. If we have to jibe in thirty knots of wind it'll be nothing but fun, if nobody gets killed, and by the time it's over you won't even remember who you are anymore, let alone why you lost your mind and bought a boat."

Regan almost smiled. "I can't wait."

"At the far end of Raccoon Strait we'll leave Buff Point to port and have a leisurely half-hour cruise in the lee of Tiburon Peninsula, till we drop the hook in Paradise Cove, which will be protected in this weather. We'll have a drink, eat some breakfast, and take turns napping and standing watch. Dawn's at six o'clock, sunrise is an hour later, though today we may not see the actual entity. We'll still have a bit of the flood midmorning and plenty of wind to go home on. If the entrance to the harbor is all cut up, we can go sailing again till things settle down. Altogether we'll have more fun tonight than most people have in a lifetime. What do you think?"

"Let's go."

Regan drove until, not half an hour and three nautical miles later, about a mile east of Angel Island, they tacked, and Captain Ron took the helm. Close-hauled on starboard with the port rail under, they bucked their way south-southeast, to the leeward of Point Blunt and Alcatraz, heading straight for the lights of San Francisco with the waning ebb nudging them westward. *Wind over tide* is what the sailors call it, wind going one way and tide the other; it can make for wet sailing, which some people think of as fun, delivered in a small enough dose.

There was no shipping, large or small, there wasn't a light on the bay that wasn't stationary—the light on Alcatraz, for example. They had the bay to themselves, a stout ship underfoot, and all the time in the world, early on a stormy Monday morning.

"It really is hard to credit," Regan marveled as they closed on the city. "Six million people in the Bay Area, and only two of them are on the water. What's the world coming to?"

"No good end," muttered Captain Ron. He fanned one hand and passed it over the view, east to west, from the lights of the Oakland container port, along the illuminated span of the Bay Bridge, to Treasure Island, the ferry building, two or three of the tallest buildings on the West Coast, Coit Tower, Fisherman's Wharf, Fort Mason, the dark stretch of Crissy Field, Fort Point, all the way to the yellow nebulae of the sulphur lights that flank the six lanes of the Golden Gate Bridge, four miles west. "Although," he added, "from this perspective you'd like to believe that some good might come of it after all."

After another half hour of steady sailing Ron said, "Ready about?"

Regan took up the lazy sheet. "Ready."

"Helm's alee."

And as they tacked, the rain arrived with great force, obliterating much of the view. By means of short, close-hauled tacks, they worked their way west along the city front, visibility limited but reasonable. The tide donated about fifteen minutes of slack to their progress, but they were taking both wind and rain on the nose.

About halfway between Aquatic Park and Fort Mason they tacked into a long beam reach, bearing midway between the north tower of the Golden Gate Bridge and the inland blur of Sausalito.

Now they had rain coming aboard in sheets. Both sailors sat on the port locker, their backs to the weather.

"I forgot to figure this in!" Ron yelled above the racket, watching a continuous cataract of fresh water, captured by the spread of the mizzen, plummet from the clew onto his knees, and thence into the cockpit.

"You're fired!" Regan yelled back.

"It looks like Bridal Veil Falls!"

"You're rehired!"

A roller came along to lift *Boy Toy*, then shrug her off, as she fell into the trough behind, deep enough to lose the wind and appreciably slacken the sails.

"That might have been the biggest swell I've ever seen inside the Gate," said Ron, as he corrected the helm. The darkness turned a shade darker. "Look to port."

The lights on the Golden Gate Bridge were nowhere to be seen.

Regan realized that she was looking at a wall of water. "Yikes!"

"Just about perfect!" yelled Ron, correcting the helm as the next swell lifted the sails into the wind.

The mizzen cataract appeared to redouble its effort to fill the cockpit. Regan thrashed her boots in the rainwater as if she were on a stationary bicycle. "Perfect!"

When *Boy Toy* topped the next swell and Ron saw where they were: "Okay, boss, prepare to fall off under gale conditions."

"*Prepare to fall off under gale conditions.* What's that mean?"

"It's time for you to take the helm."

Regan looked at him.

"Come on," Ron said. "Switch positions with me."

He scooted forward on the port cushion and Regan jumped aft to take his place.

"We're going to fall off the wind," Ron shouted, "into a broad reach, maybe even a dead run! It's not a jibe, nor do we want it to be, but it will feel like one. As we top the next roller, ease the helm over as we ease the sheets. Otherwise she'll want to stay on her current point of sail. When were done we'll still be on port, but with the breeze over the port quarter." He slashed the edge of his hand at the new vector, to starboard. "In the course of this maneuver, not only will the skipper be steering, she will also be easing the mizzen." Ron freed the mizzen sheet, led it under the away horn of its cleat, and handed Regan the standing part. "Try not to burn a stripe through the palm of your glove."

A gust heeled the vessel. Regan held the helm. The starboard rail dipped under, but *Boy Toy* heeled no further.

Ron moved to the starboard side. "I'll be slacking the jib." He bounced his hand off the standing part of the working sheet, between the cleat and the winch, sufficiently taut that it might have passed for a stick of wood. "Keep your sail to leeward of a right angle to the wind, keep the bow to weather." He unwrapped the working sheet until its standing part passed but once under the away horn of the cleat, as it passed from his gloved hand to the winch. "Ready?"

"Ready!"

As the next eastbound roller lifted the boat: "Fall off!"

Regan eased the helm to starboard as both of them eased sheets. The swell carried *Boy Toy* eastward as the bow fell away from the wind.

"Feel it?" yelled Ron.

"Yes!" she replied.

"Ease sheets. Ease the helm. Ease sheets. Center the helm. Ease, ease, steady as she goes . . ."

Now, wind over her port quarter, *Boy Toy* was seething

straight for the half-mile gap between the Belvedere Peninsula and the western tip of Angel Island, the entrance to Raccoon Strait, surfing the swells as they passed under her, having smoothly affected a course change of some seventy-five degrees in thirty knots of wind.

"Steady as she goes, boss!" exclaimed Ron. "Make fast. Nice!"

"Likewise, I'm sure," Regan said. "Skipper," she added, and they high-fived a couple of sodden gloves beneath the mizzen boom.

Ron lifted his eyes for a thoughtful gaze at the main truck, rainwater running over his face. "We should do this more often!"

"Yes!" Regan shouted back.

A swell passed beneath the hull. Regan corrected to port. The jib slacked as *Boy Toy* settled into the trough. Regan corrected to starboard. Again, a following swell lifted *Boy Toy* into the wind. Regan corrected to port. Both sails filled with a crack, and the starboard sheet parted. The bow veered to port. Regan threw her weight onto the wheel. "I can't hold her!" she yelled amid the racket of the flailing jib.

"Don't try!" Ron seized the mizzen sheet. "Give her her head!"

Regan let the rim of the wheel spin. As the *Boy Toy* swung to port, broadside to gale and sea, Ron hardened the sheet so that the mizzen pushed the stern to leeward. The next swell turned *Boy Toy* broadside to the wind, and she might have broached. But Ron eased the mizzen as she rose so that, though yawing downwind and into the trough between swells, she had only her hull and but a little sail area to present to the wind as the next swell lifted her. She climbed the following swell and, on top, more or less righted, Ron hardened the sheet so that the mizzen carried *Boy Toy*'s stern into the lee.

Worked thus, two or three swells later, the vessel lay bow to windward, stern by the lee, both jib and mizzen flogging like guns firing at will, the entire operation slowly driven backward by wind and turning tide.

"Now what?" Except that she had to shout to be heard, Regan put the query in an entirely reasonable tone.

"I need to go forward and get that sail under control," Ron shouted back, "before it destroys itself."

Regan regarded the scene at the bow. In the streaming dark, it looked as if the shadows, lines, and shapes of the inanimate world had come alive to conduct a knockdown brawl, with appropriate sound effects, strafed by tracers of rain as the works flailed in and out of the red and green of the running lights. The flogging canvas, fore and aft, sounded like a regiment of enraged taiko drummers.

"Let's start the engine!" Regan shouted.

"I thought you wanted to go sailing!" Ron shouted back.

Regan looked at him.

"Besides, that's three grand worth of sail up there." Before she could dismiss the financial angle, Ron said, "Let's try something else first. If it doesn't work, we'll start the engine."

Regan nodded. "At your orders, skipper."

"We're in irons. Understood?"

"Irons it is."

"We want to bring the bow to port. Once she's on a starboard tack, I'll take a line forward, reave a new starboard sheet, and we'll be good to go."

"But how do we get out of irons without a foresail or the engine?"

Ron pointed. "We bowse the mizzen boom to port. The breeze will push the stern to starboard. As soon as the wind comes over the starboard side, we sheet both sails to port and Bob's your salty uncle."

"Heading right back where we came from," Regan pointed out, casting an eye into the darkness.

It struck Ron that back where they'd come from was the last place Regan Ellis wanted to go. "We'll make a U-turn soon enough!" Ron shouted above the din. "With this fresh breeze we have all the boat control in the world!"

When Regan smiled, raindrops pelted her teeth like bird shot. Fresh breeze indeed.

"Take three wraps on the port winch and get the slack out of the sheet."

"Done . . ."

"Where's the goddamn winch handle?" The winch handle wasn't in its holster, low down on the forward side of the mizzen mast.

They felt around in a couple of inches of brine until Regan found it under a tangle of wet lines. Handing the crank to Ron, she belayed the tail of the port jib sheet around the away horn of a cockpit cleat, so as to pass the better part of the load to the boat's superstructure rather than her own, to prevent the sail flogging the sheet forward.

Meanwhile, Ron retrieved a four-part bosun's tackle from the rope locker. He clapped one block to a loop of line midway along the mizzen boom, the other to a dock-line cleat abaft the cabin, and led the purchase across the cockpit to starboard, took three wraps around the starboard winch, and inserted the sprocket of the winch handle. "Ready, boss?"

"At your orders, skipper."

Ron hove away on the tackle, forcing the mizzen sail to port, against the gale. As the rattling sail took the wind, the pressure pushed the stern of *Boy Toy* to starboard, which had the effect of turning the bow through the eye of the wind. Air began to flow over the starboard side The foot of the No. 4 cracked over the foredeck, starboard to port, its clew trailing a twenty-foot spiral of wounded sheet.

"Sheet home!" ordered the skipper. "Lively, now!"

Regan hardened the port sheet. If the jib had wrapped the forestay in the interim, it would have been a different story. But the stalled sail shivered to leeward until the fabric took the wind and ceased its flogging, and Boy Toy cracked into a starboard reach. Ron released the tail of the bosun's tackle and hardened the mizzen until its boom lay just a little to port of the centerline of the boat. And all went silent, excepting the maelstrom, as Boy Toy galloped through wind and tide and the teeming dark with a phosphorescent bone in her teeth, her new course nearly parallel to the span of the Golden Gate Bridge, whose lights cast an ochre pall high into the mist, not two miles west of their position.

"It worked!" shouted Regan. "It worked!"

"Dang," said Ron, as if no one were more surprised than he.

"I haven't had this much fun," Regan replied, clinging to the wheel, foulie hood and drenched hair streaming to lee-ward, "since I totaled my first Jaguar."

"Touch the wood," Ron cautioned, tapping three fingers to his own head. "We don't want to be walking home tonight."

Regan touched three fingertips to the mizzen mast. "Consider it touched, captain!"

More work lay ahead. Gripping the helm, Regan lodged her feet in the corners afforded by port and starboard lockers where they met the cockpit sole, while Ron cranked in the jib until its high clew hovered above the forward deck, where he might get to it without hanging over the side. This pointed

Boy Toy as close to the wind as she would sail, and it was correspondingly rough.

He jumped to the starboard side and, drawing aft what was left of the parted sheet, discovered the cause of the failure. "Look at this."

"It's been cut . . ."

Ron described retrieving the two sheets after they'd blown over the side at the dock. "It must have fouled some piece of junk on the bottom." Rather than throw the rope end over the side in disgust, he properly hanked it.

He was stowing the coil when Regan said, "Both sheets were fouled together?"

Ron gave this a thought, then crossed to the low side and eyed the working sheet. After the winch, he found no sign of damage to the line. Forward of the winch, the line was taut as a length of chain. He ran a hand along the sheet as far forward as he could, and there it was. Perpendicular to the length of the line, an incision cut perhaps a third into its diameter. It felt like an open wound. Under the present load, it couldn't last.

Ron rummaged the rope locker for a length of synthetic line that, though a mere quarter-inch in diameter, featured an extremely high breaking strength. He joined the ends with a Zeppelin bend, forming what's often called a strap or choker—a loop. Clipping his tether to the genoa track, he crawled forward alongside the house and, despite his outboard half occasionally dipping in and out of the passing stream, rove a lateral tension knot, so-called, in this case, a *klemheist*, about the sheet forward of the incision. Backing to the cockpit, he took a turn about a free cleat, threw in a trucker's hitch, bowsed down the doubled quarter-inch as hard as he could, and made it fast.

"If she goes," Ron said, "this will hold it." Since Ron Tagus was in charge of *Boy Toy*, each rope in the locker had a piece of tape on one end with its length inked onto it. By the light of the binnacle he selected a pair of lines. "Now I go forward, see . . ."

As he spoke, the sea walloped the starboard topside, just forward of the chain plates, lifted five or six feet above the bow, and collapsed onto the foredeck. Six inches of brine sluiced along the windward cockpit combing.

"You're going to the bow in this shit?" Regan frankly asked.

"You just keep that steady hand on the helm," Ron said, throwing a stopper knot into a line, "and I'll be fine."

"One hand for you," Regan shouted pedantically, "one hand for the boat! Little old me would be hard put to get you back tonight!" She dipped a finger in the remaining inch of water, beyond the combing. "Fifty-three degrees and all that."

"It's not complicated. You hold this course. I jump forward and bend on a new sheet. Which reminds me." He touched the breast of his pfd. "Knife."

"To cut away the old sheet?" Regan realized. "Because the knot will be too wet to capsize."

"Too wet and too slow. Then, new sheet rove, I come aft, and we tack."

"After which you take a new sheet forward on the port side and we do it all over again."

"Except for the tack." Ron pointed at the jury rig. "After the port sheet has been switched out, we fall off into *right back where we started.*"

"Bob's your salty uncle."

"Indeed," Ron muttered as he crawled over the starboard locker.

"One hand for you," Regan shouted, "one hand for the boat!"

She perched on the locker with one seaboot hooked into a lower spoke of the helm and a hand atop it. *Boy Toy* was bucking, wind and tide on her nose, and plenty of water coming aboard, but she needed to be close-hauled so the rigger could access the clew of the jib. Any other point of sail and the clew would be hanging out over open water. Ron crawled forward on his belly, leading the new line through the after and forward turning blocks, clipping, unclipping, and reclipping his tether as he went, and keeping a weather eye. Only once did a sea lift and pin him to the side of the house, but by then he had reached the main shrouds and had plenty to hang onto. It was wet work and progress was slow, made slower by the awkwardness of working in gloves, and the pitching of *Boy Toy*, which afforded Ron the odd moment of near weightlessness. Gradually he disappeared into the teeming gloom, only to reappear in the lurid green of the starboard running light, to disappear again as he crawled and skidded past the mast, forward of the house, until, arriving beneath the clew of the sail, he was diagonally across the boat from Regan and lost to her sight. Five or six extra feet of sheet passed forward through her gloved hand, then stopped. She considered locking the helm, in case another hand was needed, but *Boy Toy* couldn't be asked to hold a steady course in these conditions by herself. And two people in trouble would do no good at all. Even as Regan had this thought, the forward half of *Boy Toy* sailed over an invisible hollow in the water, then dropped in with a crash and buried her nose. A wall of water backed the jib despite the high bias of its foot, throwing the bow to starboard. But with a little help from the helm, *Boy Toy* labored up and the sail took the wind on starboard. A foot of brine coursed along three sides of the house, past and into the cockpit.

Legs athwart and both hands on the wheel, Regan's leeward

boot filled with seawater. After a long time Ron reappeared and rolled over the starboard combing onto the locker, his watch cap missing, his hair, though short, plastered to his skull, the cuffs and collar of his foul-weather gear leaking seawater.

"Ready to tack!" he yelled, flat on his back. "What's so goddamn funny?"

Regan, simply thrilled to see him again, shook her head, rainwater streaming down her face. "I haven't had this much fun," she shouted, "since I totaled my *second* Jaguar!"

The sea smacked the starboard topside abaft the main chain plates, lifted a human's height above the combing, and crashed onto the house. As water coursed over the companionway hatch and into the cockpit, Regan freed the winch handle from the port-side winch. "Ready about?"

"Wait! Switch sides!"

They did so. Regan took the winch handle, sat to starboard, and disentangled the new sheet from the lines on the cockpit sole.

"Take the helm!" Ron shouted, and she did so. He clipped to the genoa track and crawled forward to the conjoined jury rig. "Ready about!"

"Helm's alee!" Keeping an eye on the little Turk's head rove onto the rim of the helm, which marked its centerline, Regan rolled the wheel fifty degrees to starboard.

Boy Toy responded immediately and turned her bow through the eye of the wind. The mizzen boom clanged over. The jib backed with a smack.

Ron hacked the port sheet forward of the klemheist knot and the working end shot ahead, into the darkness. "Jib's away!"

Regan hauled the slack of the starboard sheet till she met some resistance, took three turns about the winch, belayed the after end of the rope under the away horn of the cleat, and inserted the winch handle. Ron appeared in the cockpit to center the helm. Cranking the winch, she made fast.

"Okay," Ron shouted, "close-hauled on port! Good job! Sit to the high side!"

As Regan sat to port and took the helm, Captain Ron unhanked the second length of line, threw in a stopper knot, took a deep breath, and clambered to the port side. "Steady as she goes, boss."

"Aye aye, captain." Ron disappeared up the port side of the vessel, now the high and windward side, clipping and reaving and crawling and holding on and achieving weight-lessness as he went.

Regan fed the new line into the block on the after car. Ron reappeared in the lurid red of the port running light, crawled across the foredeck, into the glare of the green star-board light, then hauled himself up the shrouds, his seaboots braced against one corner of the house and the lower turn-buckles, in and out of water up to his knees, one hand lifting a knife into the night. This point of sail was much like the previous one, rough and wet. *Boy Toy* pitched through waves and swells, bucking both wind and tide. A wave smacked the port topside and lifted perhaps ten feet above the deck, its un-derside rendered as ruby as the throat of a giant trout, before neatly dividing itself about the shrouds and collapsing across the foredeck, seething along the decks and the roof of the house with the sound of big surf eagerly coming ashore.

Athwart the helm, feet planted wide, Regan's other boot filled with seawater. Above all the noise she couldn't hear Ron grunt as he crawled back along the port side of the house in the dark, clipping, holding on, unclipping, as he came one or two feet at a time. Arriving at the cockpit, he clipped to the turnbuckle at the foot of the forward mizzen shroud and rolled over the port combing onto locker, streaming brine.

"I'm blowed," he croaked, scrubbing the palm of a sopping glove over his glistening face. "Son of a bitch." He pushed himself into a sitting position and took the helm with one hand and the mizzen sheet with the other. "Ready to fall off?"

Regan freed the working sheet, leaving the standing part captured under the away horn of the cleat. "Ready!"

Choosing his moment, Ron eased the helm to leeward as they both eased sheets. It felt as if *Boy Toy* were pivoting about her righting moment, and soon enough, she was creaming along on a broad reach, making for the green and red lights that mark the entrance to Raccoon Strait, with rain, wind, and tide at her back.

Ron belayed the mizzen sheet and sagged against the port shrouds, one foot working a spoke of the wheel, breathing heavily. "Time for a whiskey, boss."

Without a word, Regan slid back the hatch and dropped below, to quickly reappear bearing two glasses half filled with whiskey. She stood on the companionway steps, and they touched glasses.

"Cheated death again," Ron said, as he downed half his drink. Adding, "More or less," he quickly finished the other half.

Regan watched him without tasting her own drink. "Hey."

"Hey what?"

"What happened to your eye?"

Ron flattened the fingers of his free hand over his left eye, then looked at them with his right eye. Regan waited. Ron made a correction to the helm with his foot.

"That parted sheet was whipping around like a snake on amphetamines. I could hear it but I couldn't see it. As I climbed up the shrouds I figured I'd keep my back to the wind, plus or minus the odd ton of brine boarding the vessel. I was just getting the blade inside the loop when goddamn if the bitter end didn't come from dead aft and pop me in the eye like it was born to the task." Ron circled his empty glass. "What are the chances?"

Regan frowned. "Wait a minute. You were cutting away the parted sheet? Are you telling me this happened on your first trip forward?"

"Correct." Ron angled his good eye. "You gonna use that drink?"

They traded glasses.

Ron downed his second drink at one go. "You'd think it would help a little," he scolded the empty.

"Can you see out of it?"

"No."

"Let me—"

Ron peered forward.

"Hey." She touched his cheek.

Ron turned to face her. "The lens is gone," he said. "Not that I'm an expert."

A band of rain swept the boat, southwest to northeast, blown horizontal by the wind. Regan looked north past Ron and toward the lights of Sausalito. She looked south toward the lights of San Francisco. Far to the east, obscured as they were by a vast density of airborne water, she could barely see the lights of Berkeley. Making landfall in the present conditions was out of the question. However they worked it, they were hours if not an entire day from any sort of medical attention.

"What are we going to do?"

Captain Ron shook his head. "Nothing."

"Goddammit," she said softly.

"One eye for the boat," he said, "one eye for me."

An hour later they dropped the hook in the quiet shelter of Paradise Cove. Fourteen hours after that, just after sunset, *Boy Toy* tied up in the Berkeley Marina. A month later, *Boy Toy* was rechristened as *Sedna*, an Inuit goddess of the sea. Not quite one year after the events related here, *Sedna* headed out the Golden Gate and took a left. Less than a day later, a big winter storm roared down the coast.

Neither the ship nor her crew was seen again in Berkeley.

PART III

Company Town

THE LAW OF LOCAL KARMA

BY SUSAN DUNLAP

Gourmet Ghetto

W hen Sergeant Endo Maduri talked about the case later he'd start off, "That was the last time Shelby and I rode together." It made the guys on the force uncomfortable, but Maduri didn't care.

"Where'd you nab him?" Maduri had asked Callahan that night.

The patrol officer had the suspect on the ground. She jutted her chin toward Walnut Square. "On the walkway."

Maduri raised an eyebrow. The original Peet's Coffee and Tea sat at the corner of Walnut and Vine. The walkway looped behind it. "He the perp?"

"Witness said perp was in a brown hoodie, mahogany color." She eyed the suspect's puffy black jacket. "Close enough in this light?"

At five thirty p.m. chilly mist was turning to icy fog. The shops fronting the Walnut Square walkway were closed. Few Peet's Coffee addicts even considered cutting through the walkway from Walnut to Vine. Even fewer were likely to clamber up the Everest of cement steps in the other direction.

Certainly not Jeremy Lampara.

Jeremy Lampara was not ascending any steps.

He was lying dead on the Vine Street sidewalk. White male, middle-aged, blood thick on the chest area of his camel's hair coat.

"Camel's hair?" Maduri said aloud.

"Classic Jeremy Lampara," Detective Harry Shelby snorted.

"The flipper? The guy who owned that building over by campus? The place that got torched?"

"More to the point, someone got him." Lampara wasn't likely to get sympathy from anyone in Berkeley, least of all Shelby. Lampara was lucky anyone bothered to put a sheet over his face to keep dirt from blowing up his nose. Not that he was going to be blowing it again.

"Gonna be one bitch of a case," Maduri said.

"Unless we can run down the perp pronto."

"Perp's gone."

"*Gate, gate, paragate.*" Shelby liked to drop in Buddhist talk. Liked to make the team ask what it meant.

Maduri'd been on the team awhile. "Perp's gone, gone, gone beyond, eh?" He motioned at the suspect Callahan was holding on the ground. "You sure the perp's gone."

"Twenty says he is. We'll take your car."

"Huh?" Maduri wanted to say: *Take my car for what?* But he wasn't willing to give Shelby that too. He waited.

"Single witness, that kid over there," he nodded at a thin, sandy-haired white kid in an inadequate white T-shirt and jeans, standing next to a blonde in a gray *CALIFORNIA* sweatshirt.

"We got just one witness? At Walnut Square? There are more people standing around holding lattes than that."

"Not this late. But Brian Janssen is what we got. He saw the perp shoot, saw him run. We're going to circle the area, hope he can spot him."

Fat chance. If Janssen didn't spot the perp, this whole investigation was going to be a field day for the press: *Cops' Cordon Catches Nothing! Cops on Scene 90 Seconds After*

Shooting; Killer Long Gone. Maduri could just imagine! *Real Estate Developer Shot Dead Outside the Original Peet's Coffee and Tea.* There'd be columns detailing the laws Lampara had charged through like a rhino clearing a papier-mâché doorway. There'd be lists of the ordinances he'd skirted, interviews with the tenants he'd evicted, pictures of the buildings he'd demolished, op-ed after op-ed about the shoddy construction of his shoddy new condos. And the fire!

And then there'd be the Shelby connection. And the question: did Detective Shelby give Lampara's killer a pass?

Shelby sighed. "Small chance, but all we've got." He nodded toward the tall, skinny kid and said to Maduri, "Brian Janssen, nineteen years old, sophomore at Cal, lives up by campus by the building that burned. He saw the fire guys carry out the victim. Saw the vic's cartons on the sidewalk soaked from the fire hoses. If the poor fuck'd left an hour earlier he'd be home in LA now."

Maduri shot a glance to make sure no reporter had heard that. They'd be hard enough on Shelby if the perp vanished. From habit he slid into the patrol car and leaned toward the computer screen. Nothing there he didn't know. He turned on the engine as Shelby lowered his butt into the car and shouted, "Left on Shattuck!"

Two cars, lights and sirens, squealed to stops across from Peet's. The crime scene van idled in front. An unmarked Maduri knew to be the medical examiner's blocked the sidewalk.

Maduri turned on the engine, checked the side mirrors then the rearview, and did a double take.

Janssen was in the backseat, with the blonde in the CALIFORNIA sweatshirt beside him.

"Who's she?" he half shouted even though it was quieter in the car with the doors shut.

"Lisa Kozlovski," the girl said.

"You saw the shooter too?"

"No, I was down the block, on Walnut, when I heard the shots. When I got here the man was dead. I mean, I think he was dead. He was on the sidewalk, all bloody. Dead."

Maduri raised a questioning brow to Shelby.

"Mr. Janssen wanted Miss Kozlovski to accompany him. He thought it would be interesting for her."

"Help me to think," Janssen sputtered.

Maduri had to jam his jaws together. Half the department would be circling the area. Every cop of the force would be dragged back in. And Brian Janssen was like a twelve-year-old on a date. Like he had Maduri and Shelby driving him and his date to the movies. The girl was a knockout blonde, three levels above what Janssen could ever hope for. But suddenly the kid had a novelty to offer. *Want to ride in the back of a cop car? In the cage? Look for a murderer?* Maduri didn't expect Janssen to spot the shooter—then again, he figured if this deer-in-the-headlights kid was managing to sit thigh-to-thigh with this blonde, he had to be sharper than he looked.

Janssen nudged her.

"Would you leave the doors unlocked?" she asked. "Uh . . . I'm a little claustrophobic."

You, not him, huh?" But Maduri just said, "Sure." As he clicked the lock, a patrol car Code 3'd around the corner, its sirens screeching in Maduri's ear as it passed inches away.

"Damn sirens," Shelby grumbled. "Know why they blast your ears off?"

It took Janssen a moment to realize the question was to him. "Uh-uh."

"New cars! They're so airtight; music blaring inside. Drivers don't hear the sirens anymore. Not ours, not the fire trucks."

From Janssen's guilty expression Maduri figured the kid was one of those drivers.

Dark night, pedestrians in black, some under umbrellas. The white Christmas lights snaking up poles turned the dark blacker. Maduri hung the left onto Shattuck. If the perp was planning to escape on BART he'd be running down Shattuck toward it, or jumping on a bus. Or hiding in the Arts and Crafts Co-op standing over a sculpture he had no intention of buying. Or he'd have hidden in the hundred and one spots BPD was not going to uncover on a dark, foggy December night. He'd have gone . . . anywhere.

Janssen would want to be the hero. Maduri slowed the car. "On the sidewalk, there! In front of the French Hotel!" He pointed to a white guy in a hoodie that could have been mahogany but was more likely black. "What about *him?*"

Janssen shot a glance at the girl before turning toward the window. Maduri noted Shelby's mistake—he'd sat Janssen where he'd have a clear view out the passenger window. He should have put the girl next to window and let Janssen look over her since that was the way the kid was looking anyway.

But Janssen was staring toward the dark figure moving into the Andronico's supermarket parking lot.

"What so you think?"

"No. Not him."

Maduri caught the kid's hesitation. "You sure, Mr. Janssen?"

Janssen shrugged. In the rearview Maduri could see him shiver and slide closer to the girl, who looked none too warm herself.

"Sorry about the car. Heater repair isn't high on the department's budget plans."

Janssen started to put an arm around the girl's shoulder

but she gave him a quick head shake. "She's from LA," he said quickly. "It's like Nome here for her, right?"

She nodded.

"It's like Nome here period tonight," Shelby said. Back at the scene, officers were standing in the cold, laboriously interviewing every man, woman, and child, writing every name and address, double-checking spelling, triple-checking e-mail addresses, getting colder every minute. Getting no closer to tracking down the perp.

"Mr. Janssen? That the killer?" Maduri said as a hoodie'd figure cut into the parking lot heading to the store or on out the other exit to Henry Street. Maduri hit the gas, swung a right, circled around and into the lot from the back. "There he is. By the first line of cars. Do you see him, Mr. Janssen? Is that the killer?"

Janssen dragged his attention from the blonde and looked out the window. "Nah, not him."

"Are you sure?"

"Not him."

"Not him how?"

"How . . . what?"

Maduri glanced in the rearview mirror in time to catch the boy's smart-ass grin; the sarcasm was for the girlfriend. *Only witness,* Maduri reminded himself yet again. *Have to keep him on our side.* "How's the killer different, Mr. Janssen? Shorter, taller, fatter? More hair, less? Different clothes?"

"There was something . . . odd . . . about him. He was a little guy."

"How little?"

"Five two, maybe."

Five two doesn't even make the chart! Probably he meant five six or five eight. Janssen was a good six feet. From his view anyone under five eight was a shrimp. "Short, huh? That all?"

"He seemed spooked, you know, like he couldn't decide which way to go."

"But he ended up running down Vine to Shattuck, right?"

Janssen just nodded, shrugged at the girl beside him.

"That right, Miss Kozlovski?"

"To this street? Sorry, I don't know this part of the city. My boyfriend's car—"

"*Former* boyfriend," Janssen put in.

In the rearview, Maduri saw her jaw go tight. Janssen did not. The kid was, Maduri thought, an idiot. He eased the black-and-white out of the parking lot back onto Shattuck just as a fire engine hit the siren behind him. He jerked to a stop.

Shelby shot him a glance that said, *You get to the point when you block out even that. Not good!*

"The shooter, Miss Kozlovski, how would you describe him?" Maduri was yelling over the fading siren.

"By the time I got there," she yelled back, "he was gone!"

"Citizens of Berkeley," Shelby grumbled as the siren faded away, "they bitch about everything. But a guy guns a man down and trots off and not a single concerned citizen bothers to follow him."

Maduri shot a panicked glance at the detective. *Don't give up, damnit!*

As if she caught his vibe, Lisa Kozlovski said, "Maybe this will help. I heard someone say you wouldn't want to meet him in a dark alley—"

"Which you took to mean . . . ?"

"Bigger. I mean like more substantial. I'd say bulky too"— she turned to Janssen—"don't you think, Bri?"

Janssen hesitated as if he was scanning the still shots in his mind before agreeing with her. As opposed to the decision he *was* weighing. Hesitantly, he placed his hand on her thigh, the way Maduri used to test the burners for heat on the ancient electric stove.

"Mr. Janssen?"

"Yeah."

The girl poked an elbow into his rib and he grinned, seemed to be squeezing her thigh, though Maduri couldn't be sure. "Yes, officer, she's right. He was stockier. That's why it was so odd, see, that he was bouncing around trying to decide what to do. Only a minute. Less than that, I think. I was looking at the guy lying on the sidewalk."

Maduri shot a glance at Shelby, but the detective was off in his own world.

Maduri pulled into the intersection and hung a left. Circling back on Walnut, paralleling Shattuck, eyeing the ivy-covered hurricane fence that surrounded a block of university plantings. Good place for a perp to leap into. But dicey if anyone spotted him. Maduri aimed the spotlight at the vines, on the small chance it'd jolt the perp. Nothing.

Janssen's head was turned toward the vines, but what he was eyeing was the girl.

Look for the perp, damnit! Maduri forced himself to inhale slowly. "Mr. Janssen, I want you to do an exercise for me. While you're scanning the sidewalks, run through what happened when you got to Peet's."

"When I arrived on the scene?"

"Yeah, exactly. But keep looking out the window."

"Like patting my head and rubbing my stomach."

Patience! "Sure. So . . . ?"

"Well, you know, I got coffee and left and—"

"What was Peet's like—crowded, noisy, half-empty?"

"Pretty empty. I only had to wait behind one guy in line

before I ordered, and he was just getting regular, not like Lisa
and her macchiato." He grinned at her, raking his fingers softly
up and down her thigh.

"Keep checking the sidewalk, Mr. Janssen."

"Oh, yeah, sure."

"So you got your coffee—"

"Espresso." His head twitched toward her but he caught
himself before letting his gaze leave the window. "It was in a
paper cup. I walked outside—"

"How did it strike you out there?"

"You mean, set the scene?"

"Exactly. You're doing great." The car was back at the
Peet's corner now, on Walnut. Crime scene tape was strung
across the entry to the Walnut Square walkway. Tech lights
shone off shop windows. The bark of radios cut through the
buzz of talk.

Maduri hung a left onto Vine. Janssen was on the passenger side, looking toward the far side of the street across from
Peet's as he would have been when he came out the door with
his espresso. In front of the coffee shop, the scene techs were
laying down markers. Maduri didn't want Janssen seeing that,
coloring his memory of the scene.

An update flashed on the computer screen. Shelby'd read
it, said nothing.

"So, Mr. Janssen, light? Dark, warm, cold, crowded . . . ?"

"Well, you know, it was getting to be night. I remember
now I was surprised. I mean I wasn't in there more than a
couple of minutes, but it seemed lots darker when I came out.
And, you know, wet, like now. Like moist, but not raining."

"You're doing great. Were there people on the sidewalk?"
*Where was the suspect Callahan nabbed? Anyone else? Anyone
who could be the killer?*

"A couple, I think. Like I said, it was dark and cold and no one was hanging around, not like they do in the morning. These were, like, people going someplace."

Maduri stopped at the light at Shattuck. "Where was Lampara, the victim? When you came out. Before the shots."

"Dunno. He could have been . . . I didn't pay attention to him till I heard the shots. Till I heard him groan. When I saw him go down."

The girl squeezed his arm, but for the first time he didn't seem to notice her.

"Tell me about it. *See* it. No, don't close your eyes. See it in your mind. Keep looking out the window." Maduri turned left onto Shattuck as he had minutes earlier. "That guy, in front of the Cheeseboard? Did you see him at Peet's?"

"No," Janssen responded so quickly it surprised him.

"Go on, Mr. Janssen. You walk out of Peet's. You're holding your cup. Did it have a lid?"

"It was just an espresso. I wasn't going to be drinking it that long."

"Okay, so you walk out . . . ?"

"I come out the door there on the corner. I turn left, downhill. I get, like, to the Peet's window, no farther. Like three steps from the doorway. I hear—wait!—I hear someone yell, 'Mr. Lampara!' and then the shot."

This is it! Maduri struggled to keep his voice even. "What did it sound like? Man, woman, high, low, accent? *Hear it now!*"

Janssen was trying, trying to hear. Shelby was swallowing any reaction; Maduri'd seen him do that before when the witness was on the verge of something.

Maduri was trying not to tell Janssen not to squeeze his eyes closed.

Janssen was *thinking*.

"Don't think! *Remember!*"

Janssen jerked.

Shit!

"Nothing special. I mean,' it was like a growl, like right next to him. Just those two words: *Mr. Lampara?* Like a question.*" Janssen's jaw was quivering.

"Five thirty at night. How'd the killer just walk away?"

Did Shelby realize he was muttering aloud? Or was he just losing it?

Whatever. Maduri knew it was all up to him now. He checked the rearview. The girl was looking out the window; the boy's expression was blank, his shoulder moving up and down in response to his hand on her thigh.

"I'm not surprised," Shelby continued. "Lampara's well known in this town. Well hated."

Janssen and Kozlovski cocked their heads toward him. Almost in unison.

"You know what the Law of Karma is?"

"Sure," Janssen said.

"Right. It's the one law citizens in Berkeley respect." Shelby uttered a weary chuckle. It was an old joke at the department. "I've been on the force a long time. I used to laugh when the new guys whined about driving up one block and down the next every morning, eyes out for a parking spot, them hauling themselves out of bed half an hour early to do it, to find parking within a mile of the station, then having to run to make the squad meeting. I didn't respect the Law of Karma then, so I laughed. Then they bitch about coming back at the end of shift and finding a parking ticket on their windshields! *Rite of passage*, I'd tell them, and I'd still be chuckling when I walked the four blocks home to a sweet two-bedroom cottage I was renting there . . . Lampara, he taught me about karma. Evicted me. Flipped my house."

Now Shelby drove an hour in traffic each way to the lesser house he could afford in the lesser town. The best he could say was that by the time he got there, he only had an hour or two to listen to the wife go on about the ugly streets, the bland neighbors, the boredom. The exile.

"Lampara was just beginning then," Shelby went on in that musing voice, almost like he was inviting them all inside his head. "That was before he could buy four-plexes, eight-plexes, four-story places—and slumlord the tenants out. Mostly near campus. And then there was the fire last month, the grad student who died. You live near there, don't you, Mr. Janssen?"

The girl jumped. Had Janssen squeezed her thigh that hard?

"You live near that apartment of his that burned, right? You must've heard the sirens, seen the engines roll in, the water, heard about the shitty wiring that sparked it. Didn't you?"

"Yeah, but . . . Yeah."

"You live across the street, right?" Shelby said. "Did you see the fire from your window, Mr. Janssen? Did you watch? Did you know the guy who died? In the flames? The smoke? Was he your friend, Brian? Did you see him at the window, trying to break the glass, Brian?"

Janssen was shaking, trying to get words out.

"Did you see his suitcase on the sidewalk? Taxi for the airport? To fly to LA? To get married? Did you see that? Did you know that? Did you, Brian?"

"Stop it. Just stop it, now!" The girl wrapped her arms around Janssen and pulled him to her. She was shaking too.

Maduri shot a glance at Shelby to see if the old guy had a

plan or if he'd just lost it. If all those hours on the freeway had wadded into rage. Or if it wasn't that. If, maybe, it was the boy who'd died in the fire. But all he saw was the back of Shelby's head. Shelby was staring hard out the window, or just staring blankly. He said to Janssen, "Black, could be brown, hoodie ahead walking fast. What do you think?"

Now Janssen was staring hard, wanting it to be the suspect.

"Wait, wait! Slow down," the girl said. "Think that's him, Bri?"

"I don't know."

"Can we get closer?"

"Not without spooking him."

The computer flashed. Shelby leaned toward it. "Wait! They've got something."

Janssen stretched up to look over the seat.

"The guy on the street"—Lisa Kozlovski pointed frantically at the window—"what about him?"

"The jacket!" Shelby said. "They found the coat. Puffy hoodie. Bloodstains."

Maduri flipped on the flasher and siren and pulled into the left lane. From inside the car it shrieked so loud that Maduri wanted to slam his hands over his ears. "Where'd—"

"Behind a fence on Walnut. Brown hoodie. Reddish-brown!" Shelby was reading off the computer. "Go! Let's go!"

Maduri hung a hard U.

The back door popped open.

Janssen slid across the seat, grabbed for the cage wire, caught himself.

Lisa Kozlovski was gone.

Maduri slammed on the brakes. The crash from behind shocked him, sent Janssen into the cage. Sent Shelby into windshield.

The EMT van didn't stop. Maduri was trying to make the call; he was cradling Shelby's head. Lights flashed white, red. Sirens screamed.

A patrol officer pulled up, Maduri didn't get his name. He flipped him the keys, muttered "Witness" toward Janssen, and pushed into the van with Shelby.

Later, after Shelby went into surgery, after Shelby's wife arrived from the distant town she hated, after a wave of cops flooded the waiting room and then another when they got off their shift at eleven, and after the surgeon came out to say that Shelby would live, but not walk—only then did Maduri think of Lisa Kozlovski and how easy it would have been for her to shoot Lampara, circle around through the Walnut Square walkway, chuck her mahogany hoodie, and stroll up to the scene.

And then—he shook his head—all she would have needed was a way to get clear of the scene, pick up her *former* boyfriend's car, and drive off.

WIFEBEATER TANK TOP

BY J.M. CURET

West Berkeley

1.

I survived a ten-year stint at San Quentin. I did exactly what I was supposed to do—kept my head down, my ear to the grindstone, and my mouth shut. I stayed alive and made it out. One week in West Berkeley and it's all shot to hell.

You hear the cops tell it: I'm probably getting exactly what I deserve. But cops can be sons of bitches. My PO, Greg, hooked me up with a small studio apartment in a run-down two-story complex on 9th and Bancroft and a night-shift janitor job at the pharmaceutical company on 8th Street.

"You know why I'm sticking my neck out for you, Red?" he asked me.

"Not really, Greg. I'm just grateful for the vote of confidence, to be honest."

"I'm helping you because there's something about you. I don't know what it is exactly, but there's something about you that gives me hope. Don't fuck this up."

I'm not a bad guy per se; I've done some things I'm not particularly proud of, who hasn't? So I've dabbled in illicit drugs, methamphetamines mostly. So I've gotten into some stupid physical altercations with stupid people. But mainly it's been about being at the wrong place at the wrong time with the wrong fucking peeps. I thought those days were behind me. All I had to do was go to work, piss in a cup every once in a while, and stay invisible. I really thought I could do it too, and then I met Teena.

I saw her leaning against the shabby wooden fence out back. She had dark frizzy hair that went past her shoulders, and bright red lips. I was taken by the shape and lines of her tanned arms and legs, and by those big brown eyes. She wore a flower-patterned sundress that was on the verge of being obscene, and sandals that exposed the turquoise polish on her toenails. She held a pack of Newports in one hand and a lit cigarette in the other. I knew she could see me taking her in, and that suited me just fine.

"Hello there!" I yelled through the open window. She looked to see if the coast was clear enough for her to speak. That should have been my first red flag.

"Hello yourself," she said. No smile. No charm.

"Can you see me?' I asked.

"Uh, yeah?"

"I just moved in."

"You mean you just got out," she said in a nasty tone.

"Excuse me?"

"That piece-of-shit studio you're in is for ex-cons, who usually become ex-ex-cons pretty damn quick, so more than likely, and hopefully, you won't be around too long." With this she flicked her cigarette stub on the ground and stomped it out, both gestures done rather violently. She was spunky. I liked her.

"Sorry to disappoint you, but I'm planning on sticking around for a while. You might want to reconsider. I can almost guarantee you'll gain dividends."

"Yeah? Well, you should be real careful about who you talk to around here. And by the looks of you, I can guarantee you're going to end up like every other loser that's lived in that studio."

"You don't have a clue about me."

"You can't fuck with tried-and-true. The odds are against you."

"Poetic. You're deep. You're wrong about me, but you're deep. My name's Red, what's yours?"

"Is that why you did time? 'Cause you got red?"

"It's a long story. I'll tell you if you give me your name."

She let out a heavy sigh, put her pack of cigarettes in her front pocket, and walked to the staircase door leading to the apartments above. Just as she opened it, she looked over at me and said painfully, "My name is Teena, two e's. When you see me around with my man, don't act like you know me because you don't. It'll be best for everyone involved."

"Got it. I don't know you and you swear you know me, Miss Teena."

"If I were you, I'd move. ASAP."

I showered, shaved, and headed for work. Teena was out in front of the building, still in that merciless little dress. She was talking to a female who couldn't have been older than seventeen and already looked like her best days were behind her. "Hello again, Miss Teena. Twice in one day. There is a god," I said. After a few steps, I turned to look back and noticed she was smiling.

"Damn! He's pretty fine," said her friend.

"He's all right," Teena scoffed.

The way she said it that made me feel warm and fuzzy all over. I thought I had a chance.

2.

I barely slept and spent the following afternoon hoping to

catch Teena out back. I was mad at myself for how many times I peeked out my kitchen window and for feeling disappointed every fucking time. Later that evening I saw her. She was being strapped to an ambulance gurney, blood trickling down her face. She had a bloody rag on her head, and was screaming at the top of her lungs,

"You motherfucker!! You're gonna fucking get yours, you'll see!! Hit a woman?! You're not a fucking man!"

The four police officers on the scene stood around, looking aggravated.

"Just tell us who did this to you so we can do our job," said one of the officers towering over her as she was being placed in the back of the ambulance.

"Fuck you too, pig! You ain't shit! Fuck all y'all!" she yelled.

She was hauled off.

I immediately figured she was protecting her man. I felt a knot in my stomach realizing what she was willing to go through to shield someone who beat on her. I felt my face flush and I wanted to find out who this fucking guy was so I could put a dent in his skull.

I scanned the crowd. I tried picturing the kind of man who had what it took to conquer and keep Teena, the kind of guy who would hit a broad.

"Any of you upstanding citizens want to tell us something?" asked one of the officers. Nothing. "Yeah, I didn't think so. Have a nice night, everyone." The boys in blue got in their vehicles and drove away.

"What happened?" I asked.

"Yo! Mind your fucking business, jailbird!"

Everyone dispersed like roaches when the lights came on. I glanced up quickly and couldn't make out a face. The voice came out of the dark. I put my hands in my jacket pockets and headed for work.

"Yeah, that's right. Step the fuck off and mind your business. You'll live longer," came the voice again.

Now Teena's man knew what I looked like and this gave him an advantage over me. This pissed me off and I wasn't scared. That was the problem.

Seeing Teena with her head busted only morphed my dislike for this joker and stoked the flames of my yearning for her.

I shook it off and went to work half hoping I'd never see Teena again, and half hating myself for it.

3.

Imagine my surprise the next afternoon when I spotted Teena smoking a cigarette, barefooted, leaning against a beat-up Toyota Camry resting on four cement blocks directly in front of my kitchen window.

She wore a wifebeater tank top without a bra, denim shorts more risqué than the dress from the day before, dark shades, and an A's baseball cap. I decided to tempt fate and take out the garbage.

I hadn't really been there long enough to accumulate any significant amount of trash, so I filled up a Grocery Outlet plastic bag with shit I could gather from around the pad: a few empty bottles of St. Pauli Girl, some charcoal sketches I'd been fucking with when I was locked up that were doomed from the start, and the ripped-out pages of a Spanish-English dictionary some other inmate gave me as a getting-out present. I topped it off with bunched-up paper towels and toilet paper. I left my door slightly open thinking it wouldn't take long.

As soon as Teena saw me step through the back door of

the building, she eyed me, blew smoke from her mouth the same way one might blow a kiss into the wind, and put her cigarette out. For a split-second I thought she'd bolt, but she lit another Newport and stayed put.

"Looks like a heavy load you got there, Red," she said placidly while I threw the bag into the dumpster.

"Well, hello there, Miss Teena. You remembered my name. "

"It's an easy name to remember."

"I'm happy you're here. I didn't think I'd see you so soon."

I expected some witty banter or even a *fuck you*, but instead we stood there in awkward silence, me by the dumpster in my sweatpants and *UC Berkeley* T-shirt, and her a million miles away looking small and vulnerable and beautiful.

"Are you okay?" I asked heartfelt, my voice almost quivering.

She tossed her cigarette and used her hands to push herself off the car and walked toward me. My heart raced. I started sweating. She grabbed my right hand and led me back into the building and straight into my studio. Once inside, she let go of my hand and started to undress.

"You sure you want to do this?" I asked.

"I could ask you the same thing, but I don't really feel like talking, or thinking. Do you have a condom?"

I nodded yes. She removed my shirt and without untying the strings pulled down my sweats, bringing my boxers down as well. Kneeling before me, gently, she took me inside. Her mouth a continent of tenderness, her lips awakening the stars in me. I felt like I would come and pass out at the same time. Then she stopped abruptly. "Don't," she said.

I thought I was going to have a stroke. I grabbed her hips, raised her to me, and kissed her for what felt like three days.

I could taste the long night on her busted lip, like crumbs of bitter and sweet dried blood, raw, like heaven.

4.

I laid her on my mattress, took her cap off, kissed the cut on her forehead, and worked my way down the length of her body, stopping at her breasts. I then lost myself between her legs. Next thing I knew, I was lying naked, drained and dreary, with my hands locked beneath my head, hoping she'd never leave.

She got up and grabbed her shorts.

"This can't ever happen again," she said as she dressed.

I didn't understand. But then again, it made perfect sense. "Yes," I said. "You sure run hot and cold though, Miss Teena."

"Whatever. And stop fucking calling me Miss Teena, you sound like a fucking retard."

"Did you like it?" I asked.

"What just happened here was a mercy fuck, and a fuck you to my poor excuse of a man," she said, sidestepping the question.

"Are you sure this is one-and-done? 'Cause I'm pretty sure you enjoyed it. I know I did, but I'm betting you enjoyed it too."

"Red!" Teena yelled. She turned to me, her face softening. She whispered, "Shut the fuck up, okay?"

I knew then I'd see her again, so I shut the fuck up.

She left and I felt hungry. I still had a few hours to kill before my shift, so I figured I'd get a pizza pie, eat a few slices now, and save the rest for later. I chose not to wash up. I wanted to keep Teena on me.

5.

I grabbed a slice of pizza from Paisan, and walked back, taking

Dwight. As I turned onto 9th, I could see the flashing lights of the Berkeley PD, three squad cars strong, right in front of my building. I picked up the pace imagining the worst possible scenario—Teena's man murdered her and dumped her in my apartment. I thought maybe I should have taken that shower after all. But it wasn't Teena the cops were trying to resuscitate. It was her friend slumped over on the sidewalk, some nasty shit coming out the side of her mouth. She was being questioned and slapped around by a couple of police officers. I could hear the sirens of the ambulance on its way.

There were a lot of curious people about. I looked around for Teena, but she was ghost, and rightly so.

As I passed the cops and the girl, I said, "Never a dull moment, huh, fellas?"

"What did you say?" asked one of the officers.

I kept walking.

"Hey!" came another voice. When I turned to look, two cops were headed toward me. "My partner asked you a question. We heard you say something and we'd like you to repeat it. Can you do that for us?"

The focus of the crowd shifted.

"I said, *Never a dull moment, huh?*"

The cops looked at each other. They'd done this before.

"You just moved in, right? Apartment 5?"

I didn't answer.

"Is this one of Greg's?" asked the smaller cop.

"Yeah. I'd say two, three days, if even," answered the other. Then, directing his attention toward me again, "You were out here yesterday."

"That true?" asked his partner.

I said nothing. I felt like spitting in their fucking faces.

"What's the matter? Nothing smart to say?" said the taller cop.

"Can I be excused, *Dad?* I'd like to eat my pizza before it gets cold, and I need to get ready for work." As I scanned the crowd, I noticed a few people holding up their phones. This was not good.

"A workingman," he said, like he was impressed.

"Thanks for your help, sir! You know how to get ahold of us if you have any more information. G'night," said the smaller cop loud enough for everyone around to hear.

Motherfucker. I wanted death to take them both right then and there.

6.

I opened the door to my apartment and the disheveled sheets on my bed and the lingering scent of Teena had an intoxicating effect on me. I closed my eyes until it passed. I hadn't even made it to the kitchen when I heard the knock. I was hoping it was Teena, but the knock itself told me otherwise. I opened the door anyway.

"What up, jailbird?" said the man I assumed was her man. "Mind if I come in?"

He didn't wait for my response; he just moved around me and entered. He had two long braids in his very blond hair, and a few gold teeth scattered in deliberate locations in his mouth. His jeans were hanging low enough to show red basketball shorts. I was surprised by how white he was. I mean, I know the hood has all types and poverty and hustle can be colorblind, but this cat epitomized the definition of *caricature*. I just wasn't expecting it. I figured it would take him all of two hours inside to get with his Aryan brothers.

He walked straight into the kitchen and sat on the counter. "Damn, dude. It smells like you just got freaky up in here. Was she good?"

"I'm sorry. Do I know you?" I didn't want to give anything away.

"Yeah, motherfucker, you know me, just not officially."

I waited for him to say he knew about Teena and me. I clenched my teeth and stopped myself from clenching my fists. I could see the butt of his Glock 9 protruding from his waistband.

"I'm the one who told you to keep walkin' yesterday. Remember?"

Between the cops and now this piece of shit, I wanted so badly to beat him into oblivion and dump his body at Aquatic Park.

"Yo, you better stop lookin' at me like that, jailbird. I didn't come here to hurt you, but you keep givin' me those dirty looks like you wanna do me harm, I will sure enough end you right here, right now. You feel me?"

I wasn't feeling him at all. "What do you want?" I asked.

"I want to know what you and the po-po talked about out there. I saw you was chattin' 'em up."

"What business is that of yours? I don't even know you, and I couldn't give less of a fuck."

He hopped off the kitchen counter and tried staring me down, pushing his chest out. I didn't budge.

Through my window I noticed Teena walking out into the parking lot. She lit up a cigarette. She was checking us out and I suddenly felt brave.

"Whatever you're going to do, I suggest you do it quick. I'm fucking hungry and really need to get ready for work."

He grinned. "I know you just got out and shit, and you don't really know how things work around here, so I'ma fill you in. My name's KJ. I live upstairs in 15. I'ma talk straight and keep it a hundred: this ain't the joint, my brother. Out here you will get done in a motherfuckin' heartbeat and it'll be a few days before your body's found, if they find it. I got too much shit goin' on up in here, shit that can't be compromised, you feel me? So when you, or anyone else around here, be talkin' to the cops, it gets me a little nervous. And when I get nervous . . ." He touched his pistol for effect. "So, I'ma ask you one more time, nice-like. What were you talkin' to the cops about?" And now he pulled the Glock from his jeans and held it in his right hand.

"Hey, baby! What you doin' in there with that ex-con, baby? He fuckin' with you?"

"Mind your business, Teena. Go upstairs."

"Okay, baby. Don't get all crazy though, there's still people out front."

"Don't tell me what to do, bitch! Go upstairs!"

I thought about rushing him. I knew I could take him physically, but with the gun in his hand it was too big of a risk.

"I said some smart-ass remark when I walked past them, and they got all pissed off so they tried scaring me. But it didn't work."

"Hmm. Yeah. You don't look like you scare easy."

"I don't."

"Is that Paisan pizza?" he asked, putting the gun back in his pants. "That's some good-ass pizza, yo. Probably cold by now, though." He surveyed my apartment, like he was figuring out where to put his shit from Ikea. "You got this place lookin' a lot better than the last mofo who was up in here. That guy was a fuckin' slob."

He made his way to the door, keeping an eye on me and his finger on the trigger of his gun. He stopped short of it and said, "Yo, I know you got a job and shit, but I'ma put it out there anyway. You ever want to make some real money, I mean *real* money, you come talk to me. I could always use someone like you."

"What do you mean *someone like me?*"

"You're a hard-ass dude, bro. I'm sure motherfuckers think twice about messin' with your ass. Plus, you seem like you pretty smart, quiet, clean. Anyways, you know where I'm at. You ain't even gotta worry about fuckin' up your parole either, since I ain't got no felonies or anything like that, you feel me?"

He finally opened the door, and just as he was about to exit he turned to stare me down again. "Two more things. One: don't let me hear you been talkin' to the cops again, I don't give a fuck what the reason. And two: next time Teena goes out to smoke back there, pretend you don't see her. Have a nice night, *Red.*"

7.

Fucking Teena. She must have told him something. This vexed me plenty, sending my mind places I try really hard to keep it from going. Were they toying with me? Did he know Teena and I fucked? Was he the one behind our little afternoon delight? Whatever the hell game was going on, I decided I wasn't playing.

Turns out it's still pretty easy to get a gun in Berkeley. Everyone I used to know is either dead or doing time, so I was lucky enough to have an acquaintance on the inside who told me about a spot I should visit if anything came up.

A bar called the Missouri. All I had to do was drop my buddy's name to the doorman, and the process would be underway. I decided not having any money wasn't going to deter me.

The Missouri is nestled right on the corner of San Pablo and Parker, close enough for me to walk to, check out, and still get to work on time.

It was the kind of place a guy like me could get into some seriously regrettable shit.

The fella at the front door was clad in black jeans, boots, a black bomber jacket, and black baseball cap. He even wore black gloves and shades, which seemed like overkill, but hey, I guess everybody has their part to play, right?

I walked straight up to him and didn't waste any time. "Hey, I'm a friend of Shorty Lee. He told me you could help a brother out."

He gave me a once-over, and took a look around. I gave him my best poker face. "You want Eddie. He's here tomorrow."

"Oh," I said, feeling relieved and a little pissed. "Can I give you my number and—"

"Fuck outa here with that shit, man," he interrupted, sucking his teeth. "This ain't no motherfucking dating service. Bring your ass back here tomorrow and talk to Eddie."

I nodded in agreement and left. I didn't want to hurt my chances of getting a weapon. I knew like I know we breathe air that I needed it.

I went to work and did my best not to think about killing KJ.

8.

I woke the next morning to persistent tapping on my kitchen window. I sat up in bed and saw Teena.

"I tried your door but you didn't hear me. Open up and let me in. I have to talk to you."

"Your boyfriend with you?"

"You ain't funny," she said. "Get up, I'm coming around. It's important."

"I bet," I mumbled.

With some reluctance, not too much, I admit, I got up and opened the door. Even half asleep I noticed Teena's areolas threatening to break through her tank top. I was about to get back in bed but Teena grabbed my arm, pulled me to her, and kissed me, pressing up against my morning wood and making me wince. It was damn near impossible for me to push her away. Damn near.

"Teena. What the fuck?"

"What? No more *Miss Teena?*" she said, feigning hurt and sounding like a cross between a cat woman and a goddamned demon.

Suddenly my head was burning, thoughts about being played causing a fire whirl inside of me. I could feel my blood boil. I wanted to grab her by the throat and squeeze. I took hold of her hair and kissed her instead, and then we fucked.

Afterward, lying in silence, I heard a noise coming from the back of the apartment complex. When I looked up, I saw the silhouette of a man moving by the window.

"We really need to talk," I said softly, as I stroked Teena's face with the back of my hand, pushing away hair from her closed eyes. I wanted her to know that I wasn't angry with her, that I knew she was with KJ out of necessity and survival and circumstances beyond her control, and that I would figure something out so we could be together and—

The knock on the door startled us. Teena immediately stood up and scrambled for her clothes. I jumped up off the bed, walked to the kitchen, and grabbed a steak knife, the only knife I owned.

"Open up, Red, it's Greg."

Greg?

"Uh, now's not really a good time for a house call, Greg. Can you come back later?"

"Sorry, Red, I can't do that. I've got other appointments today and I can't alter my schedule."

I couldn't, for the life of me, remember a text message or phone call about a scheduled visit from my PO, but I'd been preoccupied. My first thought was that I'd missed it somehow. But there was something in his voice that turned my gut.

I looked over at Teena and she was pale. Her bugged-out eyes pleading with me not to open the door.

"Red? C'mon now, I'm sure whoever's in there will understand. A urinalysis is part of your parole agreement, buddy. Now be a good sport and open the door so I can do my job."

I always found the phrase *against my better judgment* oxymoronic. How much better can your judgment be if you're going against it?

"Okay, Greg, give me a minute," I said.

"Don't let that motherfucker in here, Red," she whispered, trembling.

"Don't worry. I won't let him see you."

"No. You don't fucking get it. I know that voice, Red. I fucking *know* that voice."

Just then I heard my door open.

"Fuck!" said Teena. She dashed into the bathroom and hopped up on my toilet, trying to get the tiny window open.

I turned back toward the front door and got hit with the butt of a gun on my skull.

I dropped, barely conscious. Greg stood over me. KJ was right behind him.

"You just couldn't do it, huh, Red? Just couldn't keep your hands out of the cookie jar?"

Greg looked inside the bathroom. I wanted to say something, but couldn't. "And you. You had to go and fuck this whole thing up."

"Yo, Greg, is this really necessary, man? Doing her, I mean?" asked KJ.

Instead of answering KJ's question, Greg raised his gun, pointed it at Teena, and then I heard the distinct sound of a bullet traveling through a silencer.

I heard the thump of a body drop. I rolled my eyes and could see Teena on the floor, her tank top already soaking in blood.

"KJ, it's not my fault you can't control your women. I have enough on my plate dealing with Cindy's OD and keeping your ass out of jail as it is. Go grab the saw and acid from the car. Discreetly, if you don't mind."

I tried to move. Greg shot me in the stomach.

"I thought KJ told you there was stuff going on here that couldn't be compromised, Red. I thought you were smarter than this. Then again, I've been known to be wrong about people."

9.

I survived a ten-year stint at San Quentin. I did exactly what I was supposed to do, kept my head down, my ear to the grindstone, and my fucking mouth shut. I stayed alive and made it out. One week in West Berkeley and it's all shot to hell. I'm fucking dying here.

IDENTITY THEFT

BY SUMMER BRENNER

North Berkeley

> *What you are to do without me I cannot imagine.*
> —George Bernard Shaw, *Pygmalion*

The first thing he did was cut her hair. He cut as gently as possible, but when she screamed and jerked away, nearly causing him to stab her cheek, he gagged her, then tied her hands to the back of a chair and her feet to a table leg. When he finished, there was a pond of hair at his feet. He swept and vacuumed and saved a few strands in an envelope. The second thing, he burned her clothes. The embroidered blouses and shawls, the hand-loomed pants and skirt, the head wraps, he had no choice. They were clothes that looked distinctive. They could easily be remembered. If she managed to get out, someone could identify her. People in Berkeley were curious about all things ethnic. No doubt a handsome young woman in ethnic garb, looking lost and far from home, would attract someone's attention. If she didn't stop them, they might approach her to ask where she was from. They might offer to get her help. Instead of her own clothes, he had bought jeans, T-shirts, and sweaters in the teen department at Macy's. Dresses would have to wait. He'd bought socks in case her feet got cold, two pairs with rubber grips so she wouldn't slip. A salesclerk picked out bras, panties, pajamas, and a fluffy robe. "Nothing sexy," he told her.

Later, when it was appropriate for her to go outside, he would get her a winter coat and a rain jacket. At the pharmacy, he purchased toiletries: sanitary napkins, rose-scented deodorant, dental floss, an electric toothbrush, etc. Next, he took away her flimsy plastic shoes. They aroused feelings of disgust in him which he couldn't explain. Barefoot she was less likely to run away. He also locked up her jewelry (the gold earrings and shell and bead necklaces) and documents, including her passport. He couldn't bring himself to destroy the documents. He told himself that entirely wiping away her past existence, like the name of her hamlet and family, was inhumane. He locked up the signed contract with her mother and the sales receipt for nine hundred dollars, which was a way to protect himself—that is, legally. Finally, he taught her *yes, no, goodbye, hunger,* and *thirst* in English and sign language.

In advance of her arrival, he'd had a portion of his attic renovated. The new soundproof walls had been painted pale blue, a color reputed to induce calm. He'd debated about a window, knowing that to gaze at trees and sky and hills was a great pastime, a source of spiritual renewal, especially for a child accustomed to the natural world. But in the end, he thought a window would only make her sad. The bed and dresser were new. The sheets were pima cotton, the duvet goose down, the pillows hypoallergenic. The bathroom had hot running water and a flush toilet, luxury conveniences for her. He'd considered installing a tub with the shower, but he feared she might try to drown herself. He placed a small bookshelf in the corner of the room with early readers, a pictorial dictionary, a simple atlas, and copies of *National Geographic*. He put a clock radio on the console and tuned it to KDFC, the classical music station. As far as he knew, she never changed the station or turned it off.

Most of the day, he sat near her at a small library table. They didn't attempt to communicate, only sat. He read. He graded his students' papers. He worked on the outline of a presentation he was to deliver at a conference in July. He wasn't sure what she did. Eventually, he would find a way to have her tell him her earliest impressions. But for now, he hoped his presence was reassurance that he was taking care of her.

He prepared her meals himself. In the future, he might have to resort to frozen food, veggie burritos, Cheese Board pizza, or soup from Poulet, but the homemade fare was part of the way he welcomed her. He was a good cook, an avowed vegetarian since he read Lorca's *Poet in New York* in college (". . . the terrible cries of crushed cows fill the valley with sorrow where the Hudson gets drunk on oil . . ."). His students loved to be invited over for mushroom stroganoff and shepherd's pie with green lentils. It was during his own lifetime that the preoccupation over food provenance had gone from fringe co-ops to mainstream. Berkeley had been in the vanguard of the food revolution. *In the vanguard of many revolutions*, he often said with pride.

She wouldn't touch any of it. That he expected. His food and customs of eating were foreign. The last time he gave her something to eat, she'd slept for eighteen hours. Hoping to counter her fears, he set the table in her room for two. Two plates and bowls, two forks and spoons (no knives), linen napkins, glasses of water, cups of coffee at breakfast, iced tea at lunch, and a carafe of red wine at dinner with a single glass for himself. In the center of the table, he put a hand-painted vase with daffodils (in his humble opinion, *the most cheerful flower in the world*). At every meal, he demonstrated how to use the napkin and utensils. As he ate, he smiled. He made a grunt or two of pleasure. For three days, she ate nothing, but on the fourth morning, she unfolded her napkin and put it in her lap, then dipped her spoon in a bowl of hot buckwheat cereal that he'd mixed with manuka honey and roasted almonds. One spoonful, then another. After she finished, he patted her hand, conveying both approval and gratitude.

Meanwhile, he documented the details of their encounters in a database. He planned to write a book with the current working title of *Pygmalion's Paradox*. But whether it was ultimately called *Paradox* or *Plight* was unclear. It was *she* who would determine the course of the relationship, and thus, the final title. She was the variable, he was the constant.

The long weekend was over. The days had passed without dramatic incident. She'd decided not to starve herself, which alone counted as success.

On Monday morning after breakfast, he made the sign for walking. On his fingers, he counted out the hours he'd be gone. Five or six. Then he pointed to the clock and tried to explain with the numerals when he would return. As he left, he bolted her door on the outside. It was a risk, he knew. If there were an earthquake, or fire, or landslide, she might not survive. Fire season was over, but with the recent heavy rains and flooding, and the ground hard from several years of drought, the runoff was tremendous. Two nearby streets had recently been blocked with debris. Asphalt had cracked and caved. A neighbor's foundation had been compromised. Around town the roots of a dozen large trees had loosened, causing them to fall. There'd been one fatality when a tree crashed onto the roof of a moving car. Above Tilden Park, six families were ordered to evacuate before their houses slid down a hill. Where he lived, there were several tiers of houses above him, road after road that circled through the hills, each positioned with steep slopes into its downhill neighbor's yard.

And his house, built in 1898, was positioned at the lower end of the spiral with only brick pilings for a foundation. However, his house had survived earthquakes, fires, and landslides for over a hundred years. He trusted it would survive another day.

He put the *Times* into his satchel and walked down the hill, turning once to wave at the large brown-shingled house as if *she* could see him and wave back. From La Loma, he dropped onto Virginia Street where he paused to view the sparkling bay and dark hills of Marin. From where he stood, he saw almost nothing manmade. No sign of highways or blocks of commerce and housing, only the Golden Gate Bridge and perhaps a ship or barge. Bridge and barge were not enough to mar the view. *Prelapsarian*, he called it.

He entered campus through the North Gate. Rain-washed, it looked especially beautiful, everything shimmering in the cold blue air. The sylvan paths, the towering redwoods, the bare knobby limbs of the plane trees, and the Japanese magnolias dotting the grounds with their voluptuous winter blossoms. When the long, solemn chimes of the Campanile rang out like a muezzin's call to prayer, he felt summoned to a higher purpose. The chimes, the brisk air, the pungent medley of bay laurel and wet leaves, the students on skateboards and bikes, the fresh, smiling faces, he was buoyed by their insouciance as if he'd fallen in love. He guessed it was the nearness of *her*.

His buoyance typically terminated at the entrance to Tolman Hall and the elevator ride to his office on the third floor. It galled him that the magnificent discipline of psychology, whose discoveries rivaled twentieth-century physics in its understanding of the universe of human behavior, was housed in one of the ugliest buildings on campus. And that mining, the most destructive of all human endeavors, should occupy the university's most elegant building with palladium windows and a pantile roof. He took it as a personal affront, but when he remarked on this "disgrace" to the department head, his comment was deemed a joke. A good joke that passed among his colleagues so that they started to mutter *disgrace* under their breath whenever they passed him, and break out in laughter.

He was popular with students, his courses famous for their eccentric syllabi. The readings for this semester's seminar, The Psychology of Slavery, included *Story of O*. In his generation, no other book was so eagerly devoured (except Laing's *The Politics of Experience*). Now, it was a rarity to find a student who'd heard of it.

Today's question under discussion—*Are there happy slaves?*—sprang from a chapter in Frederick Law Olmsted's *The Cotton Kingdom*. Before Olmsted became the country's premiere landscape architect, he was hired by the *Times* to chronicle the South and its peculiar institution. He wrote as a journalist, an agronomist, an abolitionist, and periodically described the plantation of a "good" master, whose slaves lived in sturdy housing with adequate food, bonuses in dollars and provisions, and free time to cultivate their own gardens and engage in crafts to earn extra money. Consequently, they worked harder, with fewer whippings, for their *good* master than their fellow immiserated slaves.

One student suggested that "happy slaves" was inherently racist. Another countered that slavery was colorblind until Europeans invaded Africa. A third remarked that in ancient texts, citing the *Iliad* and *Gilgamesh*, slaves were honored to serve a noble master, causing another to protest, "Those were servants, not slaves." At one point, he suggested they unload the terminology of master-slave, and substitute it with free versus unfree. At the lowest end of "unfree" were war slaves, work slaves, prisoners, orphans, captives, even a battered wife or child. But what actually constituted free? What were its physical, mental, and ontological parameters? Or was it easier to define freedom by its restraints on the individual or collective, such as prejudices, expectations, prohibitions, impositions, desires, customs, and laws? These were questions that had absorbed him for the last two decades.

After class, the seminar usually adjourned for a few minutes and reconvened at Caffe Strada. "I'm sorry to disappoint you today," he said, apologizing to the loyal group awaiting him. "But I have . . ."

"We understand," a student said.

"A puppy," he said.

"What kind? What's its name?" they asked.

He was surprised by their enthusiasm.

"It's a little mutt I'm taking care of . . . Aimee," he said.

"If you need help walking Aimee or anything," a girl offered.

Aimee was the name he'd chosen to call her. Not only was it his mother's name, but those two long vowels (a and e) were sufficiently elementary for a dullard to pronounce, if dullard she proved to be. However, he was certain from the first and only time she'd looked him in the eye that he had read her correctly. And in making his final selection, it was not her lovely face, or sheen of her skin, or strength of her well-formed limbs, or straight white teeth, but the spark of a deep intelligence. What she had called herself and what she was called by family and friends—her name would be the last thing expunged. After months or perhaps years, the person of Aimee would override her past.

When he went to her mother to negotiate, by way of

introduction, he'd announced to the family that he was a tenured professor at a university in California with a doctoral degree in psychology. He also mentioned he was an accomplished pianist and fluent in German and French. And although he had prepared an explanation of his intentions, no one was interested. He guessed they normally met hustlers and pimps and would assume he was a liar.

They were liars, too. He'd been told she was eighteen, but he estimated fifteen or sixteen; she was malleable and frightened, the youngest girl of eleven children.

"You making baby?" the mother asked, giving him a wink. Prostitution and fertility were the reason that men came.

Her question horrified him, as if he were a common trafficker. "No, thank you," he said, baffling whoever heard him.

The lush mountains, the simple communal life, the tearful farewells, the exchange of money nearly changed his mind. But he rationalized. Throughout his life, for whatever he wanted, he'd been taught (albeit, expected) to rationalize.

Zipping his jacket, adjusting his blue-and-gold Bears beanie, and winding his muffler around his neck, he now walked out of the campus across Hearst Avenue alongside a mob of students en route to La Val's for pizza and beer. He recalled the defunct art cinema behind La Val's where he'd seen WR: *Mysteries of the Organism* thirty-plus years ago. At the time, he'd been interested in Reich and thought he might build an orgone box in his backyard. Another unrealized scheme.

"Dreamer," his mother used to say instead of *loser*.

He continued to climb Eunice to Virginia, and struggling uphill, he reached the corner of La Loma and the small concrete staircase built as a parapet, its sharp right angle offering a corner where he could stand. Every afternoon, he stopped there to catch his breath and watch the western light on the water. He was always tired and less hopeful than in the morning.

"Aimee," he cried softly, and hurried home.

DEAR FELLOW GRADUATES

BY MICHAEL DAVID LUKAS

Indian Rock

First of all, I think it's only appropriate for me to extend a hearty congratulations to my fellow graduates (and to all you proud family members)! I've been there with you these past four years and I understand how you all must feel, sitting up there on that stage.

But as much as I would love to recount all the ups and downs of the past four years, as much as I would enjoy reminiscing about Spirit Weeks past and shedding a tear over the last days of our youth, a higher duty calls me to task. What I present before you, in this, my last column as editor of the *Berkeley High Jacket*, is a tale that needs to be told, burns to be told, even if some people out there (Mrs. Eliason!) won't be happy I'm telling it.

By now, some of you (especially all you proud family members) might be wondering: *Who the heck is this guy? What is he talking about? I thought this was the graduation edition of the* Berkeley High Jacket.

I can assure you that this is indeed the graduation edition of the *Berkeley High Jacket*. In the rest of these pages you will find the traditional fare for such an issuance. On pages 6–9, you can see where your dear child and their friends are going to college (as if you didn't already know!). On pages 12–15, you can read a variety of melancholy farewells to our fair school. And so on and so forth.

If you would rather not read this story, you are obviously free to turn the page. But I can assure you that you will be glad to have read it.

The events in question began late one Wednesday night a few months ago (actually, technically, it was early Thursday morning). As the editor of this fair paper, it was my responsibility to drive the finished proofs down to our printer in Fremont once every other week. It's a long drive, and on my way home, I would often stop at a little park near my dad's house.

You may be familiar with Indian Rock, around the corner. You may also know Grotto Rock, a few blocks up the hill. Chances are, though, you've never heard of Mortar Rock, which is why I like it. There's almost never anyone there.

On the night in question, I was coming home particularly late. The moon was high and white and the streets were empty. I parked across the street from the rock and climbed to the top, which is when I noticed the two men in a beat-up white Volvo.

There are any number of reasons why two men might be sitting in a beat-up white Volvo across the street from a park at two thirty in the morning. But these two seemed a little shady. They were both uncommonly large, with Nordic features and a slightly dented appearance that seemed out of place in the neighborhood. Was I stereotyping? Yes, my fellow graduates, I was. And, like any good Berkeley High student, I felt bad for succumbing to my biases. But as we will see, my biases, in this case at least, were spot on.

After sitting quietly on top of the rock for five or ten minutes (not smoking a joint or anything like that), I realized that there was someone else in the park with me: a tall, gangly man bent over a trash can. It took me a moment to process that this man, digging frantically through the trash in a public park at two thirty in the morning, was none other than my English teacher, Mr. Balz.

As most of my fellow graduates know, Mr. Balz is not your typical teacher. He can recite *Beowulf* by heart in Old English. He often delivers Shakespearean monologues from atop his desk. And once he dedicated an entire period of my Bible As Literature class to the poetry of Liz Phair. I can't say I'm the biggest fan of Mr. Balz. (My own personal feeling is that he's kind of a poser.) But I also don't have any particular ill will toward him. And I've always thought that the jokes about his name are a little cheap.

So there we were. Me and Mr. Balz, staring at each other across Mortar Rock.

"Michael Lukas," he said in the same voice he used to call my name off the roll sheet. "AP British Literature."

There was a short silence, then a car door slammed and Mr. Balz took off running.

Those Scandinavians were big but they were fast. Half a block down the hill, the dark-haired one caught up with Mr. Balz and grabbed his shirt while the blond one tackled him to the ground. There were some grunts and a crunching sound as bone hit asphalt. Before Mr. Balz could shout for help, the Scandinavians duct-taped his mouth, bound his wrists, and carried him to the trunk of the Volvo. You could have been sleeping in your bed a few dozen yards away (perhaps some of you were) and not heard a thing.

If I were a less reliable narrator, I would tell you that I leaped into action right then and there. I would say that I put my dislike for Mr. Balz aside, hopped in my dad's Subaru, and sped after the Scandinavians on a wild chase through Tilden Park. But the truth is, after watching all this transpire, after seeing my AP British Literature teacher tackled, stuffed into a trunk, and driven to who knows where, I did nothing.

I drove home and spent the rest of the night with my covers pulled up over my head, praying the Scandinavians hadn't seen me or heard my name. Sometime in the dark hours of the morning, I decided that the most prudent course of action was no action at all. I would keep this whole thing to myself, wipe what I had seen from my mind, then finish up the school year and head off to college.

But, as Mr. Balz often said, the truth will out. That next morning, when I saw Sarah Meyers at the bus stop, I couldn't help but tell her.

"Wait, *what?*"

"They put him in the trunk and drove away."

Sarah stared at me, squinting, like she wasn't sure I was even real. "What?"

Most of my fellow graduates probably know Sarah Meyers. For those who don't, I would describe her thusly: She has bright red hair. She does not suffer fools, gladly or otherwise. And she always keeps a box of Froot Loops in her backpack. She's two parts Joan Didion, one part Simone de Beauvior, and one part Courtney Love. Some people say she took the SATs on acid, which may or may not be true. What I know for sure is that she aced them, and that she's going to Columbia next fall on a full scholarship.

"Did you call the police?"

"I—"

"Did you tell your parents? Did you tell anyone?"

"I told *you.*"

"And what am I supposed to do?"

"I don't know."

"Clearly."

She swung her backpack around and dug into the Fruit

Loops. "Okay," she said midchew, "here's what we're going to do. First, we're going to go over to his house and check things out."

"Now?" I had a calculus test second period, we both did. More importantly, I didn't want to run into those Scandinavians again.

"Yeah, now," she said, already walking down the hill. "OR, do you not consider this an urgent situation?"

Mr. Balz's house was on one of those tiny streets off Indian Rock Road, a three-story brown shingle with a front yard so overgrown you could barely see the house itself. The bottom-floor windows were all covered with sun-faded tapestries and the mailbox was stuffed full of junk.

"It was his grandparents' house," Sarah said, standing in the driveway. "I think his grandpa was a judge or some kind of politician?"

"Very interesting," I said. "Now, how are we going to get in?"

Sarah gave a little smile and hoisted herself up over the fence. "I just might know where he keeps the hide-a-key."

Most of my fellow graduates will probably have heard some of the rumors about Sarah and Mr. Balz. You might have heard that they went camping together last summer, took mushrooms, and stayed up late into the night reading passages of *A Midsummer Night's Dream*. You might have heard Cindy Lee say she saw Sarah coming out of Mr. Balz's house. I don't know if any of these rumors are true. They probably aren't. What I do know is that their relationship goes beyond what most people would think is appropriate. Sarah once told me she considered Mr. Balz "more of a friend than a teacher" and I know that he wrote her a recommendation letter that used the phrase *beautiful mind* at least three times.

"Is this how his house usually looks?" I asked once we were both inside.

There was mail scattered around the entryway. Half-filled mugs lined the stairs. And a huge oak dining table blocked the way to the kitchen.

Sarah turned and looked me dead in the eye. "How much of a slut do you think I am?"

"I don't," I said. "But I mean, you've been here before, right? You knew where the hide-a-key was."

"I've been here twice. Once for a study group, and once to feed his cats when he was out of town. And yes, it does usually look like this."

I followed Sarah up to the third floor and into a bedroom that seemed to be inhabited almost entirely by cats. There were litter boxes everywhere, little felt mice, and nests of old fabric. Two black cats stalked the edges of the room while an orange one stared down at me from the top of an eight-foot-high scratching post. I turned to say something to Sarah, but she was already crouched down in front of a small safe at the back of the closet.

"You're going to try to guess the combination?"

She looked back over her shoulder, still spinning the knob. "I'm guessing it's the same as it was when I was house-sitting," she said. As she fiddled with the knobs, one of the black cats doubled back and rubbed its flank against her knee. "Two, two, seventy-four." The safe popped open and she smiled to herself. "*But at the length truth will out.*" When I didn't catch her reference, she explained: "Mr. Balz's favorite line in all of Shakespeare. *The Merchant of Venice.* Act two, scene two, line seventy-four." She took out a sheaf of papers and leafed through them. After a few moments, she held up a manila folder. "Bingo."

In the top right-hand corner was one word, written in Mr. Balz's distinctive block letters: *Evidence*.

At this point we probably should have gone straight to the police. At the very least, we should have been more careful with the evidence. Instead, Sarah and I sat down in the middle of the floor and began going through the folder, piece by piece.

"This is what he was talking about," she said under her breath. "He was always saying how shady Mrs. Eliason is."

She laid out two pieces of paper (schoolwide test results, both reproduced here for your benefit) and was beginning to explain what they meant, how they might have been manipulated, and so on, when there was a crash downstairs.

"One of the cats?"

Sarah shook her head. "Come on." She motioned for me to follow her upstairs to the attic, a dusty open room filled with banker's boxes and old surfing equipment. Downstairs, there were the muffled sounds of conversation, then another crash.

"Did you take the files?"

I looked down at my hands. "I have these," I said, still holding the two pieces of paper we'd been looking at.

"Great," she said, jiggling one of the windows at the other side of the room.

"I thought you had it."

"Nope."

When the window wouldn't open, Sarah wrapped an old wetsuit around her hand.

"What are you doing?"

"Come on," she said as she punched through the window and stepped out onto the roof. "Don't be such a baby."

For those of you who have never been on top of a roof,

I will tell you this: two stories is a heck of a lot higher than you think. From where we were standing, Mr. Balz's backyard looked like it was about fifty feet down. Maybe that's an exaggeration. It probably is. In any case, it was not a jumpable distance, not by any stretch of the imagination. But don't tell that to Sarah Meyers.

I can't say exactly what happened next except that one moment she was peering through the sunlight in the middle of the roof. The next she was jumping into an overgrown hedge. There was a crash and a long silence. Then she crawled out from under the hedge. Her face was pretty scratched up and there was a massive gash on her hand. Still, she was smiling.

"It's not as far as you think," she called up.

"I don't know. It looks pretty far."

Just then, the attic door shook. There was a quick shout, a grunt, and the doorframe splintered. Another few seconds and there would be no more door.

My fellow graduates, I would like to tell you that I reacted to this situation with cool detachment. But the truth is, I fell. In the grips of fear and indecision, I lost my footing and slid to the edge of the roof, whereupon I somehow caught my arm on the gutter and dropped the fifty or twenty or fifteen feet to the ground.

I blinked. I was still alive, but my leg was on fire. No, it *was* fire. Molten pain.

"I think I broke my leg," I said as Sarah helped me up.

"If you broke your leg you wouldn't be able to walk," she replied. "And anyways, we're not walking anywhere. We're getting the fuck out of here."

She dumped me into the backseat of Mr. Balz's old Audi, and seven harrowing minutes later we arrived, mostly intact, at our destination: the Berkeley Police Department parking lot.

The woman at the front desk seemed to recognize Sarah. "Detective James?" she asked, and without waiting for Sarah to respond, she buzzed us back.

"Detective James helped me out when I was getting that restraining order against Tom Kantor," Sarah explained.

"Oh," I said, not sure how else to respond. I hadn't heard about any restraining order. I just thought they had a bad breakup.

"He's a sweetie," Sarah said. "Not Tom—he's a dick—the detective. A little rough around the edges, but very avuncular."

When we walked into his office, the very avuncular Detective James was having a little nap, leaning back in his chair, his chin tucked into the soft pillow of his chest.

"What?" he barked awake, softening when he saw Sarah. "Meyers. That little pervert still bothering you?"

"No sir," Sarah said. She was sitting up straight. Her eyes were open in a kind of vulnerable and hopeful tilt. "It's something else, something about our English teacher."

"Okay."

She turned to me.

"So," I started, "I guess it was, sir, I suppose it all began—"

"Son," Detective James interrupted me, "take a deep breath. This isn't story time. And you aren't being interrogated. Just tell me what happened. Plain-like. Start to finish."

"All right." I took a deep breath. Then I told him everything: the Scandinavians at Mortar Rock, Mr. Balz's house, the documents.

"And you gained entry to the house with a key?"

"Yes sir," Sarah said.

"The location of which Mr. Balz informed you of previously?"

"Yes sir."

"And the safe?"

"It was open," Sarah lied without blinking an eye.

"The safe was open?"

"Yes sir."

Detective James leaned back in his chair and held the documents in question up to the light. He thought for a few rattling breaths, then wrote a couple things on a yellow legal pad.

While he was writing, Sarah glanced down at her phone. Something she saw made her jaw loosen slightly. She drummed her fingers on the desk, as if trying to make out a difficult equation, then slipped the phone back in her bag.

"Here's my number," Detective James told me. He pointed to a yellowed stack of business cards on the corner of his desk and I took one. "Call me if you see those Scandinavians again."

Sarah stood up and swung her bag around her shoulder.

"Wait," I said, "don't you need us to, I don't know, help out?"

"Help out?" Detective James chortled a little. "No, son. We'll take it from here."

"But how—"

"Like I said, we'll take it from here. The case is in good hands."

"So that's it?" I asked, standing in the parking lot with Sarah.

She didn't say anything for a few moments. When we got to the sidewalk, she took out her phone and scrolled to the text she had gotten while we were in Detective James's office.

Safeway. Tice Valley Road. WC. We have Balz. No Police.

"Who's that from?"

"I don't know," she said. "But I know where that Safeway

is. My grandma used to live in the old folks' home across the street."

Back in the car, Sarah opened the glove compartment, found a Dead Kennedys tape, and popped it into the stereo. I wanted to ask what the plan was, whether we should call for some help, like maybe the police. I wanted to tell her to slow down, or at least to signal when she was changing lanes. But the music was too loud to think. All I could do was hold onto the armrest, watch the green hills of Orinda flash past, and let the lyrics drill into my skull.

> It's time to taste what you most fear
> Right Guard will not help you here
> Brace yourself, my dear
> Brace yourself, my dear . . .

"So what's the plan?" Sarah asked as we pulled into the parking lot.

"Ride the wave," I said, a lame attempt at sarcasm.

"Yes," she said, patting my knee. "Now you're getting it."

She put the car in park and scanned the lot. "Over there." She pointed at a woman standing next to a pile of watermelons by the front entrance. Then she jumped out of the car and walked straight toward her, paying no regard to cars or shopping carts.

"Mrs. Eliason!" she called out.

And there she was, my old biology teacher, the new principal of our school. Mrs. Eliason was just about the last person I was expecting to see in that parking lot. But neither she nor Sarah seemed very surprised.

"So nice to see you here," Mrs. Eliason said, scanning the parking lot behind us. "You kids wouldn't mind helping me with these bags, would you?" She pointed to the shopping cart next to her.

"Sure," I said.

We each took a bag and followed her to her car.

"I hear you two have had quite the morning."

Before we could respond, Mrs. Eliason opened up her new BMW. Sitting in the passenger seat was none other than Mr. Balz.

"Hey, guys," he said with a weak little wave.

He seemed good, as good as anyone could be after being thrown in the trunk of a car and whatever else he had endured.

"If you don't mind," Mrs. Eliason said, motioning to the backseat, "I think we've had a little misunderstanding."

I glanced at Sarah and she looked at Mr. Balz, who nodded.

"All right," Sarah said, "this ought to be good."

While Mrs. Eliason loaded her groceries into the trunk, Sarah pressed a few buttons on her phone. I thought she might be calling the police. In fact, she was turning on her phone's voice recorder.

You can find a transcript of the whole conversation on page 4. For those who don't want to read the whole thing, I'll give you the overview.

It was all a big misunderstanding, Mrs. Eliason told us. What I had seen the night before was just a prank, a little thing that teachers do for fun. And the guys at Mr. Balz's house, they were just trying to find his toothbrush. Mr. Balz nodded, but you could tell that he was just trying to make Mrs. Eliason happy. When we asked about the documents in Mr. Balz's safe, Mrs. Eliason's tone changed. She told us that no one would believe us, that she knew Detective James personally and that it would be easy to convince him that nothing untoward had happened, except for our false accusations and the documents we had faked. And, of course, something like that would most certainly reflect poorly on our academic standing, which would obviously put our college admissions in jeopardy.

She could ruin our futures with a few keystrokes. Or, she said, we could call Detective James right now and make it all go away.

"You have a choice," she said. "Either you're part of the solution or you're part of the problem."

Well, Mrs. Eliason, we've made our choice.

My fellow graduates, esteemed family members, after reading this article I hope you will be somewhat closer to the truth and can decide for yourself what you think.

Thank you for your time and congratulations again. This is your day. Enjoy it!

FREDERICK DOUGLASS ELEMENTARY

BY AYA DE LEÓN

West Berkeley Flats

Keisha waited until everyone else left the office. It was Friday night and nobody seemed to be working late. Still, she shoved her sweatshirt up against the bottom of the door, in case any light could be seen. Only then did she turn on the fluorescent light in the windowless copy room.

A few weeks before, she had swiped a contract on letterhead from a real estate agency. Earlier that day, she had borrowed a coworker's computer to write the fake lease for a rental apartment. She had copied the language off the Internet, but was anxious about any spelling or grammatical errors. Especially because she couldn't save a forged document on a company computer. She had sat at her data-entry cubicle during lunch, reading the words over and over until they blurred, proofreading it to the best of her ability.

That night in the copy room, she cut and pasted and made copies of copies, until she had a reasonable-looking forgery on fine linen paper. She squinted at it in the glaring fluorescent. It looked legit. It "proved" that she rented a two-bedroom apartment in Berkeley.

Keisha and her seven-year-old son Marchand lived in Holloway, a few towns north of Berkeley, just past Richmond at the end of the BART line. Holloway's student population was nearly all black and Latino, but the teachers were predominantly white. All of the schools were performing far below the national average, and the district was on the verge of bankruptcy. Her son had been bullied by bigger boys, and one of the teachers had been fired for hitting a student. Apparently, the administration had tolerated it for years, but one of the staff had caught it on video, and it had gone viral on social media.

That was the last straw. Keisha wasn't going to allow her son to be in a school where white teachers were physically abusive. But she couldn't afford private school. Even a partial scholarship was out of the question. Bay Area rents were exorbitant.

When she first got pregnant with Marchand, she and her boyfriend had a great one-and-a-half-bedroom apartment in Richmond. She was working at the law office doing data entry. Her boyfriend was working as a security guard at the mall. They had enough income to save for the baby. But one night, her boyfriend got stopped by the cops for no apparent reason. Ultimately, he was hauled off for resisting arrest and battery on an officer. The dashboard cams, however, had been turned off. They beat him badly enough that he was in the hospital for a week. Then he was locked up.

Keisha gave up the apartment and moved in with her mom in Holloway. She was numb with grief for the first couple weeks, then she cried for another month.

"Girl," her mother had told her two weeks before her due date, "you need to stop all that crying and get ready to have this baby."

Her ex-boyfriend's mom called after the video went viral of the teacher hitting the student. "One of my friends from church called me," said the woman who would have been her mother-in-law. "She asked me, *Isn't that your grandson's school in Holloway?*"

The two of them talked, and Marchand's grandmother offered Keisha the use of her address to get Marchand into the Berkeley public schools. They had much better test scores, and Berkeley was the first district in the US to voluntarily desegregate in the 1960s. They wouldn't have crazy racist white teachers hitting the kids.

The mother-in-law put Keisha's name on her energy bill to document her residency, and Keisha breathed a sigh of relief.

But when she went in to the district office to figure out how to register her son for school, there was much more documentation required.

All proofs must be current originals (issued within the last 2 months) imprinted with the name and current Berkeley residential address of the parent/legal guardian. A student can have only one residency for purposes of establishing residency.

Only personal accounts will be accepted (No care of, DBA, or business accounts).

Group A:
__ *Utility bill.* (**Must provide *entire* bill**)
__ *PG&E*
__ *Landline phone (non-cellular)*
__ *EBMUD*
__ *Internet*
__ *Cable*

Group B:
__ *Current bank statement (checking or savings only)*

___ *Action letter from Social Services or government agency (cannot be property or business)*

___ *Recent paycheck stub or letter from employer on* **official** *company letterhead confirming residency address*

___ *Valid automobile registration <u>in combination</u> with valid automobile insurance*

___ *Voter registration for the most recent past election or the most recent upcoming election*

Group C:

___ *Rental property contract or lease, with payment receipt (dated within 45 days)*

___ *Renter's insurance or homeowner's insurance policy for the current year*

___ *Current property tax statement or property deed*

Keisha was bewildered by the list. She wouldn't even be able to document her actual address in Holloway, let alone her baby daddy's mother's address in Berkeley.

As she stood there in the empty entryway for the Berkeley Unified School District, a mother and daughter walked in, a matching pair of strawberry blondes. The mother was talking on the phone, pulling the girl behind her. ". . . Which is exactly what I told him," the woman was saying. "The rest of the PTA needs to get involved, because this is absolutely unacceptable. Hold on—" The woman stopped in her tracks and the girl, who was looking off into space, nearly collided with her. The woman turned to Keisha. "Where's the Excellence Program office?" she demanded.

Keisha blinked, confused. "I don't work here," she said.

The woman stared at her for a moment, taking in Keisha's

multicolored extensions, tight jeans, and low-cut top. Then she turned away without a word, and put the phone back to her ear. "Where did you say the office was?" she asked whoever was on the other end, and headed down the corridor, dragging the girl behind her.

The strawberry-blond woman was the only parent Keisha saw that day. Obviously, this white lady wasn't going to let her daughter get smacked by a teacher. Or go to an underperforming school. Keisha was determined to beat the list.

At work, she cancelled her direct deposit, and started having her paychecks sent to her mother-in-law's house. It was incredibly inconvenient to have to take public transportation across three cities twice a month to get her check two days later than usual. Yet she and Marchand managed it, and his grandmother was delighted to see more of him.

But the rental agreement? That had proven to be the most difficult to fake.

"Number seventy-two?" The full-figured woman behind the counter at the Berkeley Unified School District office had large brown eyes, a neat bob hairstyle, and a weary smile.

Keisha stepped forward with her paperwork. After the look the strawberry-blond mom had given her last time, she'd had her braids done without colors and dressed in her interview suit. She wanted to look like she worked in San Francisco's financial district or Silicon Valley. Like someone who could afford a two-bedroom apartment.

But now it was registration. The district office was full of Berkeley parents wearing jeans and T-shirts, cotton separates, and ethnic fabrics. Keisha felt overdressed. Still, she filled out the various forms to enroll Marchand in second grade.

When the woman called Keisha up to the counter, she pulled out her paperwork with what she hoped looked like confidence. Marchand's birth certificate, her driver's license, and each of the required documents from the list. Two were real, but the third one was the forgery.

The woman inspected each of them carefully. Keisha's heart beat hard as the administrator's sharp eyes got to the rental contract. As the seconds ticked by, Keisha grew increasingly certain the woman would call her a fake, or worse yet, call the police. Could she be arrested for this? But just as she began to brace for the worst, the woman smiled and said she would make copies for the file.

Keisha smiled back, relief washing over her.

The woman brought back the originals, stamped her copy of the registration form, and stapled it to a packet of papers. They were in.

Two months later, she got a letter at Marchand's grandma's house that the boy had been assigned to Frederick Douglass Elementary.

The first day of school dawned overcast and chilly, like so many Bay Area August mornings. Keisha and Marchand rode a BART train and a bus to Frederick Douglass. It took longer than expected, and they arrived twenty minutes after the start of school. Keisha found Marchand's name on a list and hurried him down the hall to room 126.

The hallway was wide and bright, with daylight streaming in through the windows. At their old school in Holloway, there were always late families rushing in, parents hissing at their kids about what they should have done to be on time. But this school's corridors were quiet and orderly. Keisha vowed to catch a much earlier train. She would get Marchand to school on time from now on.

The numbers of the classrooms were getting higher. Room 118. Room 120. Along the hallway wall hung a big banner that read, *Every Month Is Black History Month*, between pictures of Harriet Tubman and Rosa Parks.

When they got to Room 126, there was a poster of Frederick Douglass on the door.

Marchand tugged on Keisha's hand. "Mommy," he asked, "do they sometimes hit the kids here too?"

"Oh no, baby." She kneeled so she could get down to his level, and put one hand under his chin. "Nobody gets hit here," she said, glancing up at Frederick Douglass. It was the classic unsmiling portrait in a bow tie, with his salt-and-pepper hair combed back and a dark goatee. "That's why Mommy worked so hard to get you into a good school. Now come on, sugar, we got to get you into your class."

She opened the door with an apology in her mouth—full of *late BART train* and *I promise to do better*—but she was startled into silence. Twenty-three faces turned to her, expectantly. All of them were white.

Keisha felt disoriented. This was the first school district in the nation to voluntarily desegregate? This was a school named after the great black abolitionist?

Keisha looked closer. No. Not all white. That girl by the window with the blue hair was Asian. That boy on the far end might be Latino. And that girl looking up at her, with the sandy hair and the missing tooth, was definitely mixed with black. But every single kid in the class would pass the paper-bag test.

"You must be Marchand," the teacher said warmly to her son. She was a slender young woman with a messy blond bun on her head. Miss Keller.

Keisha watched her son walk shyly forward into the class. "Give Mommy a hug goodbye?" Miss Keller prompted.

Numbly, Keisha hugged her son and stepped out into the hallway, wondering what she had forged her way into.

RIGHTEOUS KILL

BY OWEN HILL

Gilman District

The Gilman District, newly named by realtors, was mostly industrial a few years ago. You'd go there for Urban Ore if you needed a broke-down couch to replace your more-broke-down couch. There was a body shop and a good Mexican restaurant, perhaps too good because it brought in too many urban pioneers on the hunt for good manchamanteles. From famous red mole to the Gilman District. There goes the neighborhood.

I had been coming to West Berkeley since the aughts, yes, for the mole, but also for the books. SPD for the poetry, and Jeff Maser's place for used, rare modern firsts, just to browse and occasionally to sell something. I do a little book scouting, although not full time like in the old days. It just doesn't pay, and I get a little freelance work as, believe it, an unlicensed detective, something I sort of backed into that now pays the bill at Berkeley Bowl and for the rent-controlled studio southside.

I finished my enchiladas and the imported Coke, then went by SPD to get Marvin some Kevin Killian and for Dino *The Collages of Helen Adam*, because he wouldn't have heard of her but he would appreciate the way beauty recognizes itself, and he would love the captions, *"remember how I warned you when you're praying too late."* I don't usually show up bearing gifts but

Marvin had said, "It's kind of a party," and I knew Dino would be there, Dino Centro. O Dino Centro.

Walked a little farther, down to 10th Street where Marvin had bought that house, cheap, when nobody really lived down there. The neighborhood wasn't especially dangerous, but dark, away from stuff, desolate as a staircase. Barely six figures at the time Marvin bought the house, just back from Central America. The money came from "somewhere" but "wasn't much." Marvin, the most Marxist of my Marxist friends, moving within and without radical subsets, dropping hints like, "I was in Athens and this crazy guy I know planted a bomb in a police station. I almost didn't get through customs!" Marvin, homeowner. Lovable guy. Best friend.

I knocked, door open, walked in the house that smelled a little like a cat box. Furniture that recalled places where you lived in your college years. It was a nice house nonetheless, forties vintage, what they call Arts and Crafts though I think that's a wider definition now than it was. Urban Ore and Ikea furnished, nice walls though, because for some reason Marvin liked to paint. This time the walls were very light with a bluish tint. I once asked Marvin what color it was and he answered, inexplicably, *vanilla hots*.

The "party" was mostly on the couch, blue Naugahyde, or, in the case of Dino, on the floor up against a matching ottoman. They were in black, awash in blue walls and furniture, except Dino, as usual, in seersucker. It was always seersucker or white linen, any season, with a gray sweater under the jacket in cold weather. It wasn't cold so it was a blue oxford button down. Just Dino, Marvin, and Patti O'Hara. I hadn't seen her in a couple of years.

My first impression, after that couple of years, was that she had been working out. Muscles bulging from a black wifebeater. "Still boxing, Patti?" and she went into her stance because she did, in fact, do some boxing. So, my best friend and the two people in the world I would most like to sleep with. Okay, a party, I guess.

Marvin hadn't yet read the Killian and so was suitably impressed. Dino: "I am astounded, dear Clay," and then a wet kiss. Life is good sometimes.

Dino went into the kitchen and came out with a shaker. Negronis, my favorite drink, not really Marvin's though. He favors bourbon-based cocktails. I wondered about the occasion. Was I the guest of honor? Decided to let that one go. Why argue with Boodles and Campari, and why interrupt Dino Centro midshake?

Cheese Board snacks and smart talk. Conversation turned to the high cost of living, everybody leaving Berkeley. Where do we go? Bay Area out, East Coast also too expensive, flyover states opioid and Trump-soaked. Emigrate? Marvin suggested Montevideo but not yet. Too many friends still here, and there were "battles to be won and lost."

This from Marvin, soldier for the revolution even when there isn't one.

And then, third drinks in hand, talk about the neighborhood, those cheap-rent war stories. You could get a whole house for a few hundred! I paid a hundred bucks, down the street, for a walk-in closet in a house full of commies! True civilization starts with cheap rent and ends with gentrification. I wasn't aware that the CEO of TalkLike had moved into the neighborhood. This set off a negroni-infused discussion of "the pig down the street" at high volume.

"You have to see this place! From warehouse to palace! An oppressor work space in Berkeley. Fuck Berkeley." From Patti O'Hara, leaning a little too close to my ear.

Marvin suggested that we all "go for a stumble" and have a look at the CEO's "bunker." We helped each other off the couch, Dino's scent mingling with Patti's in the warm late afternoon. We walked past SPD and in a sort of circular way toward Gilman. The gourmet burgers, the free-trade coffee, the vegan joint, the Whole Foods. Chunky guys with beards, buried in their devices.

It was looming, almost as big as the Whole Foods down the street. Truly bunker-like although too tall, maybe three stories. Military-style brushed chrome, brick facade, blackout windows. There was still a loading-dock entrance in keeping with the industrial chic. A place to house the Tesla, perhaps. Workers used to sweat in places like this. Now they're luxury homes. Where are the sweaty workers? I wondered what it was like inside, curious, but also a little queasy, that way the hoi polloi view the aristocracy. *And the poor love it / and think it's crazy.* We looked up at the thing like apes before a mono-lith, then walked silently back to Marvin's place.

Plopped on the couch between Dino and Patti, the min-gling scents a little stronger, feeling sleepy but a little excited. Marvin in the kitchen making coffee, humming, then, "Well, we could blow it up," followed by, "You can't blow up all of capitalism," from Dino, who has a smidgen of the capitalist left in him.

Dino almost asleep on my shoulder, oxford shirt unbut-toned, Patti lying head in my lap, legs over the couch arm. Dino, "A little graffiti wouldn't hurt," then Marvin, booming from the other room, "A bullet in the head would send a bet-ter message," and Patti, "Well, we all have guns."

Coffee, kisses goodbye, and I returned southside, back to the Chandler Apartments, at the corner of Telegraph and Dwight. Fed the cats, worked at some poetry. A perfect Sunday.

* * *

Following Wednesday, I was out buying books and the phone buzzed. Dinner at Marvin's. Got into the old Honda Civic and headed out to the Gilman District. Happy to find that it was the same group. Marvin cooking pasta. Eggs on the counter so I guessed carbonara. He was pouring an Italian white, kind of thin but in a good way. We started downing it like water. There was some music on and Dino and Patti were dancing. A nice group. Pasta and lots of jokes. Some pot with a silly name, something like Purple Urkel, but maybe I have it wrong. We were on the couch again, sides touching sides, and I was thinking about the different ways you can melt into somebody's flesh, how the luckiest accident of birth is to be bisexual.

My brain came up for air. Marvin back in the kitchen making coffee. Said something about a neighborhood association, but not an official group. They would like us to talk to the CEO, a sort of delegation. I spaced out again since I don't live in the neighborhood. My corner of Southside is still scruffy. Gentrification is months away. When I zeroed back in, they were talking about fleets of luxury cars and drones flown from the roof. The kind of thing you'd expect from techie CEO types. I was beginning to get bored, but then they asked me to go along because he had a bodyguard and an extra presence could help. I used to box Golden Gloves and I stay in shape, and occasionally I need to defend myself when doing my "detective" work, but I don't look like a bouncer either.

I was feeling a little floaty and thinking that the walk would do me good. The Gilman District isn't pretty. I guess somehow that's part of its charm, or always was, but now it's different. Couples making midsix figures or more sucking up the urban experience, then spitting it out cleaned up and with a get-off-my-lawn mentality. Live-work castles full of toys, set among the junkyards and bad roads.

For some reason we were walking close together, lots of touching. At some point I turned into Dino, kissed him, and all at once everybody giggled. I felt something hard in his pants—not the thing I was looking for, though. A handgun. Old joke. Dino lives, um, outside the law, so no surprise, but I was hoping for something sweeter.

And again to this palace that rose gleaming from the squalor yet was somehow uglier than the street where it lived. Patti stepped back and faced a security camera, announced us. Gilman District neighborhood watch. The warehouse-style door opened slowly, old-fashioned pulley, and it seemed that someone had called central casting and found a goon. Square jaw, shaved head, you know . . .

Patti sucker punched him, then kicked him going down. Great pair of boots! I wondered where she found them. The action seemed very stylized, or does now in retrospect, like a scene in a Melville policier. Her short hair shook just right and I zeroed in on the back of her neck. I wanted to fuck her.

They seemed to know the way upstairs. Recognizance? Looking back, I'm surprised that I went along. I've been through cases and capers with these people, but I didn't even know the circumstances. I knew he owned TalkLike. Tried to remember his name. Something vaguely Swedish.

No need to describe the enemy. "You're either at war or you're not," Marvin told me later. The guy had no idea. They played with him for a while, doing up the neighborhood association drag. *We'd like you to turn down the security lights, we'd like to see you at the meetings.* He smiled and clichéd for a while, then was "tired" and would like us to go.

I turned to go, then looked back and Patti was Ingemar

Johansson, Hammer of Thor. She had donned a single black leather glove, left hand. Solar plexus, then again a kick to the CEO's head. Dino pulled out the handgun. Three shots. Who would hear shots in a bunker? And then, who hadn't heard shots in this neighborhood?

I felt some panic. I had touched the desk, possibly something else. Thought about DNA and started to sweat.

"Shall we go?" This from Marvin, and so we did, but not before Dino hit the bodyguard with a couple to the head. Did it kill him? Wouldn't it have to?

We go, but not fast. Just walking. I shoot Marvin a puzzled expression.

"Don't look so worried. A fixer will be along soon to clean up our mess, and, yes, they'll break the cameras. It's all set." And then, walking ahead a little, "We piss on them from a higher place."

It isn't easy to get to Marvin's roof, not simple like mine. You have to crawl out a window and lift yourself on a makeshift ladder, and after all that, the view isn't much, just a bunch of buildings, the view of the bay blocked long ago by upscale rental properties. We did it anyway. It was a warm night, rare for Berkeley, and we needed a little air. We didn't talk about what happened, we just sat there close until it got cooler, then went downstairs and showered. When there's shooting and fighting, you need to wash it off. Marvin disappeared into the kitchen and I bathed with Patti and Dino. This was our after-party, skin and soap.

Came home late, fed the cat, looked out my window at the traffic triangle where Telegraph meets Dwight then runs south into Oakland. The usual scene, homeless guy playing conversational solitaire, a couple of sleeping dogs, a couple of lumps under ratty sleeping bags. I reflected a little on the day's "work," if that was what it was. Revolutionary fervor would have carried Patti and Melvin, but Dino must have been paid. My motivation was a mystery even to me. Sometimes you just go on your nerve.

I didn't have occasion to see Marvin for a couple of weeks. When I did it was to do a book buy in Concord, art books and a few decent novels. After we did the deal, we stopped at a nondescript brewpub. "Okay, Marvin, what was up with the home invasion."

A shrug, then, "It's a small step away from your other adventures but we wanted to take you there. It isn't your first righteous kill and it won't be your last. You wanted it, based on the guy's style and his toys. You got the gestalt and went along. If we weren't old pals I'd say this is the beginning of a beautiful friendship. We will piss on them from a higher place."

We finished our burgers and beer, got in his van, and headed back to the Gilman District.

Acknowledgments

Thanks to Liz Leger, Zelda, to the editors and publishers at the late, great Creative Arts/Black Lizard for reprinting the best of classic noir, and to Moe's Books, Berkeley's Taj Mahal.
—O.H.

Thanks to composer Milo Francis, my best friend. Thank you, man, for the soundtrack recording for *Oakland Noir*. Thanks to Rick Moss and Veda Silva with the African American Museum and Library at Oakland. To Calvin Crosby and the wonderful team at NCIBA, and to all the independent booksellers, for their support. Special thanks to Maria San Antonio and Bill Barham, for always having my back, and for the fried chicken. To Zach Embry, for all the inspirations and conversations. To Foster Douglas for overseeing the web and social media, and for the groovy Piedmont Avenue sound system. To Alice De Parres and Michael Ross, my angel network! Thanks to Bonnie and Michael Stuppin of the Alexander Book Company, for your incredible support and care. Thank you, Michael Calvello, for allowing our time together at Owl & Company to be so life-changing and rewarding. And thanks to Johnny Temple, for believing in me, a bookseller with a dream.
—J.T.

ABOUT THE CONTRIBUTORS

Nye' Lyn Tho

LUCY JANE BLEDSOE'S short story collection, *Lava Falls*, came out in 2018, as did her most recent novel, *The Evolution of Love*, which takes place in the East Bay. Her fiction has won an *Arts & Letters* Fiction Prize, a Pushcart nomination, and an American Library Association Stonewall Book Award. Bledsoe has also participated in two National Science Foundation Antarctic Artists & Writers Fellowships, a Yaddo Residency, and a California Arts Council Fellowship.

Michael Weber

SUMMER BRENNER is the author of a dozen books that include crime fiction, poetry, youth novels, and short stories. Her novel *Nearly Nowhere* was translated into French by Gallimard's imprint Série Noire. About *I-5: A Novel of Crime, Transport, and Sex*, R. Crumb wrote: "It has a quality very rare in literature: a subtle, dark humor that's only perceivable when one goes deep into the heart of this world's absurd tragedy, or tragic absurdity."

Elizabeth Burchfield

THOMAS BURCHFIELD'S nomadic life began in Peekskill, New York, and eventually led him to the Bay Area. He's the author of the Prohibition-era gangster noir *Butchertown* and a contemporary vampire novel, *Dragon's Ark*. His film reviews and articles have appeared in *Bright Lights Film Journal*, the *Strand Magazine*, and *Filmfax*. When not working on his next novel, *Captain Zigzag*, he is communing with nature, and hanging with his wife, Elizabeth.

Diana Sanchez

J.M. CURET (AKA JOSE MARTINEZ) is a poet, writer, member of the Berkeley Writers Circle, and current student at the Writers Studio San Francisco. His short stories include "Wifebeater Tank Top" and "Papi's Stroke," for which he received an honorable mention for *Glimmer Train's* Short Story Award for New Writers in 2018. He lives in the San Francisco Bay Area where he teaches high school English and lends his voice to several local salsa bands.

Anna de León

AYA DE LEÓN teaches creative writing at UC Berkeley. Her 2020 novel *Operation HOLOGRAM* explores FBI infiltration of African American organizations. Her previous works include *Side Chick Nation*, the first novel published about Hurricane Maria. She is currently working on a black/Latina spy-girl YA series called *Going Dark*, and writes about race, class, gender, and culture at @AyadeLeon and ayadeleon.com.

Judith Davis

SUSAN DUNLAP is the author of twenty-five mystery novels, featuring San Francisco stunt double and Zen student Darcy Lott, Berkeley police officer Jill Smith, forensic pathologist–cum–private investigator Kiernan O'Shaughnessy, and PG&E meter reader Vejay Haskell, She has also written many short stories and a suspense novel, *Fast Friends*. Dunlap has taught hatha yoga, worked as a paralegal, and been on the private investigative defense team in a capital murder case.

Oscar Bucher

BARRY GIFFORD is a recipient of NoirCon's Anne Friedberg Award, and was the founder of the original Black Lizard Books, for which he was given the Maxwell E. Perkins Award by PEN West. He is the author of the world-famous novel *Wild at Heart: The Story of Sailor and Lula*, among many other books, and cowrote the screenplay for the film *Lost Highway*.

Terri Carrion

OWEN HILL is the author of two crime novels, *The Chandler Apartments* and *The Incredible Double*, and he coedited the *Annotated Big Sleep* with Pamela Jackson and Anthony Rizzuto. Until recently he lived in the Chandler Building on the corner of Telegraph and Dwight in Berkeley.

Javier Calvo

MARA FAYE LETHEM's work has recently appeared in the *New York Times Book Review*, *BOMB*, and *A Velocity of Being: Letters to a Young Reader*, a best-selling collection of letters and illustrations. Her forthcoming translations include novels by Patricio Pron, Max Besora, Javier Calvo, and Marta Orriols. She splits her time between Brooklyn and Barcelona.

Irene Young

MICHAEL DAVID LUKAS is the author of the international best seller *The Oracle of Stamboul*, a finalist for the California Book Award, the NCIBA Book of the Year Award, and winner of the Harold U. Ribalow Prize. His second novel, *The Last Watchman of Old Cairo*, won the National Jewish Book Award for Fiction and the ALA's Sophie Brody Medal. He was born in Berkeley, lives in Oakland, and teaches at San Francisco State University.

Tristan Crane

NICK MAMATAS is the author of several novels, including the Lovecraftian murder mystery *I Am Providence* and the supernatural thriller *Sabbath*. His short fiction has appeared in many anthologies and magazines, including *The Best American Mystery Stories* and *The Year's Best Science Fiction & Fantasy*. Mamatas's fiction and editorial work have been nominated for the Hugo, Bram Stoker, Locus, and World Fantasy awards.

Andrew Aldrich

KIMN NEILSON is a longtime Berkeley bookseller and editor. Her translations of the poet C.P. Cavafy appeared in *TRY!* and an article on Elizabeth David in *PekoPeko*. "Still Life, Reviving" is an offshoot of a longer piece she is working on about Berkeley in the years 1980 and 2000.

David Lüttschwager

JIM NISBET has published twenty books, including the classic noir title *Lethal Injection*; six volumes of poetry; and a single nonfiction title, *Laminating the Conic Frustum*. Current projects include a fourteenth novel, *You Don't Pencil*, and a complete translation of Charles Baudelaire's *Les Fleurs du mal*.

LEXI PANDELL is a freelance writer and former *Wired* editor from Oakland. Her nonfiction work has been published by the *New York Times*, the *Atlantic*, *Condé Nast Traveler*, *GQ*, *Playboy*, *Creative Nonfiction*, and others. She is an alumna of the UC Berkeley Graduate School of Journalism and was recently awarded the Wellstone Center's Emerging Writer Residency for her novel-in-progress. She also hosts Desert Salon, an annual writing retreat in Joshua Tree, California.

Sunshine Combs

JASON S. RIDLER is a historian and writer. He is the author of the Brimstone Files series, over sixty short stories, and several works of military history. A former punk rock musician and cemetery groundskeeper, he is a teaching fellow at Johns Hopkins University and a creative writing instructor at Google, YouTube, and other locations. Ridler is currently working on his forthcoming book, *Harvest of Blood and Iron*.

SHANTHI SEKARAN is a writer and educator in Berkeley. Her latest novel, *Lucky Boy*, was named an Indie Next Great Read and an NPR Best Book of 2017. Her essays and stories have also appeared in the *New York Times*, *Salon*, and the *LA Review of Books*. She's a member of the San Francisco Writers' Grotto, an AWP mentor, and teaches writing at Mills College.

JERRY THOMPSON is a bookseller, poet, playwright, and musician. His work has appeared *Zyzzyva* and the *James White Review*. He is the coauthor of *Images of America: Black Artists in Oakland*. His fiction and prose have appeared in various anthologies including *Voices Rising*, edited by G. Winston James, and *Freedom in this Village: Twenty-Five Years of Black Gay Men's Writing*, edited by E. Lynn Harris. He is the coeditor of *Oakand Noir*.